MAS͟TERWORK

MASTERWORK

John Miglis

Lippincott & Crowell, Publishers

NEW YORK

FIRST EDITION

Designed by Vikki Sheatsley

Library of Congress Cataloging in Publication Data

Miglis, John.
  Masterwork.
  I. Title.
PZ4.M6316Mas   [PS3563.I3715]   813'54   80–7862
ISBN 0–690–01894–0

---

80 81 82 83 84 10 9 8 7 6 5 4 3 2 1

This book is dedicated to the Adelman family,
Enrico, Jenifer, Vanessa,
Alexandra, and Jonah.

Acknowledgments

This book could not have been written without the assistance of Messrs. P. Gottmer and W. Polack. I would also like to thank Luitsen Kuiper, Chief Restorer of the Rijksmuseum and co-author of the *Report on the Restoration of Rembrandt's Night Watch,* for sharing his time and knowledge with me.

Author's Note

One Sunday in the fall of 1975, a man whom the newspapers later dismissed as a lunatic walked into Amsterdam's Rijksmuseum and, with a serrated knife, destroyed the museum's single most priceless work of art, a wall-sized group portrait by Rembrandt called *The Night Watch.* That insensible moment of seemingly wanton violence is the basis for this work of the imagination. Outside these covers, none of the characters are real.

Between the light and the dark there is something which partakes of both. Therein lies the secret of enchantment.

—Leonardo da Vinci

Part I

THE DESTRUCTION

1

The hypnotic sway and clack of the speeding train had lulled van Rijks to sleep, and it was that same maddening combination of movement and sound that now drew him out.

Opening his eyes, he saw a small boy, perhaps three years old, between his spread legs, with a plump, dimpled hand on each knee. The boy bounced wildly, oblivious for a moment of van Rijks's gaze, treating his knees as though they were part of a gym set. When the boy looked up and their eyes finally met, he greeted van Rijks with a delighted squeal that turned his face crimson.

"Milos!" a woman's voice barked. Milos froze; the smile drained quickly from his face. "Milos, stop bothering that man."

Milos sauntered back to his seat beside his mother, pausing briefly, defiantly, to bounce between two armrests.

"No bother," van Rijks mumbled up the aisle after the child. In that first instance of opening his eyes, he had almost called Milos his own son's name, and now his chest filled with a hot fluttering of anxiety. Johannes, he said to himself. Then he repeated the name.

He closed his eyes again, but all he could see on the inside of his lids was Milos's blond ball of a face beaming up at him.

He could hear the mother reprimanding Milos and offering him a bit of salted licorice at the same time. It was the same way he had meted out discipline: equal parts of whip and sugar cube. He would have bet, right then, that Milos was her only child.

The first hour on the train had been bad for him. The coach

had been completely empty and the heated air smelled intolerably of dust. His mouth tasted of dust too. He had brought nothing to read; nor could he have concentrated long enough to get through a paragraph anyway. He would have given away all the sketches in his portfolio for someone to talk with, forgoing in an instant the purpose of his trip for the distraction of conversation. He had informed Neel, his wife, that he was going to Amsterdam to sell his sketches at the Dam on the Queen's birthday, hoping also to pick up a commission in the bargain, and after that he would stay around for a few days to unwind. What he didn't tell her, couldn't tell her, was that if he didn't get away for a while, he was going to explode. He might even kill her.

Van Rijks looked absently out the window as they streaked past the newly blooming tulip fields—acres of bright red, yellow, pink, and white bulbs laid out in infuriatingly precise patterns between irrigation canals, stretching to the sharp gray line of the distant horizon. From the sky, the colors must have formed a spectacular tableau, and he wished that he could somehow suspend himself with palette and canvas and brush and do justice to that geometric beauty. Instead, in a week or two, he knew all the flowers would be mercilessly hacked down and sold by the handful on the street corners of Amsterdam, Utrecht, The Hague; and by the gross in the spring flower auction. And all of them, all the colors of these infinite fields, would end up wilting in pale vases full of putrefied water.

In the distance, too, outlines of the idle blades of windmills formed dark skeletons against the monochromatic gray sky. Scatterings of listless cattle milled in an endless spring drizzle. But these sights moved too quickly past him, and it seemed as though he, in the train, were somehow still and everything outside a fleeting panorama.

Finally, he was left to look at the only thing that did not move —the reflection of his own face captured in the double thickness of glass in the train window. At first it startled him because it was not the face he was used to looking at. His hair was gone; he had insisted one night that Neel shear it with a pair of scissors. While he held the mirror on his lap, he had watched the reflection of her pale face, her red-lined incredulous blue eyes. And since he had abandoned Neel, he had decided to stop shaving. The bearded face, now caught in the glass, looked ragged; the eyes misty. The face seemed strange and distant to him, as if it matched perfectly the way his insides felt—form and content merged into total confusion.

He brought down his paint box and sketch pad from the overhead rack. The fluorescent light of the coach and the double thickness of glass gave his reflection a wan color and surreal depth. He remembered an M. C. Escher print in a book he kept in his studio of a goateed man staring into a crystal orb in his outstretched hand, the man's black-and-white image convex, the details of background excruciatingly distorted. Using a piece of charcoal, van Rijks rapidly sketched the train window and part of his seat. With pen and ink, he then carefully printed the warning sign at the top of the glass, sketched his large ragged-looking face, and, underneath, chalked in its dim reflection on the second level of glass, like the faint shadow of pentimento bleeding through an aged canvas.

As he squinted at his reflection to see the detail of his new thick beard, he found that his face was contorting involuntarily, stretching comically as he had often done to amuse Johannes, his neck muscles cording thickly like stiffened snakes. He became suddenly terrified at this total lack of control and, in a panic, slammed closed the sketch pad.

"Milos," he whispered loudly.

Four seats up, Milos poked his head above the seat. He wore that same brilliant smile; black licorice spittle dribbled from the corner of his mouth.

"Come here."

Milos sprang from his seat, and as he did, his mother's arm shot out to grab him. "Milos," she called.

"It's all right," van Rijks said. "He's really no bother."

She peeked around at him, then smiled self-consciously and turned away.

5

"What is your name?" Milos asked.

"Rembrandt," van Rijks teased, recalling his attempt at self-portrait, and the other self-portraits in his portfolio that he intended to sell. "My name is Rembrandt, the artist."

Milos's face screwed up in puzzlement. He tried to repeat the name but made a mess of it.

"You can call me"—he paused for a moment, recollecting the fields they had recently passed—"Tulip. Can you say that?"

"Tulip," Milos squealed, running back down the aisle. "Mother," he said excitedly as he reached his seat, "that man is called Tulip, like the flower." Then he climbed on the seat, gave a sharp yelp, and jumped. He ran back to van Rijks.

"Climb up here," van Rijks said. He helped Milos onto his knee and began playfully bouncing him. He sang, "I have a little boy named Milos/He comes from a crack in the wall/If he eats his meat and vegetables/He'll grow up strong and tall."

"I don't come from a crack in the wall," Milos said, suddenly indignant. "I come from my mother. In here." The child pointed to his belly.

"Of course you do," van Rijks said, patting Milos's small rounded back. "Of course you do." They both giggled; then he began singing the song he had made up for Milos again, more softly. He did not feel desperate with the child sitting on his lap, only immeasurably depressed. He wanted to keep him there, to hold on to him forever.

"Do you want me to draw your picture?"

"Sure." Milos jumped from van Rijks's lap and scrambled back to his mother's side.

Van Rijks, taking some chalk and his pad, followed Milos.

"May I?" he asked, indicating the seat in front of Milos's mother.

"Yes," the woman said, looking out the window. Her feet were drawn up under her; her shoes, side by side, were on the floor.

"My name is van Rijks. I'm an artist," he said. "And I would like very much to sketch you and your son, if you don't mind."

"I don't mind," she said, "but I'm afraid you won't find the

6

subject matter very interesting." She laughed uncomfortably.

Of course she minds, he thought. Her hair was pulled back on her head, tied with a green ribbon. A small crop of pimples dotted the bridge of her nose, and she kept covering the blemish with her index finger as she talked. Milos bore her sharp blue eyes, her small nose. Her lips were thin, almost purple against her pallid complexion.

Van Rijks shaded the upper corner of the page, lightening as he moved toward the center, quickly dabbing his thumb to his lips, then smudging the chalk so it looked like a wash. Then he framed her shoulders, the curving line of her back, her feet tucked underneath. Milos squirmed impatiently beside her.

"Are you finished yet?" Milos said, rocking as though he had to urinate.

"Not yet," van Rijks said.

When he outlined the woman's head, the angle seemed the perfect suppliant position for the eyes he was about to draw. Until recently, the eyes of each face he had drawn had been flawed, no matter how well crafted the rest of the composition. It was the greatest frustration and greatest failure of his art: he knew the secret, knew how the eyes exhibited the range of grandest and most pitiable of human emotion, knew even more about their magic than most celebrated artists; but he could not render them. And so he took to copying others' work because eventually he could not bear the flaws in his own. He had even shared his ideas with his young students once, about the use of the eyes in art. "Light enters through the eyes," he had emphasized to them, "and, through some magic of chemistry and supernatural beneficence, transforms into the seen image, projects somewhere in the brain, as if on a movie screen—a dog, a cat, a tree. . . ."

"But," he continued, "the obverse, for the artist, is just as true." He told them that states of emotional being sprang well-like up through the nerves in the spinal column, gathered in the mind, and manifested themselves in varying intensities around the eyes. That, he explained, had accounted for a person who *looked* sad, or happy, or worried.

The trick, and what had always given him trouble, had been bringing to life these observable states accurately and consistently.

Now, he thought, I have captured *her* pitiable look—the bone-weariness of tired eyes and aching, swollen feet, the singular embarrassment of her acne—in two shadowed ellipses that could as well be showing her soul.

"What is your name?" he asked the woman, obscuring the line of her chin with a little spit, then wiping his blackened thumb on his slacks.

The woman covered her acne. "Mrs. Bouman."

"I am going to sell some of my work in the Dam this weekend, Mrs. Bouman." Then he added, "With a little luck."

"I'm sure you will," she said. "You get along quite well with children. Do you have any?"

"I'm a copyist, you know. No style of my own. I might not sell a single drawing." Her question repeated itself in his head. He watched his fingers speed up, racing to catch the palpitation in his heart. He sketched in Milos, resting obliquely across his mother's lap, his lips riveted to his mother's exposed breast. The conversation must not turn that way. "Turn your head a little, please. You can give this to your husband when I'm finished." His voice broke on the last word, and he was no longer able to watch what his hand was drawing.

"That would be nice."

"Let me see," Milos said, springing across the seat and jarring van Rijks's elbow.

"Stop," he snapped at Milos. Mrs. Bouman shot him a hard look.

"Aw," Milos whined, "that doesn't look like me."

"Can I see?" Mrs. Bouman asked.

He stared at his drawing. The picture of the woman was surely Milos's mother, but the child at her breast had somehow transformed into Johannes. God, he had not wanted that again. It was as if his own eyes had conspired to mislead his hand.

He remembered the first time he had drawn Johannes's face

8

after the child's death. He had told Neel that he had been sitting in the school yard at lunchtime, sketching the face of one of his students. But when he looked down, he had seen Johannes there, filling the page with his plump apple-red face and grotesquely sad eyes. He had captured a moment in his son's life so truly that he felt the sadness inside himself, and he began to tremble. What worried him most, though, was that he had no recollection of actually drawing the face. When it was completed, he felt as though he had come out of a trance, to see it for the first time.

Neel had insisted that he see a psychiatrist. And he had gone, so afraid had he been at this manifest vision. But after the first session, he stopped. He went to his studio instead, though he had lied to Neel about still going to the doctor's.

Mrs. Bouman looked embarrassed at the sight of her breast so graphically depicted at the mouth of a strange child. "I know I should be grateful," she stammered, handing him the sketch back, "but . . ." She quickly slipped her feet into her shoes and began buttoning her blue serge overcoat. "Put your coat on, Milos."

"I didn't mean to offend you." Van Rijks looked down at his sketch, and his heart shuddered. He could hear screaming, though the sound never reached his lips. His brain felt pressured, as if it had swelled against the inside of his skull. The child he had sketched at Mrs. Bouman's breast looked dead, gaunt-faced, hollow-eyed dead. He began to sob. Milos asked his mother what was wrong with Tulip.

"I don't know," his mother said, taking down two suitcases from the overhead rack. "But we should go."

"Please," van Rijks said. "I'm sorry." He wiped a line of mucus from his nose with a handkerchief, quickly breaking off his sobs. "I'm all right. It's just that . . ."

"Milos, go look out the window." She pushed Milos up the aisle, handing him the bag of licorice.

"What's the matter?" Mrs. Bouman asked, sitting down. "Did you lose your child? Is that . . ."

"Yes," he said. Lose your child, he repeated to himself. That asshole psychiatrist had used the same euphemism. He died, damn it. "He died," he said.

"Long ago?"

"I don't know about that." He could feel a wave of sobbing coming on; he contracted the muscles in his chest, pushed downward, and looked out the window. He tried to give her an accurate answer. "It was about a year ago," he said. Then, "But it feels like it could have been yesterday." He knew when he had lost his sense of time, knew the exact moment, but he would be damned if he would tell her. It was none of her goddamned business.

He felt her hand patting his knee—as if *he* were the child—and jerked his eyes from the window, his knee jumping as though he had been pricked by a pin.

"I'm sorry," he said. "I liked your child, and I wanted to draw him, but I don't want your sympathy. I want to be left alone."

He rose quickly and returned to his seat. He heard her call Milos, watched her gather her bags again. She and the child then pushed through the doors into another car. After she had gone, he walked back to her seat. The drawing was folded in half, lying on the floor. Bitch, he thought, picking it up.

Outside, the tulip fields had long since disappeared. Acres of rails moved past him, laid out as precisely as the tulip fields. The windmills had become tall stacks now that billowed dark smoke, and the listless cattle had become small darting delivery trucks. The conductor whisked through, calling, "Amsterdam. Centraal Station."

The air on the platform still held a winter chill. He raised the collar of his coat, tied his scarf, picked up his cardboard suitcase and black leather portfolio, and walked into a cloud of steam that rose from under the train and floated heavily down the platform. The steam felt warm, smelled thick with dirt, but it insulated him briefly against the chill. For an instant, in that opaque whiteness, he did not care whether or not he ever came out the other side. He felt safe, unthreatened by his own thoughts, for the first time in ages, mindless. Except for the dirty smell, he imagined heaven to be this way—warm and misty and white. When the cloud dissipated, he saw Milos and his mother hurrying ahead. She craned her head and, when she saw him looking at them, quickened her steps. *Lady, I didn't do anything to you. All I wanted was for your son to be mine, and he was for that short time we sang and I caressed the bony line of his back.* He quickened his pace too, trying to catch her, not knowing what he would do or say when he did. All he knew was that he didn't want her to leave him. Or, more precisely, he didn't want the child to disappear.

Inside the busy terminal, he lost her among the files of luggage-laden travelers. A booming hollow voice echoed among the high rafters of the terminal, announcing in several languages the arrivals and departures. He considered having her paged, but he remembered that she was married, and that her husband was no doubt meeting them. Finally, he pushed through the front doors, crossed the bus and tram lines in front of the station, and entered the Tourist Information Office to secure himself a room for the weekend.

After paying one fee for having a room found for him, and agreeing to another for the room itself, and after an argument with the young girls who worked behind the V.V.V. desk, in which he accused them of conspiring with the hotel owners to raise prices during a holiday weekend, he went back to Centraal Station and put his luggage in a locker. He needed to find a café where he could start drinking, where he could lose the edge he had acquired on the train that made him grind his teeth.

He caught a tram in front of Centraal Station and, without paying, rode it up the Damrak to the first stop. Then he walked a half block, passing a camera store, a sex shop and cinema, and the American Express office, till he found the Café Zwart. The last time he had come to Amsterdam, he had done his drinking in the Zwart because he had felt comfortable there. And now he needed to feel comfortable as much as he needed to get drunk.

Though the evening had gotten chillier, he sat at a small table on the patio and ordered a jenever. Neon lights up and down the darkening Damrak were flashing reds, yellows, whites, blues; it looked as though some mad artist had succeeded in transferring

11

the colors of the tulip fields to his palette, then mixed them in a careless drug-induced state and splashed them along the tourist strip. Across the street, where the water taxis that prowled the canals were filling up with tourists every fifteen minutes for night cruises, lights flashed like the curvilinear entrances to enticing carnival rides. Citroëns, Mini-Coopers, Mercedeses, and Volkswagens—bright red and white lights blazing back and front— zipped past, the intermittent howling of horns accenting the drone of Friday-night traffic.

Soon the patio in front of the Café Zwart filled with young lovers, snuggling into each other against the chill and sipping snifters of brandy. He felt miserably out of place. One couple asked if they could share his table and he gruffly turned them away. He needed to calm down, but the lights, and the noise, and now the crowd were beginning to press in on him, making him as edgy as he had been before he had followed Milos and his mother, frightening them. He could not believe he had actually done that; if he could somehow find them now, he would beg their forgiveness.

Another couple asked him for the extra chairs around his table, and he got up, cursing them under his breath, and went inside.

"Pils," he yelled to the bartender above the din. He held up one finger. The bartender ran the tap, then slapped the head of the beer away with a flat wooden stick as it overflowed the glass. "One guilder fifty."

The bar was packed, and though he had been sitting outside for a small eternity, he could not recollect seeing a single soul enter.

Nor had he heard the commotion they made. Thunderheads of gray smoke clouded the dim globe lights hanging from the ceiling. A group at a table in the corner was singing "Happy Birthday" to Queen Juliana. The song moved like a wave through the bar, catching up everyone except him in its swell. He hung his coat on a hook, sat on a barstool, and drained his glass. The bartender, standing Prussian-erect, stone-faced, watched the singers.

12

"Another," van Rijks yelled, holding up his glass.

The bartender turned away and began washing glasses in a steel sink.

The man beside him nudged his elbow. "How old is she?" He was a thin, speckle-faced man with dark-rimmed, tinted glasses. His speech seemed slow from drink, and he looked directly into his glass as he talked and not at van Rijks.

"Who?"

"The Queen."

"I don't know." Van Rijks tossed his coaster into the sink where the bartender washed glasses. "Give me another, will you?" he said adamantly. The bartender looked as if he wanted to break his neck. This was the wrong night to come here, van Rijks thought. The whole city seemed as if it were on the verge of going mad, and he felt closer to it than anyone. "She's twenty-three," he said to the little man.

"You're crazy." The man idly stacked some coins on the bar in front of him. "She's in her friggin' seventies."

Van Rijks paid the bartender, then sipped at his fresh glass. "So I was a little off."

"I get it," the man said. He laughed at van Rijks as though he had made a joke. "You're all right."

"I am?"

A plump dapper man, dressed in a herringbone-tweed jacket and matching cap, left the table in the corner where all the singing had begun. He joined another man, sitting alone, who had a head too large for his small, bent body. His whiskey-mottled cheeks hung like sacks of soft cheese, and the fat over his lids weighted his eyes half closed. Van Rijks took out a pen and quickly sketched the man as a resting bulldog on the cocktail napkin in front of him.

"You an artist or something?"

"Yeah," Van Rijks said.

"You're a bastard!" the bulldog shouted as the dapper man approached his table.

"And you're uglier than a Moluccan whore."

"They go at it regularly, those two," the man said into van Rijks's ear. "My name's Molen."

"Glad to meet you," van Rijks said. He pushed away from the bar and quit the Café Zwart.

Before he reached the corner, Molen was jerking at his sleeve. "Hey, what's the matter with you? Did I insult you or something?"

"No," van Rijks said.

"Then why'd you insult me?" Molen squared himself off on the curb, blocking van Rijks.

"Sorry. I just didn't want to stay in that bar. I was looking for a quiet place to drink." It seemed only fitting that the next thing to happen would be little Molen taking a swing at him.

"Why didn't you say so? You an out-of-towner? I'll show you a place." Molen relaxed, slapping van Rijks playfully on the shoulder.

"What time is it?"

"Early," Molen said. "Early."

"I'll buy you a drink, then," van Rijks offered. He did not want to be alone now. He felt strange, and he did not know why, as if everything were a bit off center, like a wheel out of true. The sidewalk seemed soft underfoot, and light from the streetlamps suffused balls of hazy yellow light.

Molen took him to a small café near the station, so van Rijks could get his luggage and make the walk easily to the Hotel Kap, where he was to stay. They talked for two hours, drinking jenever, then beer. Van Rijks paid for each drink over the mild protestations of his new friend. He listened distractedly as Molen puffed out his chest and told stories about himself. He called himself a hustler by trade. He worked a couple of girls in the red-light district. Sometimes he would sell hashish, or cocaine, and once in a while LSD on the streets and at the Dam to tourists who heard they could buy whatever they wanted for the right price. There was nothing much van Rijks liked about the small, speckled, weasel-looking man in dark glasses sitting in front of him, except that he was occupying time and keeping him from think-

14

ing about Neel, and Johannes, and Milos, and the bulldog at the bar, and all the unfitting ironies that were beginning to fight for primacy in his mind. Molen promised to show him a good spot where he could set up his work at the Dam tomorrow, and before van Rijks finally left for the night, he and Molen agreed to meet first thing in the morning.

Outside, Molen pressed a small foil-wrapped package into van Rijks's palm. "You're an artist," he said. "Take this. It'll help you relax tonight."

"What is it? What does it have to do with being an artist?"

"Never mind. Just chop it up with a razor and put it up your nose. It'll get rid of your depression. Besides," Molen said, "I never met an artist that didn't like it."

Instead of walking to the Hotel Kap, van Rijks hailed a cab. The hotel's narrow, high-gabled brick front faced the Keizersgracht, one of the city's main semicircular canals. The water, with the pungent smell of raw sewage, lapped against the old houseboats moored to the quay. Cars were parked close together on the cramped street with their front bumpers hanging over the water.

The woman who ran the hotel took one look at him as he came through the door and, shaking her head, said, "I thought you were coming when the V.V.V. called; I waited, but I rented your room when you didn't show."

"I have money," van Rijks said, pulling a handful of brightly colored bills from his pocket. "Give me anything. It's late." He realized then, as he was straightening out his money, that he had spent more than fifty guilders on drinks with Molen. The little weasel really was a hustler.

A pinball machine was jammed into the corner of the small lobby, its bright colors flashing off the wall like summer heat lightning. An imitation zebra-skin couch was pushed up against another wall in front of a color television set. A foul-smelling cloud of cigarette smoke ringed the woman's head.

"I have a small room at the top," she said. "It isn't fancy, twenty-five guilders, like they told you at the travel bureau. Includes breakfast."

"Give me the card."

"It's not as big as the other one," the woman said defensively. Her wavy brown hair was sticky with layers of spray. Her skin was the texture of worn, overstretched canvas; her breath was rank.

He signed his name as Rembrandt van Rijks and paid for two nights.

"The third night is twenty-two guilders and my name is Mrs. Kolb." As he took the key from her, she said, "Hey, wait a minute. What kind of joke is this?"

He took the card back from her and stared at his signature. It was true. He had written Rembrandt. He went upstairs without answering her.

"Shit," Mrs. Kolb said, spitting the word after him. "I get all the birds in this town. Breakfast is over at nine. A minute late and you don't eat. And I don't want any trouble out of you."

His room was at the top of three flights of stairs. He found it at the end of a dark hallway, across from the water closet. There was no shower on this floor, and the hall smelled as musty as an old closed-up attic. When he opened the door and turned on the light, his heart nearly exploded.

From the doorway, he saw a three-quarter bed and a small porcelain sink. Nothing more. A large tattered rug doubled for a bedspread. A forty-watt bulb hung from a single cord in the ceiling. If he stretched his arms away from his sides, he could touch both walls.

"It's the Queen's birthday," he said. He threw his suitcase on the bed and propped his portfolio and paint box against the wall.

But his acceptance of the room was not to be that simple. This hotel room seemed identical to the studio in Leiden. During his last year of teaching, he had rented the studio above a fish shop. He spent long hours there examining his ideas about painting, working hard at them on canvas. After he'd abandoned Neel, he simply moved in with a hot plate and all the clothes that would fit into a single suitcase.

16

There had been a radio in the room, but he took it down to Stolk, the man who owned the fish shop and his apartment. A single mattress on rough springs occupied one corner and half the length of wall of the small room. His easel stood in front of the window, and he indulged himself by buying a small worktable where he could sit and sketch or spread a newspaper before him and read by the late sun.

What had ultimately precipitated his moving into the studio was not just his hatred of Neel but the fact that he had been fired from the school where he had taught for five years. One day he had simply been called into the headmaster's office and quickly dismissed. His students' parents, who paid well for their children's education, had reported him a lunatic. "Off the wall," several of them had told the headmaster. They claimed he had been committing blasphemy in front of their children. "What is this nonsense, calling on God to pay some debt to you? Scarring your soul? What kinds of things are those to say to children?" the headmaster had asked. Had he done it? Of course he had. But why? I cannot tell you, van Rijks had thought, but I could paint it for you. "I don't know why," he had lied. Then, lamely, he offered, "I'm getting sick, maybe."

At first, he did not tell Neel he had been fired. He simply went to the studio instead. He understood that it had been bad for his students and he felt guilty about that. It had gotten so that he could not stand in front of the class without the children's faces transforming—one at a time—into Johannes's face. Or he would find himself scribbling some lesson about primary colors on the blackboard, and the distinct grip of Johannes's failing hand seemed to clutch his own and change the handwriting to an indistinguishable child's scrawl.

He had visited the psychiatrist, then, and quit him the same day. He would provide his own therapy. He knew that if he could establish some routines to pull himself around, he would be able to work, and so once every three days he shopped for food and used the public bathhouse. Occasionally he brought back a book

17

but could not bring himself to read it, so he stashed each one in the closet. He cooked two meals a day for himself.

But in that room he struggled with two things. The first was that children were death to him now. All it took was a puzzled look, a squeal of laughter, or an instant of frightened incomprehension showing about the eyes at an adult's scolding voice to send him reeling back to those same moments with Johannes. And the resonance of those moments served only to remind him of what he no longer had. When he saw joy, he remembered the absence of joy. He knew this certainly, had it confirmed again the moment that child had sought out his attention on the train. He had felt the brittle frailness through the thin bones of Milos's delicately curved back, and he'd had to fight back the groan that swelled in his throat.

Milos had not been Milos then. He had become Johannes, resurrected from the sweat-soaked sheets, his eyes no longer glazed with fever but full of an infinite blue sparkle. And that moment had brought back to him his abysmal weakness, exactly as it had felt that night as he watched his son succumb to the fever. He had prayed harder than he had ever prayed before for the fever to leave Johannes, that it somehow be transferred to him, who no longer possessed the boundless possibility of innocence. It was not fair to kill children; they had not lived long enough to have done wrong.

The other part of his struggle arose out of the first, and he had assigned an unendurable concreteness to it. At the instant of Johannes's death, he had not been in the room. He had gone into the bathroom to relieve himself. When he returned to his vigil, he found his son, breathless, eyes widened with neither shock nor pain but with a puzzled look that seemed to see some final truth.

He had sat there, for how long he did not know, staring at that face, empty of everything but the last inscrutable vision those eyes had seen, and he began to pray again. Until he realized that even the prayers meant nothing. Then, trembling as if a palsy had seized his limbs, he reached over to Johannes's face to close the lids. His hand shook so violently, though, that the tips of his fingers poked into the eye itself, and for a moment they stuck. A revulsion that jarred him like a severe electric shock coursed up his arm and settled in the very center of his belly. Everything inside him turned to stone coldness, as if he had touched the boy's fleeting soul, and he started to howl. Even now, he carried the feeling of dry pressure from the gelatinous eye on the tips of his fingers, as if they were immutably scarred; he could feel it as clearly as he could now show on any face he chose to draw the deepest recess of its tormented soul.

All this he turned inward, as though the possibility existed that it could be buried inside him, never to resurface. He shunned all his visitors in his new isolation—Neel, the headmaster, an elder from his church—everyone, except Stolk.

Each Friday, Stolk knocked on his door. He always carried two bottles of Amstel beer. Van Rijks would pay the rent immediately, and Stolk would pour out the beer in two small cups to celebrate the end of another week.

Stolk was a stocky man, not more than five years older than van Rijks, but he looked as though he were approaching his sixties. He wore his blood-smeared white coat and white hat in the shop, but when he collected the rent he wore a nylon shirt and sports jacket. His hair had thinned, and he combed it from one ear, over the top of his head, to the other.

On one of his early visits, van Rijks had asked him, "Do you ever get rid of the smell of fish? This whole room smells of fish now."

"My wife says the same thing to me." Stolk looked hurt. "She won't give me a kiss till I soak the smell away in the tub." He palmed the pale skin of his balding head. Then the look on his face changed to a toothy clownish grin. "I'm part fish anyway, didn't you know?" He held out his hands and inspected them, as though he expected to see translucent scales appear.

"Well, here's to the smell of fish," van Rijks said, raising his cup. "It's better than the smell of sour milk."

Stolk looked puzzled. Van Rijks knew why he had said that, but he could not explain himself to the fishman, any more

19

than he could make him know what fever, debilitating fever, smelled like. It smelled like sour milk. If only he could paint that image. . . .

A part of him wanted Stolk to understand, believed that Stolk *could* understand, and yet he felt he would burst before giving words to what stuck in his throat.

"He was a natural artist, you know," van Rijks had told him. "Of all the children I've taught, my son showed the most natural talent. Sure, all parents say that about their children, but Johannes was different. He explored multi-media effects at four years, mixed acrylics at five. He did watercolors at the easel with a sure, confident, steady hand."

Stolk never stopped smiling his pathetic smile. "He must have made you very proud."

"I used to think," van Rijks continued, "that it was not my destiny to be a great artist myself, I've always been more of a copyist. But I had it in me to raise another Vermeer or Rembrandt. He could have been good enough. You could see it. The time and the country and art were ready for it. And now . . ."

"You shouldn't dwell like that on your sadness. It will pass," Stolk offered lamely.

"It will not," van Rijks snapped back. That was why every child's face he drew turned out to be Johannes.

Stolk went into a detailed explanation of how to clean and cook fresh eel, as if he had heard nothing that van Rijks had told him, then left.

On later visits, van Rijks showed his new sketches to Stolk, sketches that were not in any way copied from others. They were horrific studies of anguished faces—mostly children—with undulating skulls, hollow eyes, grimacing lips. Often staring incredulously in the midst of chaotic cityscapes, their eyes, blank as slate, were painfully prominent.

These pictures disturbed Stolk. After looking at them, he would say, "Why don't you paint something happy? Stop thinking so much about it."

Eventually, Stolk stopped coming for the rent. One day, van

Rijks found an envelope shoved under his door with instructions to drop the rent in the mail slot of the fish shop.

He took Stolk's absence as an insult and stopped buying his fish downstairs. He would panfry some chopped beef or pork and eat it with a can of sauerkraut or a plate of boiled rice. He grated bread, then sautéed it with chopped mushrooms and garlic; he even made soup, boiling down a potful of lentils, throwing in the leftover cabbage, carrots, and a bone from the butcher shop. He could not figure out where he had learned these things, but they came easily. He did not need Stolk for company, nor Neel for cooking. He would live quite well with his memories.

He began painting more, using his window, a mirror, and the last light of the sun for a series of self-portraits. He decided that work was the only thing that would pull him out of his tailspin. His clothes became messy from wiping his brushes or charcoal-covered hands on them. He filled his sketch pad, used up all his canvases, and finally began working on the wall itself, as though it were a fresco he had been commissioned to paint.

Each night as he fought to sleep, he would stare at the faces he had drawn on the walls. Then he would pull himself out of bed and pace the room till his legs ached. Sometimes he went two or three days without sleep.

And now, in the narrow room in the Hotel Kap, watching the slow swaying of the naked bulb caused by God knows what movement, he thought that the only thing missing was the frescoed wall from Leiden bearing the crowd of glinting eyes. Their laser-like stares seemed to generate a light of their own as they looked off in infinite directions.

No, he could not so easily give himself up to sleep. He thought if he opened his portfolio, he could release all that torment into the room and feel quite at home. But he was going to sell it all because he was low on money, and those that he didn't sell he would destroy with fire.

He spread the foil packet that Molen had given him on his paint box, took a razor blade from his toilet kit, and chopped some of the white powder as Molen had explained. *What is it?* It'll relax you, Molen's voice now taunted him. He could do the powder and try to relax. Or he could open the portfolio; but if he did, he might never sleep again. He knew that now. He shoveled some of the crystals onto the edge of the blade and put it to his nose. Then he repeated the process, feeling his eyeteeth and throat go numb.

Immediately his heart began to pump faster. His nose burned and his eyes began to tear. "Goddamn that bastard, Molen," he said. "Goddamn them all."

2

Pieter Beckum sat at his desk in the restoration studio at the top of the Rijksmuseum's east tower, staring blankly at a personnel report in front of him. An inordinate number of sirens had shattered the still morning on the street below; the shrill, grating noise had set his teeth on edge. Light poured through the huge window behind him; it was a leaden gray that promised a cold steady drizzle for the remainder of the day.

Fifteen minutes earlier, he had interviewed a young student from the University of Amsterdam, sent to him by a former colleague for a period of apprenticeship. He would have to reject the boy—and, worse, he would have to explain why to his friend. There just was not enough work to keep another apprentice busy. Also, he hadn't had an independent commission in months. He was forced to drag pieces out of the vaults to keep Demmie working—cleanings, relinings, and retouchings of minor works of little value. Not since Vermeer's *The Letter* was slashed from its frame by some blackmailing thieves had he had a challenge worthy of his background.

Even the museum appropriations committee had sensed the lull in his department. Recently, they had given him trouble in getting supplies. The sales desk, cafeteria, and movie theater all got their money ahead of him. The committee cut his budget by one third and increased the others proportionately. He even resorted to pleading with the Director General. "Let me pay my apprentices a stipend to keep them going while there are no masterworks." The Director General had flatly refused: "It's all a matter of economics." Two of his apprentices had left within a week—one to a small museum in Paris, the other to the Maurits-huis in The Hague. He couldn't blame them. Had he been in their shoes, he would have gone also.

At first, he felt embarrassed to have to inform his colleague of his distressing state of affairs, as if word would spread through the museum community like a summer fire through dry grass. But he knew, too, that it was not simply economics that made him reject the boy—Theillen was his name. If he had had all the money in the world, he would probably have denied Theillen.

He began making notes for the letter of rejection. He had never taken on a university-trained apprentice. Like himself, all his students were sent from master restorers, not schools. He believed, somehow, that universities eased an apprentice's hard way, and he would never really be happy with one in his studio.

And Theillen did not have the attributes of a restorer. In that brief interview, Pieter saw things that no master restorer would tolerate in his studio. For one thing, the boy showed too much impatience. He fidgeted constantly in his chair; his fingernails were chewed to the nub. He knew they were silly things to pick on, but they added to his overall feelings about the boy. No, he would not have done at all. The business of restoration required an obsessive patience (something universities could not teach); it was tedious, and, he had to admit after so many years, sometimes boring work. A boy like that would make mistakes, and God forbid if they were on a Caravaggio or a Vermeer.

He had had no such feelings of foreboding about Demmie de Graaf before he took her on. Though he had never accepted a woman apprentice before, nor for that matter ever heard of one, she had turned out splendidly after her first year. She had come highly recommended after working with a master restorer in England whom he had long admired. She had put herself through school without the help of her parents or stipends; she did well on her examinations; she was fluent in three languages and spoke with uncanny insight about art.

24

In the apprentice's studio next door he could hear her now, humming a song that had become popular on the radio this spring and played in all the cafés. It was a lilting, melancholy tune, perfect for the drizzly grayness of the day, perfect too for creating an imprecise longing in the pit of his stomach.

The day he had interviewed her, he had liked her instantly. She sat across the desk from him, her back as straight as a ruled line, wearing a solid mask of self-confidence. On first sight, her frightfully wild hair made her look simply shaggy, like a sheep hound, but as he studied her practiced look of determination, he saw through the coarseness as he might see through the layers of discolored varnish of a Baroque painting. There emerged an original beauty: pale, slightly large eyes; nose a bit too short for the length of her face, but fine and thin as though she were quite used to breathing hot clean air; wing-shaped, too red lips, the bottom one a little thicker than the top.

When she had introduced herself, she had shaken his hand with the strength of a stevedore and he noticed that her hands, like her eyes and lips, were also too large. He found himself staring at them as he asked her about the Jan Steen on which she had assisted his colleague, Mr. Harmenz.

As she answered, he realized that he was not paying attention. His eyes followed her hands as they fluttered about in front of her. She seemed powerful, dignified. And yet he knew there was a vulnerability, though he could not then name it, somewhere inside her. That simple contradiction intrigued him.

The only negative mark he had recorded on his balance sheet had been for her clothes. He simply did not understand them. It seemed as though she had deliberately chosen them from the flea markets and the glitter boutiques along the Kalverstraat. She had mixed an antique blouse and skirt of contrasting colors with modern cowboy boots and long silk scarfs, and though the clothes on anyone else would look as though the person had stepped from an asylum, on her they looked extravagant, eccentric—even, he had to admit, attractive.

As he thought about her, he had to smile. This morning, when the members of their group were making their rounds before the museum opened, she had stopped them in front of Rembrandt's *The Night Watch* to present her recommendations for future work. He required each of his apprentices to do this. And true to form, she had chosen one of the most difficult of all pieces.

The morning group included two visiting apprentices from Brussels; Stan Martins, the frame-maker; and three fine-arts students from the University of Amsterdam. They had gathered about her in a semicircle, and he moved to the rear so he wouldn't make her self-conscious.

He watched her closely as she recited the litany of the painting's marred history. Her voice rose and fell expressively, as if she were onstage. "Completed in 1642, *The Night Watch* was hung in the guild hall of the militiamen who are portrayed in it. Some years later, it was removed to the Town Hall, where some fools cut in on all four sides so it would fit through the door. Two entire figures on the left-hand side were completely lopped off."

She stood a head above everyone in the group, and as she talked, waving her hands expansively, Pieter noticed she was absentmindedly stepping backward. The heel of her boot caught on the tapestry rug on the floor, setting off a high-pitched alarm. Everyone was startled, crowding into each other, mumbling "What's going on? What's happening?" When she removed her heel, the bell died.

"Jesus, that scared me," she said, laughing.

A wan-faced guard came running through the gallery door, a whistle poised at his lips, but when he saw Pieter he nodded and backed out. The group gave a nervous titter.

"Anyway," she continued, walking to the side where the two figures had been cut off, "the entire composition was thrown out of balance. If you'll notice, the two grandly dressed central figures —Banning Cocq and Lieutenant van Ruytenburch—who appear to be stepping right out of the painting, were not intended to be the center of balance, though they are now."

One of the art students interrupted her to ask what she thought the center was. She looked suddenly annoyed.

26

"Geometrically," she said, "it is that triangular portion of face on the most receding plane of action. What some critics call Rembrandt's face. Simply an eye, nose, a foppish hat. But dramatically the painting was never meant to have a precise focal point. The lines of the picture plane diffuse the focus so that the figures seem to be moving in more than two dimensions. Kind of a dramatic synthesis. Shades of light and dark; movement and rest."

Pieter interrupted to mention that there were other areas of previous damage. He told the students, "Past restorers, acting in good faith, cut out weakened portions of the painting and replaced them with newer, stronger canvas, then retouched the areas.

"The easiest way to tell the scars is by noticing that the inpainting done in this manner darkens differently from the paint on the original canvas." He showed them the darker, retouched hole in the drum in the extreme right corner. "From a distance, this is difficult to see, but the hole should never have been repaired in this fashion."

Demmie summarized her recommendations by explaining that a good cleaning was in order, because most of the extreme darkness of the painting, which people wrongfully attributed to Rembrandt's technique, was actually due to a blueing effect in the varnish from humidity and moisture in the spectators' breath. Finally, she said, "It is ironic that what gives people life—their breath—takes the life out of the paintings."

When she asked if there were any questions, the same fine-arts student, a young long-haired man, pointed to what she called the geometric center of the painting. "If you stare hard," he said, looking neither at her nor at the painting, "that face bears a remarkable resemblance to Rembrandt. Is there any proof—"

"Could be," she said, breaking off his question. Then she began to stroll toward the gallery door, as if the question had never been asked.

Pieter came around in front of the group. "Let's move on," he said. "The museum will be open soon." He would remind her, when he saw her later, that diplomacy was also part of a restorer's bag of artifice. Biology, chemistry, art history, a little detective work, diplomacy, and so on.

He lagged behind and patiently explained to the young man, more out of embarrassment for her curtness than anything else, that Rembrandt had done more self-portraits, and had painted his broad, ugly face into more paintings, than perhaps any other artist and might very well have done so here.

"I know that," the boy said. Pieter felt an unexplainable burn of anger rise in his throat. What was going on here? He did not know how, but in some way he felt he had just been made the fool.

By noon, Pieter decided he had spent enough time pining over delicate ways to tell his colleague that he couldn't accept the new apprentice. He rode the elevator to the first floor for lunch.

He sat at a small table on the north side of the museum cafeteria where the windows nearly reached the top of the high, vaulted ceiling, flooding his corner with flat gray light. The faint fragrance of fresh-cut flowers on the table in front of him made him wish that he was walking through the tree-shaded lanes of the Vondel Park with Demmie instead of listening to the excited racket from the schoolchildren having lunch across the room.

Henk, the busboy, a little balding man in a blue tunic who looked like a circus clown without makeup, stopped at his table. "Good day, Mr. Beckum," he said, clearing some dishes off the table next to Pieter's.

"Working hard, Henk?"

"Same as usual. These damned tour people are pigs." Henk's pouting mouth turned even farther down at the corners.

Pieter ignored his complaint. "Where are you and the missus taking your holiday this year?"

"Don't as yet know," Henk said. "How do you eat that stuff?" He pointed to the raw herring and onions on Pieter's plate.

Pieter shrugged. He gulped a hunk of herring, chewed it quickly, then chased it with a swallow of beer.

28

There was a commotion at the head of the crowded cafeteria line. Someone was trying to fight through, and people were resisting.

"Excuse me," an officious voice boomed. "Pardon."

Then Jan Hansson, the museum's public-relations man, burst through. He looked like a harried, fat little child pushing through a thick hedgerow, and Pieter laughed. Henk shook his head.

"I'm glad I found you," Jan said, huffing as he slid a chair beside Pieter's. His face was flushed from his battle with the crowd. His deep-set eyes danced nervously, never focusing for long on anything, and Pieter found himself wanting to ask if he was about to have an attack of some kind.

Jan shot his thumb over his shoulder. "Animals, they are. Wouldn't let a body push through even if it was an emergency."

"And is it an emergency, Jan?"

Henk looked at Jan as though offended by his presence and scuttled off to clean more tables.

Jan picked up a piece of Pieter's herring and shoved it into his mouth. "Christ, how do you eat this?" He washed his mouth with Pieter's beer.

"Put more onions on it and you won't taste the fish."

"What's the point in eating it, then?"

"Tradition."

"The Queen's coming," Jan said. "I just got a call from The Hague. It seems that our Royal Highness has persuaded the good Prince Bernhard to have her shuttled through as some sort of birthday present."

"Do I detect a note of sarcasm in your voice?"

"Just a note."

"What's up, then, Jan? She's been here before."

"It's not every day that Juliana decides to visit our house. We'll have to arrange things. Security. Media coverage."

"Why trouble me? Media's your department. And the police take care of security."

"I'm just excited," Jan said. "Did you hang the Vermeer yet?"

Pieter stabbed a silver-gray hunk of fish with a toothpick and held it out to Jan. It was smothered with raw chopped onions. "Try it this way."

"No, thanks. My stomach." He patted his soft paunch.

"Ulcer?"

"I hope not."

"Juliana's visit will give you one, if you don't already have it."

"Please," Jan said. "What about the Vermeer? It's been done for nearly two months."

"I can't hang it yet. The varnish is going to take another two weeks to dry properly."

"With that painting out, it's like having company over with the couch missing. You've got to hang it."

"I don't have to do any such thing, and you know it," Pieter said, instantly resenting Jan's obvious attempt to pressure him. "All I have to do is see that that painting lasts forever. It cannot be hung."

"You're right, of course," Jan said, his eyes settling on Pieter's plate. "But you're a prig, just the same, for not doing it." He pushed out of his chair and scurried down the aisle, disappearing through the line of tourists more easily this time.

Pieter continued his lunch, wondering, too, why the hell he was eating herring. It had no real taste, covered as it was with raw onions. Its consistency was somewhat like cold, soft cheese. *What's the point in eating it, then?* Jan had asked. *Tradition,* he'd answered, a strangely powerful word, one that allowed people to say and do things without the slightest thought. He had, for example, just rejected some boy, who may have dreamed of becoming a restorer all his life, because he did not fit with the tradition. The art of restoration itself had always been passed from master to apprentice, not taught in some university, and that, he believed, was as unassailable as divine doctrine. But another part of him knew that the blind acceptance of tradition was the cause of many an unexamined life. Routines became easy to fall into; ennui set in. And that was a living death, of sorts. He pushed the plate of herring aside, deciding not to finish it, nor ever to order it again. If he stopped to think about it for half a second, he had to admit that he really didn't like it. And Theillen? He would have to stay rejected anyway.

"Hoo-hoo, Pieter." The voice, high, lilting, and distinct, wafted to him above the buzzing of the cafeteria.

Demmie was making her way among the tables. With her tray balanced on one hand above her head, she moved with the precision of a waitress. Her tightly curled hair bounced with a rhythm all its own. She let out another "Hoo-hoo," and everyone turned. She didn't notice, nor would she have cared about them, he thought, if she had. If anyone were to examine his life, her presence in it would not make sense. But she had caught his affection as surely as if she had set a well-camouflaged trap.

He knew that soon after he took her on. She was attractive and he was attracted to her. She was also very good at her work. He knew better than to mix romance with restoration (it would be disastrous). But he had never had a woman apprentice before, and had never known a woman like Demmie, and so it had always been easy to forgo emotional relationships that might impinge upon his work. Though he had thought of himself as a man of certain answers in his self-contained world, with her he found he did not even know the questions.

Then all his confusion about how to deal with her ended six months, ago when the rough times began at the museum—when his funds were being cut, when his apprentices were leaving. She stayed with him, offered her friendship and support, and he accepted it gratefully.

Sometimes they went to the Leidseplein and sat in a café and talked: he about his problems with the Director General; she about her dancing, her boyfriend. She was easy to talk with, wonderfully open in ways that most women of Pieter's age could not or would not be. Frank, sometimes blunt, she was always honest, so much so that he often felt as if he were talking with a child who did not understand that what she had just said (too loudly) was embarrassingly accurate.

Now, as Demmie slipped into the chair Jan had drawn beside

31

Pieter, she asked, "What did he want?" She inclined her head toward the door.

"Be nice," he said.

"I am nice." She wore a forest-green leotard without a bra. A pink silk scarf wrapped her neck several times and hung to her knees.

"And speaking of being nice, you were awfully rude to that art student this morning. You should have more patience, even with stupid questions."

"He was rude to me," she countered. "He'd been trying to make it with me all morning, brushing up against me and all. I just felt like doing something cruel to him."

"Well, in trying to rectify your behavior," he said, "I ended up looking the fool."

"All due respect, but you shouldn't try to rectify my behavior." She emphasized his words. "You never told me what Jan wanted."

She had a plate of cold salad and a half liter of rosé on her tray. She forked some lettuce into her mouth and broke off a piece of bread.

"Jan wanted nothing so far as I could make out. Other than to pressure me into hanging that Vermeer before the varnish is thoroughly dried. Listen," he said, catching the scent of her perfume, "why don't we sneak away for the rest of the afternoon? I don't have any more work to do."

"You don't have to sneak away. You're not married. Besides, I can't. I have to teach a dance class."

"I'd love to watch," he said.

"You can't today, Pieter. Sorry."

Since it was the museum's policy not to pay apprentices, except for special projects, Demmie made her living by teaching intermediate and advanced jazz at a dance studio on the Prinsengracht. When she invited him to come, he took immense pleasure in watching the dancers' lines as they tried to conquer space. At very rare times, when they were really on, he believed they dealt with form, and planes, and values of light and dark, movement and rest—drama in a kinetic form—just as precisely as his precious paintings did.

God, he wanted to touch her then. Her lips shone with oil from the salad. He wanted to put his arm around her and draw her close. He knew there was nothing wrong with that, except that he couldn't bear having it spread about—among Henk, and the guards, and the cashiers—that the Chief Restorer had been seen cuddling his apprentice in the cafeteria. Demmie had mockingly called it his "sense of propriety," but he was fifteen years older than she, and propriety was something he understood as a way to get by.

What made him believe that he could touch her, what gave hope to his longing for her, a certain palpability to his desire, were two wonderfully intimate moments that had had their beginning in the studio a month before. He had been watching her varnish a small modern piece, and the rhythm of her hand with the large brush was simply too jerky.

"Why are you shaking?" he had asked.

"Would you hand me a mahlstick?"

He did. "Are you feeling all right?"

She continued varnishing, using the mahlstick—a long stick with a padded end—to prop her wrist and steady it. "My boyfriend wrote me a letter, Pieter. He said we were through. That he wouldn't travel from England any more to see me. Couldn't afford it. Economics. Shit," she said.

He placed his hands on her shoulders, feeling at once fatherly toward her. Subdued tremors quavered through her neck and shoulders.

"Think I'll get over it?" she asked. Then she stopped altogether, and though she did not make a sound, he knew she was crying.

Afterward, he had told himself that it had been the varnish fumes, no extracting fans working in the room, the faint smell of salt on her neck, the iridescent lines in the cornea of her brilliant blue eyes, the single tear that ran from the corner of her right eye to her chin as she turned to him, that had made him falter, had made him brush her glossed lips with his.

He had told her that she would be all right.

She had said, "I'm going to get drunk." And she left the studio.

That night he had searched the cafés for her, worried that she had gotten too drunk to take care of herself.

Then after he had tracked her down, he put her in his car and took her home. She'd spilled liquor all down the front of her, and as he carried her up the stairs, he had felt how wet she was. Inside, he undressed her, lingering over the removal of each item of clothing, savoring her accumulating nakedness, and put her to bed.

He had never wanted anyone so sorely in all his life. The touch of her skin was silken. There had been a moment when the thought danced through his head to take his own clothes off, to slide in beside her and touch those secret places; but he had not.

The next day, she had thanked him. She told him most boys she knew would have thrown her over the arm of the couch and had their way with her.

Yes, he wanted her, but he wanted her to make the choice.

3

Van Rijks woke up to a glaring sun in his eyes; it burned through the thin gauze curtains, and he tried to swat it away. It was such a nuisance. Then he lay still awhile and watched the silvered dust motes twirling in the column of light. He realized that he had fallen asleep fully dressed and without having removed his suitcase from the foot of the bed. Whatever Molen had given him had worked. At first, with the numbing and the loud pounding of his heart against his sternum, he thought the bastard had played a cruel trick on him; but it was morning now, and he was alive, and he had made it through the night untroubled for the first time in ages.

He rolled out of bed and, at the sink in the corner, splashed water on his face, then changed into a pair of denim pants, a long-sleeved pullover, and a bright yellow cardigan sweater. For some reason, he felt unbelievably irritated. Your face looks like shit, he thought, staring at the puffed eyes in the mirror above the sink. Drops of water glistened in his tawny beard; his head had been sheared so closely that his scalp shone through in spots as though he had the mange. Lately, he hated this time of morning, with the sun so bright that it burned through everything. The quality of light was so clear, so intense, that it seemed as though nothing could hide from it. Dust balls in the corner of the room glowed; rain spots or film on windows showed gray, like a fog; the dark rings that looped so generously under his eyes, dimmed by the night, looked like troughs of rich soil. Stolk celebrated the end of each week; van Rijks celebrated the end of each day.

Mrs. Kolb was not in the lobby when he came downstairs. He ducked through a small door and into the dining room. Three wooden tables, each covered with a red-and-white checkered tablecloth, filled the room. Mrs. Kolb was stooped over one, removing the unused place settings of those guests who she had decided were too late for breakfast.

"Sit down," she said gruffly, not bothering to turn. "It's two minutes before, but I'll get your breakfast anyway. Sit down."

"And good morning to you, good lady," van Rijks said as amicably as he could. His voice sounded tinny, and he was still a little dizzy from the drug Molen had given him. The thick tannic smell of burnt coffee filled the room.

When she finally turned, he seemed to have surprised her. "Oh, it's you," she said. "Did Rembrandt sleep well?"

He resented her sarcasm. Is it something about the way I look? he asked himself. He felt his beard. Perhaps it was missing. Then he vaguely remembered that she had gotten the name from him, something he had said or done yesterday.

She disappeared through the kitchen door, shaking her head. There was a clattering of dishes. After a moment, she reappeared with a coffeepot in one hand and a plate of ham, cheese, and toast in the other. She shoved them onto the table in front of him.

"Orange juice is extra," she said.

He felt like giving her the back of his hand. He had done nothing, and she was treating him like shit. He looked at the clock; it was just past nine. He felt a kink in his cheek and realized he was making a face. More dishes clanged in the kitchen; he could hear her cursing. Cursing him? He rolled a slice of ham and a piece of cheese together and put them into his mouth. The sound of his chewing dissolved the sound of the bitch's voice and the metronomic ticking of the clock on the mantel.

He had to meet Molen sometime this morning. That had been the last thing he remembered about last night, but he could not recall where. His irritability increased with this frustrating lapse of memory.

36

Mrs. Kolb poked her head out once, and when she saw he was not finished, she shouted, "Come on! I've got beds to make too. I'm not just kitchen maid. I do everything around here!"

Her shrill voice so startled him that he slammed his cup to the table, splashing coffee high in the air and all over himself. "And I do everything!" he yelled back. He turned, expecting to see Neel's face, but it wasn't and he became frightened with himself. He had wanted to mimic her, but it had come out too violently.

"Easy," Mrs. Kolb said, backing against the doorjamb. She ducked quickly back inside and closed the door. Then he heard the click of the latch being thrown.

Damn, this trip was turning out worse than he could have expected. All he had wanted was to clear his mind so that he could make a new start. Yet from the first instant he stepped on the train, it appeared as though anything but that would happen.

He pushed away from the table, leaving the rest of his breakfast on his plate. He could not eat now. He had not meant to yell at that leather-skinned old bag, and he felt guilty for frightening her. He wanted to knock as he passed the kitchen door, to tell her he was finished and that he was sorry, but he could not bear the possibility of finding her cowering under the sink.

A sharp pain throbbed against his temples and across his forehead. *What is it now? How much more can a man take?* He rushed back upstairs for his portfolio, paint box, and sketch pad, which he had put into carrying bags. Afterward, when he crossed the lobby and finally stepped outside, the pain vanished as quickly as it had come, which surprised him.

He walked in the crisp, cold morning air, up the Keizersgracht to the Raadhuisstraat, and turned toward the center of the city. All the narrow-fronted shops that lined the brick sidewalks were closed. He passed a group of small children playing in the cobblestone street. They were wearing bright clothes and crude paper crowns, adorned with crayoned royal jewels. Some of them were singing "Happy Birthday," while others, four abreast with arms linked, marched toward him along the sidewalk. As they approached, his chest began to tighten and blood pounded against the backs of his eyes. There was a tall girl who looked like Johannes. In any group there was always one, and he could not tell if he was seeing him or if he was imagining seeing him. He wanted to yell to them to stay away.

The children circled him. He had to fight down the pounding inside him. "Did you make those crowns in school?" he blurted. "They're very beautiful."

The tallest girl stepped forward. "Yes," she said. *She* had Johannes's face. She took off her crown, and as he stooped before her, she put it on his head. The other children burst into laughter. "You may keep it," she said and reached out to shake his hand. He released his bags. She had fine alabaster skin. He could see faint violet webs of veins showing on her neck.

When he stood up, her small hand still in his, the surge of blood caused him to stagger. His vision blurred momentarily, sending two little jags of lightning across his lids. "Where is he?" he asked her.

"Who?" the child said.

The circle of children began to sing "Happy Birthday" to him, as though it were really his birthday and not the Queen's. The tips of his ears burned, and the children's loud cackly voices, violently out of tune, upset him.

"Stop singing!" he commanded. Then he added, "Please."

The tall girl was not singing. Her eyes were wide, terrified; her mouth was agape, but no sound issued, and yet it seemed that the entire cacophony was coming from her. If only he could put his palm over her mouth, the others would stop. She squealed then, and the circle broke, scattering like a flock of startled pigeons. But he had managed to hold fast the girl's hand. It quivered in his, sending ripples of warm fear up his arm to his shoulder.

"Let go of me!" she cried. "Please!"

"It will be all right, Johannes," he said soothingly.

She tugged once, hard, against his grip and broke free, then ran to join her friends clustered down the street. "Monster!" they were yelling. "Help us, somebody!"

He picked up his bags and ran, and their screaming seemed to follow him. He could still feel the trembling warmth of the hand that had quivered in his. I have to find somebody I know. Where is Neel now? Molen? Anyone? When he finally stopped running, he was looking in the window of a small corner barbershop.

He removed the paper crown and studied his reflection in the glass. He *was* a monster: the beard, the wild eyes, the ragged hair. Fix yourself up and you will feel better. But, more important, change your looks in case those kids send a cop after you. He crumpled the crown and tossed it in the gutter.

"Can you give me a shave?" he asked the barber, who was sweeping a pile of downy hair across the floor. A neat roll of fat circled his waist, jiggling as his arms worked the broom.

He looked at van Rijks, a smile cracking his pudgy face, then said, "I can do something with the hair too, if you like. Make it neater."

"Fine."

"Sit down," the barber said. He pumped up the chair and wrapped a leather apron around van Rijks's neck. When he spoke, he talked into the mirror. "There's not much to cut on top."

"Cut it anyway."

He watched the barber study his head. Then the barber looked into the mirror, as though they were talking face to face, and said, "Rumor has it that Juliana's going to be at the Dam this afternoon. That'll be something new, you know? Usually, she stays at her—"

"Do me a favor," van Rijks interrupted. He had watched the barber talk to his reflection for only a few minutes but it maddened him. That, and the fast *click-click* of scissors at his ear. "Turn the chair away from the mirror, all right?"

"Sure. What's the matter?"

"Nothing." He was starting to feel ashamed because he had frightened the children. He did not dare go back to try to explain to them.

"You going?" the barber asked. "To the Dam?" He kept up a stream of patter about Juliana and Prince Bernhard for the entire haircut and shave as though he knew them personally.

When the barber finished, van Rijks did not look like the same man who had come through the door a few minutes ago. He ran his hands over his cheeks. In fact, he did not *feel* like the same man. He felt clean and different, new. The first thing he noticed when he stepped outside was the naked sensation of cold wind blowing on his beardless face.

The Dam was aswirl with hectic activity. The streets had been cordoned off by the police in every direction. On the Queen's birthday, everyone was allowed to sell anything he or she wanted on the streets, and people spread out their blankets and tables, side by side, all over the city, offering everything from the useless to the personal. Van Rijks had never been to Amsterdam on this day, contenting himself always to stay in Leiden or to go for a drive in the country. Children offered old comics and speed skates they had outgrown; adults sold clothes, broken appliances, pornographic magazines. Canopied stands had been set up by vendors to sell fresh herring, patate frites, and sandwiches.

Van Rijks knew it would be impossible to find Molen, so he settled himself in a clear area by the police barricades where the Damrak turned into the Rokin. He arranged his drawings—some matted and ready for frames; others, like the sketch he had made of Milos and his mother on the train, roughly sketched on poor paper, but for sale just the same. Then he turned his paint box on end and sat on it, looking at the sheer madness around him and feeling as though he had just sat down in a foreign country.

Along the back of the Square, people were jammed into bleachers half as high as the giant columnal War Memorial. Across the plaza, a gaily colored gazebo had been erected where the Queen would eventually stand to receive those subjects who had brought her gifts.

Before him, a large band, dressed in dark, antique double-breasted velvet coats and three-cornered hats, tuned their instruments. At a table set up in the middle of the crowd, several chefs baked their special pastries. By another table, men wove great straw baskets; their women close by, in starched lace hats and blue aprons, worked silk in spinning wheels. A pock-faced man with a giant red handlebar mustache stood near him, puffing on a clay pipe and carving shoes out of rough blocks of pale wood.

"Is this a birthday or a circus?" van Rijks muttered.

"Why, it's a circus, of course," said a voice behind him.

He was so stunned by hearing an answer, the right answer, that he felt hot tinglings in his joints. He jerked a look over his shoulder, and there was that weasel-faced Molen, much paler in the sunlight, small eyes deeply shadowed behind the tinted lenses.

"I told you I'd meet you here," he said. "What do you think —I'd bullshit?" He wore the same bright turtleneck and, van Rijks supposed, the same jeans that he had worn last night. They were well wrinkled.

"There's a better place closer to the center," Molen said. "Come on, let's move. You'll sell more." He started to gather the drawings.

"Leave them where they are!" van Rijks commanded. Molen froze at the tone. With measured calm, van Rijks continued, "I like it fine here."

"Yeah, well, I'm going to wander about for a bit, then." Molen started off.

Van Rijks picked up his sketch pad and opened a pen. He stared past Molen.

"I was only trying to be helpful," Molen called back to him. He looked wounded.

In the very center of the plaza, a huge mat had been laid out. Tumblers wearing white tights threw themselves tirelessly along the mat, their arms and legs splayed in cartwheels, righting themselves with a flip at the end, then beginning the exhausting journey again. Nearby, gymnasts worked uneven parallel bars, spinning, hooking, and flipping to dismount. Van Rijks sketched as rapidly as his hand could move.

A trumpet sounded, and everyone turned. A column of soldiers marched into the plaza, halting in front of the Royal Palace. The band nearby began to herald the Queen's entrance, and the doors of the palace slowly opened. Van Rijks put his pad down, stood, and moved a little closer, like everyone else, to see what was going to happen. People were packing in behind him, and he realized that he had done something stupid. He had left his work unattended. He looked back frenziedly over the crowd, trying to regain his bearings, but he was totally confused, as if the mechanism in his brain that kept vertigo from intruding upon balance had somehow malfunctioned.

He heard three sharply pitched barks from the soldiers' commander, but they did not register with him. When three deafening volleys followed in quick succession, sounding like peals of close thunder, he became so frightened that his heart shuddered. His pulse rose, fluttering like the wings of startled birds, first into his temple, then down into his belly, and for an instant he swayed dizzily. Then he began bouncing up and down to see over the people's heads, to see where he had left his work. He knew one thing: he was being pushed farther away. He couldn't figure out which way to go, and he shoved the people away from him, clearing a path. Some idiot knelt before him, glasses perched on top of his head, a camera poised at his eye, snapping away at him, and he kicked him aside, nearly falling in the process. "Asshole!" van Rijks yelled at him.

The Queen had come out the palace doors and was already in the gazebo. A line had formed in front of van Rijks, a solid stream of people circling slowly toward the gazebo. Police stood at arm's length at the boundary of the line. Finally, he could see his paint box on the other side, and he began pushing through the people. Someone was going to trample his work. Or worse.

A thin, bearded policeman stopped him as he tried to press on.

"But I have to get to the other side!" he protested.

"You'll have to stay in line, like everyone else."

"I can see them from here. Those are my drawings. I have to get over there!"

When the policeman turned to look where he was pointing, van Rijks made a wild effort to burst through. He'd seen a man standing over his drawings—a man of Molen's type—and he knew the man was going to steal one. He heard himself yelling that he had to get past, then felt himself going down hard on the cobblestones as the policeman tackled him about the knees.

He was trying to kick free, shouting, "A man was standing by my drawings! Looking around. He was going to steal one!" His heart pounded more wildly than when he had been frightened by the rifle volleys. He couldn't kick off the dreadful, clamping weight at his knees. Whistles were going off, painfully shrill. Somehow he had gotten into a wrestling match. He wanted it all to stop, but someone was pounding his kidneys now, and the hurt made him twist wildly, striking back at the uniformed figure. Suddenly he was on his feet. There were police uniforms all around him and hands tugging at him, this way and that. They were leading him away. They were going to arrest him.

People's faces turned to him. They looked angry, as though he had spoiled their whole goddamned party. And there was Molen's face. He did not look like a weasel now.

"Molen!" he called out. "Here!"

Molen pushed through. The circle of police kept him and Molen separated. "Get my stuff!" he yelled. "It's over that way. You know where it is."

Molen looked indifferent, almost as though he had never met him before.

"Molen, it's me," he said. "Remember? Please." Had he spoiled the party for Molen too? What was everyone so upset about? He was not a troublemaker.

Finally, Molen said, "What do I do with it?"

The police were pushing him into a blue Volkswagen van. One of them called him a tough and shoved him. His mind shut down. He could not even recall his hotel's name, or any other familiar place in this city. They were going to slam the door on him, and he had to make a decision.

"At the museum," Molen called out to him. "I'll wait for you there, the Rijksmuseum."

"Thank God," van Rijks said.

The van lurched, throwing him back in his seat. He did not

know what was going to happen but he was not so scared now that Molen was going to take care of his work. He was a bit bruised up, and knew the police probably were too.

He could not stop the drumming of fear in his chest. Its pitch was intensifying; he was sure the cops in the front of the van could hear it. Then he felt as if he were being deprived of oxygen, that his blood was heating up and he was about to burst. He heard his breathing, which sounded more like panting, and he could figure none of this out.

Then a reason came to him: Molen was a weasel. He would sell his life's work and keep the money, and he would never see the bastard again.

And another reason came: He had no one in the world he could turn to now, and he needed to have someone.

And another: Johannes, at five, had showed he would be a better painter than his father, and a part of him was jealous and hated the child.

And another: Johannes was dead.

And another: Where were these fucking cops taking him?

Slowly he felt his sinuses swelling and water welling up in his eyes. A tear sliced down his cheek, and he began to sob.

4

Pieter Beckum had come to the Dam this Saturday morning to take pictures. He had made arrangements to photograph Demmie's dance class with the new lens he'd bought for his Nikon; however, without giving him a reason, she had canceled at the last minute. Except for the resorts, almost every shop and business in the country was closed while, true to tradition, his fellow countrymen spilled into the streets to celebrate Juliana's birthday. He likened their devotion to his own eating of herring. It was just something Dutchmen did.

Two weeks before, when he and Demmie had spent a lunchtime walking through the Vondel Park, she had made the point that it was a disgrace to have such a fine camera and never use it. They had stopped at the café by the lake for a glass of wine.

"I use it often," he told her. "For work." It was necessary that he record every phase of each restoration on film. You never knew what you might have to go back to if there was a foul-up.

"But why don't you take pictures of beautiful sunsets at the beach?" she asked. "Or silk-white swans in a pond in front of a windmill? Or," she said, laughing, and hiking her long denim skirt up her thighs, "beautiful women?" He stared at her legs. Dancer's legs. Muscled thighs and calves honed from pale ivory.

He almost asked her to pull her skirt down, to stop being so outrageous, but he found himself laughing instead. "You're right, I suppose. Would you pose for me?"

"Only if you practice on something other than paintings and

become very artistic. There's more to life than just one's work."

She had said that to him before. That was why she pursued dance, and rode a motorcycle, and did all sorts of unpredictable things. Before he had met her, he would not have entertained such thoughts. His father had been a restorer too; he had thought and talked nothing else. Pieter had been raised to believe there *was* nothing else.

So he had come to the Queen's birthday celebration to practice with his lenses. And to observe another meaningless tradition because he had nothing better to do. He strolled among the people, snapping picture after picture. When he heard the trumpets sound, he climbed the first row of bleachers to photograph Juliana's entrance. A phalanx of soldiers filed into the Square, forming two parallel lines at parade rest. Their commander shouted orders, and they snapped their rifles up to their shoulders. They fired volley after volley; the sounds of the blasts tightened Pieter's chest.

His breathing became so ragged that he could not hold the camera still. He knew people, his age and older, whose memories of the war, triggered by the sound of a German accent or some unique association of their own, would send them reeling backward thirty years in time. Just a few years ago, one friend of his had had a nervous breakdown when he was detained at the German border; another jumped at the sound of forceful knocking at her door.

For Pieter, it was the sound of gunfire. Standing here, in the Dam, with the War Memorial behind him, he remembered his father showing him a photograph of massacred Amsterdammers, taken as the Nazis retreated from their city.

"You see that man there," his father had said, pointing. Pieter squinted. "You know him. We bought food from him."

But all Pieter had seen was a twisted figure, a black fan of blood in the gutter under its head. Then he recognized the man's eyes, the shape of his face.

"Remember that," his father had said. "That's what people are capable of." And he did remember.

46

The memories never left him, though they did not visit him so often any more. They surfaced at unexpected moments, saddened him, then disappeared, leaving their aftertaste, leaving too the knowledge of the precariousness of his own life.

He resumed taking pictures with a clear shot of Juliana's harried face and upraised arm as she signaled the beginning of the processional to the banner-draped gazebo. He fought back the dread that churned in his stomach. The line in front of him now —thousands long, five and six abreast—began its slow march.

On ordinary spring days, this plaza, overseen by the palace's giant sculpture of Atlas carrying the globe on his backstretched arms, was filled with flocks of dirty pigeons, with hippies who sold dope to tourists, with ice-cream vendors and herring men. Today there were more gypsies than Pieter could count, their heads wrapped in brightly colored kerchiefs, their bodies in even brighter clothes, filing into the line with bouquets of bright tulips to present to Juliana. The former colonies were represented too —Moluccans, Indonesians, a smattering of Africans, all carrying gifts.

He had gone through an entire roll of film before he found what he considered a decent subject. A man, whose hair was cropped so close that he could see the sheen of white scalp through dark stubble and who wore a bright yellow cardigan, was pushing people away from himself. He looked wide-eyed, perhaps claustrophobic in the extreme. He began turning, bouncing—a nearly bald head shooting up, then sinking into the crowd.

Pictures without a subject were merely snapshots, Pieter thought. Demmie would be the first to appreciate the photo essay he would do of this bird. He thought that photographers, like painters, required specific subjects, no matter how trifling, to give direction and dramatic focus to their work.

The crowd surged around the man as Pieter forced his way toward him. Ahead, the yellow sweater cut through the mass like a power boat, leaving a wake of perturbed second glances. He snapped pictures of the man's back as he separated the people around him—appearing through the viewfinder to be holding

47

everyone at bay. He bounced; Pieter worked through the crowd, holding the camera above his head, then down to focus, snapping, winding, snapping again. He caught the man's heavy-jawed profile in several shots. Pieter felt dwarfed by the fellow, who looked to be a head taller than everyone, though he wasn't. "Beautiful," Pieter kept saying, though he knew the man couldn't hear him. "Now look this way. Fine."

Then the man came straight at Pieter, moving like a glassy-eyed sea beast above the ocean of heads. Once, the man looked directly into the camera. Through the viewfinder, Pieter saw his eyes squint fiercely, madly, as though he realized some part of him was being captured, his privacy intruded upon. The man came closer. Pieter held his focus, fighting a terrific urge to flee, and as he snapped the final picture, he was knocked brutally from the man's path and stepped on. "Asshole," the man said to him.

He had bruised his elbow, but he was proud of having held his ground, because he had gotten that last picture, the one picture of fear or panic or simply madness that made the whole roll worthwhile. He could not wait to have it developed to show Demmie. He would call this series "Subject in Search of the Artist." She would get a laugh out of that. He capped his lens and packed the camera into his shoulder bag.

The man had come back again, pushing through the line near Pieter, and was now arguing violently with the police. Pieter could hear cursing, and the man began to break through again. Was he crazy enough to try to get to Juliana? Pieter fumbled for his camera. All of a sudden, the man went down, the policeman too, as though the earth had given way under them. Whistles screamed, and blue uniforms converged from every direction. The man was yelling. Pieter tried to fight his way into the crowd; he needed pictures of this melee, this absolute lunacy. The people in the slow-moving line were not even watching. They wouldn't let him through. Then the man was on his feet again, and the police were leading him away, his arms pinned straight to his sides, a dozen blue uniforms surrounding him.

Pieter tagged behind, catching one more shot as they threw the

48

man into a van. "Let go of me, you turds!" he was yelling. "I'm a Dutch citizen." Flashing blue lights came on, and the van forced its way through the crowd and around the barricades, disappearing down the Rokin with the two-tone whine of the siren shattering the festive air.

He went back to the bleachers to get a few more shots of Juliana with his new zoom lens. She wore a floppy hat and an aquamarine suit with a silk ribbon cinched at her hip. A corsage was pinned over her left breast, above her heart. Her face hinted at fatigue, but she maintained her dutiful grin as she waved to the throng who passed in front of her. Ah, the duties of office, Pieter thought. I bet she'd give half her sovereign holdings for a good nap now. He put his camera away and decided to take a nap in her stead.

As he walked up the Rokin to catch a tram to his apartment, a voice called, "Mr. Beckum." Pieter turned and searched the faces behind him. "Over here." A waving arm.

It was the boy, Theillen, from the university.

Pieter gave him a quick wave, then began walking away. He had had enough of the Queen's celebration. He had had enough of crowds.

A hand caught him by the sleeve as he stepped from the curb. He turned; it was Theillen again.

"Can I buy you a cup of coffee?" the boy asked.

"I can't," Pieter said, thinking of his nap. "I have to be some-where."

"One cup. I won't take much of your time. It's important."

"All right." He hated himself immediately for the capitulation. He knew what it was about, and it was going to be unpleasant. His elbow hurt, the crowd had gotten to him, and now he felt as though he'd just backed into a trap.

They walked up the Rokin in measured vibrating silence, crossed the canal to a small café, and sat outside with steaming cups of espresso. The Press Institute was two buildings down. Two blocks in one direction was the red-light district; two blocks in another was the Queen's birthday party. They drew equal crowds. The town was a madhouse; instead of a nap, Pieter decided, he would get out. He would pack it in for the beach at Zandvoort.

"Well?" Theillen said. He fidgeted in his seat as he had done during his interview.

"Well what?" Pieter sipped his coffee, waiting for Theillen to summon his nerve, and watched a line of tourists cross a dock in front of him and board a water taxi. A young girl, wearing a brilliant yellow paratrooper's coat, called to them just as they were negotiating their first step onto the boat. When they looked up, surprise playing all over their silly faces, she snapped their pictures. In an hour, when the boat returned, their pictures would be developed and hanging with price tags on a stand where they debarked. The girl reminded him of Demmie, the way she dressed, the colossal nerve she exhibited in her work.

"Did I make it?" Theillen asked. "I know I should really wait, but . . ."

Pieter still felt a little disoriented. There was no tactful way to tell him. "I'm afraid you didn't." He waited through a stunned moment, watching the young girl in the yellow jacket surprise each tourist.

"But why not?"

"I have filed a report with the university. Rather, I will file it Monday morning. They'll let you know my reasons."

Theillen stopped fidgeting. Pieter knew he was not going to have such an easy escape. "That's not fair," Theillen protested. "We're here together now. You rejected me. Tell me why."

Pieter suddenly disliked Theillen for putting him on the spot. He did not have an answer prepared, and now he felt himself squirming. He hated these scenes. First a lie began to form behind his lips, then a subtler truth. He told Theillen that he did not have the right temperament for a restorer's tasks. That he was a bit too nervous. That a university should teach students other things. He felt like a bully, continuing to punch at someone who had already given up.

"I'm sorry," Pieter finally said. "All that sounds worse than I

50

meant it. Also, there is very little work right now, and nothing for you to do."

Even this didn't make Pieter feel less guilty. Theillen looked pathetic. He wore only a T-shirt against the brisk weather. His complexion had paled since Pieter had given him the news. His biceps, with their pumped-up bulge, were as incongruous to a restorer's demeanor as the tattoo on his forearm. It read: "Anne Frank, 1929–1945." Where was the future of restoration? First Demmie, now him. But this boy genuinely wanted to study it, as did Demmie. And she was turning out well.

"Why the tattoo?" Pieter asked.

"It's no concern of yours," Theillen blurted. Then he flushed.

The tattoo didn't make any sense. Theillen had been born so many years after the war; there was nothing he knew about it firsthand. It should not be his nightmare.

"I had it done for no reason," Theillen said, softening. "I visited her house on the Prinsengracht once. It made an impression on me. Afterward, after seeing the room where she hid and all that, I went to a man in the red-light district who does tattoos."

"I'm sorry," Pieter said. "My decision is firm. Perhaps you should try another museum." The disappointment that showed on Theillen's face made Pieter feel as bad as he had ever felt, but he told himself, damn it, there was nothing he could do about it. He excused himself, slung the camera bag over his shoulder, and threw some money on the table for the coffee.

He stopped briefly at his apartment to pick up an overnight change of clothes and his bathing suit. It still might be too cold for the water, but he could rent a windscreen or sit in a solarium.

As he surveyed his apartment, he became very upset with himself. His clothes were strewn over the bed; a couple of towels hung from the doorknob of the bathroom. He had never been sloppy. Each thing had always gone in its predetermined place. Something in his life seemed to be coming apart—his work at the museum—while something entirely different—his relationship with Demmie—was coming together. He did not know where the balance was, or if there was any balance. It was as though every-thing carried its own set of rules, of dangers, and, finally, of unanswerable ambiguities, and all you could do was hope that the choice you made was as good as the choice you might have made.

He quickly gathered up his dirty clothes and tossed them into the hamper. He tried phoning Demmie, but there was no answer. He knew if he went by the studio she would not interrupt her class to speak with him, so he drove straight to the beach at Zandvoort.

He passed through the oak-shaded, brick streets where the cheaper pensions were, through the town with its casino and modern hotels, then up through the high grassy dunes overlooking the North Atlantic. He rented a room at a small hotel and ordered a bottle of cold Perrier and some lemon. From his porch he took pictures of lime-green, undulating knolls, punctuated by thick sand dunes and the darkening forms of old abandoned farm implements. A late-afternoon wind swept in off the water, and only the hardiest of sun-lovers stretched out on the beach below him.

He attached his zoom lens and began photographing a couple with a young child directly below him. They were huddled against a multicolored windscreen. Up the beach, four women were sun-bathing side by side on the same blanket. They had put two screens together to block the wind. With the aid of his lens, he could see that two of the women were absolutely stunning, and all were topless but one. They took turns rubbing oil on each other. For a moment, he considered boldly descending the steep stairs, but he was not that bold; the lens would have to suffice. He was glad Demmie had suggested he become *artistic* with his camera and wondered why it hadn't occurred to him. His days of picture-taking always gave him something to look forward to. On those days, when he looked through the viewfinder, the things he saw were usually elevated beyond their ordinariness. He had felt a great affinity for that man who popped his cork at the Dam this afternoon. But had he not had his camera, he would probably have looked past him as all the people in line had done, not seen the specialness of his disorientation in the three-and-a-half-inch square frame, not thought of that terribly hackneyed saying, "There but for the grace of God . . ."

Those moments of capturing life on film had become infinitely interesting to him. He took great pleasure in knowing that the images he photographed ultimately became concrete through the marriage of his own imagination and the techniques of the dark-room. He compared it to his work and found it exhilarating. To create, he thought, was more fulfilling than to maintain.

And with that thought, he imagined his father spinning in his grave, his father who had been *his* master restorer, who had lived and breathed nothing else. Pieter too had once lived and breathed nothing else. After working as an apprentice to his father, he had summoned the courage to break away. He traveled first to the Uffizi in Florence, to Paris, and then to the United States, working as a staff restorer. Finally, after more than twenty years of work and study, he attained the rank of Chief Restorer at the Rijksmuseum, the goal which had taken precedence over thoughts of love, of marriage, of whatever else young men were supposed to think about as they shaped their lives.

Yes, he thought, until now. Now his life was filled with ex-tremes of drama and boredom. He was coming to realize—through his blossoming relationship with Demmie—that all he valued might lose its substance like the fleeting spray of a comet's light when measured against what he was discovering.

5

The police turned van Rijks out of their van on the Churchill-Laan, at the foot of a huge bronze sculpture of Winston Churchill posed with his left hand clutching his lapel in a most statesman-like manner. The officers did not say a single word to him, nor did they seem to notice, or care, that he was still sobbing uncontrollably. As he watched them drive away, his sobbing stopped. His chest filled with a rage he had never known before. It felt hot and pressured, as though it might cleave into shards of raw flesh, flying off with some cosmic centrifugal force at any moment. He was completely lost and began walking up the Ferdinand Bolstraat, back into the center of the city, wondering where he had to go to meet Molen. Then he remembered the Rijksmuseum and asked a passerby for directions.

As he turned onto the Museumstraat, a long, wide, tree-lined street, he recognized the back of the impressive building immediately. Thomas de Keyser designed it, he remembered. The year eluded him. Its spires jutted ominously against the gray sky; its center skylight, a single rectangle of luminescent glass, stared squarely at him; its archway that tunneled through to the front entrance became a dark mouth. He was crying again, this time more quietly. As people approached him along the sidewalk, they suddenly shied clear. "Molen," he kept repeating. He searched for his face. Molen. *He has my life in his hands.*

Inside the archway, the dark tunnel that had swallowed him so completely, he struggled to get hold of whatever it was that had set him off at the Dam. Neel's words, "You are going to break down," whispered through the door of his studio in Leiden, echoed vaguely inside his head, and the more he tried to push them back, the more resonant they became. "You're going to crack like a porcelain vase if you don't get help," she had told him. *Where's Molen? The bastard stole my portfolio. If you don't get help.*

A million bicycles clattered through the archway, the riders chattering like magpies. Mopeds raced through too, the sputtering of their tiny engines amplified by the vaulted ceilings. Then they were gone. He was alone, and the contrasting silence was so abrupt that he wanted to scream. He stopped at one of the showcases to look at a framed print of Rembrandt's *The Night Watch*. More bicycles clattered through. More mopeds. Children's shouting. He clutched at his ears, but the sound was inside his head. The little girl with the crown trembled in his hand, the horror in her pale eyes accusing him of intentions he could never be guilty of. Monster, they had shouted at him. He loved her, didn't she know? Loved them all. Children were death to him now. He stared at the little girl with the chicken tied to her waist in the foreground of *The Night Watch*. "Molen!" he screamed. There was excruciating silence as his anguish echoed like the cyclists' chatter against the vaulted ceiling, then died away.

He rushed out of the tunnel, into the gray light of day. Buses were lined up in front of each of the double entrances to the museum. Groups of people poured from the museum's doors like so many swarming insects from the belly of a dead beast. He pushed frantically among them, searching for Molen's weasel face. *Inside. He has to be waiting inside.*

He went through the revolving doors. To the right, an elfin-looking guard in a black uniform checked tourists' coats. Van Rijks paid the two-guilder entrance fee, poked his head into the cafeteria to see if Molen was waiting there, then climbed the brass-railed marble stairs, lined with busts of past museum curators, to the galleries. He passed under a sign which read REM-BRANDT—VERMEER—HALS; passed another sign, erected by the police, BEWARE OF PICKPOCKETS.

Here, some voice inside his head intoned. *This is the place.* He was calm here. He no longer felt the supremely hot explosion building in his head and chest. It occurred to him then that the studio in Leiden and the train ride, and all the other things that had brought him this far, were calculated in an indefinable way to culminate here, as if this should be a natural place of comfort to him. He knew of no artist who did not feel comfortable in a museum of this kind. He had dreamed of having one of his paintings hung in some museum, dreamed too of having Jo-hannes's work exhibited in such a place. He shook with his own excitement.

He found himself in the great hall where tourists crowded against the long sales desk to purchase poster reproductions of the masterpieces they had just seen. He was filled with panic again, realizing that he could not remember precisely what Molen's face looked like. His hands were trembling from the impossibility of the situation. He was an artist, an observer of detail in the minut-est form, and he could not remember the face of the weasel who now held everything of importance in the world to him.

The loudspeaker in the great hall blared, announcing—first in Dutch, then in English, German, and finally French—that the museum was closing for the day and would reopen tomorrow afternoon.

Some Americans from a historical society were herded into line by their tour guide for the march out, and van Rijks quickly took off down the long hall of foreign masterpieces that led to the *Night Watch* room. *Have to find Molen. Molen.* A black-uniformed guard came toward him, cutting off his path. "Closing, sir," he said politely. "You have to go the other way."

"I'm looking for someone," van Rijks said urgently.

"There's nobody back that way, sir. I've just secured it."

Van Rijks ran back to the main hall and got in line with the tour group. As they passed the last door before the stairway, he darted inside. He found himself alone, walking through a series of small rooms that contained icons and religious statues from the Middle Ages, wall-sized tapestries adorned with elaborate scenes of suffering, rich vestments for church ceremonies, gold and silver chalices, large ivory and hand-tooled hardwood cabinets.

A voice wafted to him through one of the connecting walls. "You'll have to leave," it said in a polite, officious tone. "It's closing time. Sorry."

Van Rijks hid behind one of the large cabinets, hoping with all his energy that he would see Molen being shuffled out in front of the approaching guard. The footsteps got louder. Then three young people, dressed in tattered denims and light jackets, walked past him with a burly guard at their heels. Van Rijks slipped around behind the high cabinet and listened as the guard locked the door behind the young people, then came back to make the final check.

He approached the cabinet that van Rijks hid behind and slowly walked around it. Van Rijks circled too, keeping the guard opposite him. He could hear the guard's steady breathing, and his own. His pulse thumped wildly in his throat and he fought down the urge to cry. Then the guard doubled back around and startled him so completely that he jumped.

"Come on, now," the guard growled. "What is this?"

"A chest," van Rijks answered, staring into the glinting buttons on the guard's black coat. He hoped the joke would soften the man.

The guard clamped a hand on his shoulder, the force of his grip sending shock waves down to van Rijks's thighs, turning the muscles in his legs to cold mush. "You get out now."

"No!" van Rijks yelled, tugging free and backing away. "I can't leave. I have to meet someone here. You have to let me stay."

"There's no one here. The museum's closing." The guard came at him. His eyes tightened with menace. He fingered a silver whistle in one of his large, hairy hands.

Then something occurred to van Rijks. "Would you kick a man out of his own house?" He fumbled for the hotel receipt in his

57

pocket. "Here, look at this. This is my museum." He shoved the paper under the guard's nose. "Look at the name. Van *Rijks.*"

"I don't give a damn what your name is. Get out or I'll throw you out."

The guard took him by the arm and began to pull him, and van Rijks went limp to the floor, kicking like a child throwing a tantrum. The guard put the whistle to his lips, releasing a shrill screech. The sound crashed inside van Rijks's head and he jammed his fists against his ears. But the sound had gotten inside, as a vapor might, and it inflamed the tissue of his brain, swelling it till he felt as though sharp thorns were pricking the soft, sensitive tissue. Within seconds there were two other guards in the room, dragging him out and down the stairs.

All the while, van Rijks screamed, "You can't do this! This is my house, you turds," believing in the melee that it was indeed his house.

They deposited him on the steps of the west wing entrance and slammed the immense double brass doors behind him.

He pounded against the doors with balled fists, shouting, "Scum! Frigging barbarians!" He heard laughing behind him, but he did not turn, did not care. "You've not heard the last of me yet!"

He felt a hand patting his shoulder. "Take it easy," a familiar, soothing voice said. When he turned, he saw Molen, no portfolio, no paint box, nothing in his hands.

"Where is it, you bastard? Where's my stuff?" Molen had put him through all this. Molen had become his tormentor. It was all his fault. He started for him, his lips curled menacingly. "Where is it?" he repeated.

"Easy, I said. It's at my place. I have it all."

"Take me there. I want it now."

"First things first," Molen said. "I want a reward. Buy me dinner; it's the least you can do." Molen laughed uneasily; then van Rijks joined him, the vibration of his own laughter suddenly lightening all his feelings of fear, and the terrifying anxiety that had rumbled through his chest. This bird, he thought, isn't so bad after all.

They ate near the museum in a basement café called de Fles. It was dark; the walls were painted a chocolate brown and what little light there was from the overhead lamps was muted by the leaded Tiffany shades. When the waiter came to take their order, van Rijks said, "The best you have. After all, it's the Queen's birthday, and the king—that's me—shall, you know"—he made an obscene gesture with his hand—"tonight."

The waiter laughed and said, "Yes, your majesty. Steak and salad all right?"

They ate in silence. Molen wolfed his meal as if he hadn't eaten in a week and might not have a meal this good for another week. Van Rijks knew Molen's game. Molen was a greedy pimp who made his livelihood exploiting the lost who came to this city. But that was all right tonight. Van Rijks himself was one of the lost, and a face as familiar as Molen's was now—even if slightly repugnant in its dark, close-eyed shiftiness—was something he could feel comfortable about. Molen's face, which he was etching indelibly into his memory so he would never again forget it, gave him a sense of sanity, as Stolk's brief visits to his studio had, a sense that there was something he could count on.

"I want to get laid," Molen said, wiping his lips on the sleeve of his shirt. "How about you?"

Van Rijks grunted. Molen had put him in a good mood, and though he hadn't thought of sleeping with another woman since Neel, it seemed particularly attractive now.

"Buy me a whore in the district. I don't want one of my own. I can get that any time."

"I want my drawings," van Rijks said. "First." He would try to sell them at the Waterlooplein flea market tomorrow.

"What's your rush? They're safe. They're not going anywhere."

Van Rijks counted the bills in his wallet.

"Buy me one. I'll get you one of mine free."

They rode a tram down the Vijzelstraat to the Mint Tower.

The tower was brilliantly outlined against the darkening night by a thousand tiny white lights. A carillon played out the time. As they sat on the canal wall listening to the tune, sharing a full bottle of jenever, the music made van Rijks giddy.

The streets of the red-light district were close, dark even with streetlamps, foul-smelling. They walked past a house where a fat black woman sat half naked at a window. Her breasts, swelling moonlike out of the top of her corset, were paler than the rest of her skin. She tapped her ring against the window—long, insistent, beckoning taps. Van Rijks stopped to stare at her. She winked and puckered her thick purple lips. He was starting to feel frightened again. The sated, warm feeling from their meal left him. He could feel anger beginning to bubble through his limbs.

In the next window, an old woman old enough to be his mother sat working a crossword puzzle.

They passed another window. And another. Molen walked quickly, as anxious as he had been with his meal—looking, as he had said, for the right one. Young ones, old ones, skinny ones with glasses, with great sores on their faces. *You are in hell for sure now,* some voice said to him. *Molen is your tormentor. You've descended into the steamy pits of piss and shit and the foul fish odors of the flesh.*

They passed a brightly lit club where a thin, dark-skinned man stood calling to passersby. Lively music blared through speakers high above his head. "Live show," the dark-skinned man called to van Rijks. "Real fucky-fucky, twenty-five guilders. Real fucky-fucky." At the entrance to the club, lighted color pictures showed naked black men twisted into all manner of positions with naked white women.

"Where are you taking me?" van Rijks said, his voice fluttering with anxiety.

Molen turned to him. "What's the matter? You don't like girls? Why are you rushing me?"

Van Rijks pulled a hundred guilders from his pocket. "Here," he said. "Take this. When you're done, meet me at the Café Zwart."

"You don't want one of my girls," Molen said, shoving the money into his pocket.

"I want Neel."

"Neel? I don't know any Neels. What's the matter with you? You look sick."

Van Rijks backed away. "Café Zwart," he said.

"You sick?" Molen asked.

"Go fuck your whore!" van Rijks shouted. "Café Zwart."

Van Rijks ducked into an alley. There seemed to be an endless stream of men coming at him, brushing against him in a space no wider than his shoulders. They soiled him as they brushed by; they grunted like animals, their breath coming to him foul as death, foul as the fever that had soured Johannes's mouth.

In the dark, he stumbled in dirt where cobblestones had been torn up. What was he doing here among these assholes who followed their cocks from one window to the next? The thought that he was just as bad as the worst of them made him laugh. But why else had his life turned out so? They would not look into his eyes as they passed him, shielding their guilt and their sins with chins jammed into their chests. He felt that he too should be hiding something.

A small Oriental man, wearing an overlarge leather coat, stood in front of an open window. Above it there was a bright red bulb. Inside, a blond woman sat in white satin bra and panties, her legs daintily crossed. A ghoulish black-light inside made her underwear and hair glow with phosphorescence.

"Give it a whirl, mate," the Chinese man, blocking his way, said in an English accent.

The woman leaned out from her stool, grabbing for his arm. "Fifty guilders, Mac," she whispered. "And I'll do anything for you."

"Suck the Devil's dick, then," van Rijks countered, surprised at his own vulgarity.

Finally, he passed out of the alley into a narrow street. The darkness was everywhere. He longed for a familiar face. Not Molen, this time, but someone compassionate. Stolk. Or Neel, maybe. He had done badly by her, and he would tell her so, if only she'd turn one of these corners and bump into him. But what would she be doing here among these whores? Somewhere in the back of his throat an ugly violence struggled with a consuming desire to cry. Neel had to take his hand, lead him out of here, comforting him as they went. *It's all right. You'll be better. I just want you to see the doctor.* She was giggling at him now, patronizing. She was more capable of that than Molen. *Crack like a porcelain vase.* Neel did not know that her simple warning had become a taunt. Darkness was everywhere. He was trapped in an infernal labyrinth. A tapping above his head drew his attention. He expected to see Neel, her shock of red hair tied behind her head, sitting at the bedroom window watching what went on in their street below, as she had done each evening before the news came on the television. A woman leaned out over the sill. "Thirty guilders," she said. "Best in the district."

"Where's Neel?" he called up to her.

"You're drunk," the woman called back, one breast popping out of the cup of her bra. "Beat it."

"Where's Neel?" he repeated. "She told me she'd be here tonight!" He could hear himself yelling with all the air in his lungs but could do nothing about it.

A crowd of short, foreign-looking men gathered near him. They were all dressed the same; they were laughing at him, pointing.

"You're ruining my business," the woman at the window said. "Go find your whore around the corner."

"She's no whore, you fuck!" he yelled back. "And she's up there. You can't hide her from me."

The woman vanished suddenly, reappearing with a pan of scalding water. She heaved it and he sidestepped the steaming torrent as it spattered the pavement. The men who had gathered were laughing hysterically.

A rush of hot water flooded his brain. He yelled, "I'll show you, you whore! You devil's asshole . . . piss on me." He picked up a stone and threw it at her. She dodged and it smashed the window next to her, sending pieces of glass showering to the pavement. The light came on in the room and a man's voice yelled, "What the bloody hell's going on out there?"

The whore he had thrown the rock at began screaming as though she had been stabbed, the high shrill scream of a woman possessed. It was like the screech of the guard's whistle at the museum, and he covered his ears, but he could hear it still. It pricked his skull like millions of tiny needles.

A rumble of heavy feet thundered up the alley. They were coming for him. He ran. He ran through the darkness of the close streets, through the islands of dim yellow streetlight, the sounds and smells of whorehouse sex all around him. The rumble of feet got louder, seemed closer. There was no escape.

Then he stopped. He was in front of an empty lighted window. The door was ajar. *Go in.* He heard the feet again. The bastards were going to overtake him. He jumped inside and closed the door behind him, panting like a frightened cornered fox. They would beat him if they caught him.

When his eyes focused, he saw a thin woman, her back to him, arranging some paper towels on a small table by the sink. The room smelled dank with perspiration, sour breath, and sex. "Fifty guilders," she said, without turning to him.

He could no longer tell if the echo of feet was in the alley or in his head. He reached into his pocket and pulled out a fifty-guilder note. She snatched it from his hand, and he quickly drew the drapes.

The room was no bigger than the one at the Hotel Kap, than his studio in Leiden. He felt the pressure building in his head. "You're not Neel," he said. "But you'll do."

"I'll be Neel for twenty minutes," she said flatly, "if that's what you want."

She was nearly as tall as he was, and quite attractive. Despite the coolness of the evening, she wore a red-and-white candy-striped halter top and denim shorts. Her shoulder-length blond hair was lacquered into place; bangs hid her eyebrows and accentuated her almond-shaped brown eyes.

"What's your name?" she asked, putting the money in a small cigar box on the table.

"I don't have one," he answered. "What's yours?"

"Agenata." She peeled the top over her head. Her nipples stood like two small dark pebbles against the brown of her large areolas. Her breasts were almost perfectly flat. "Or Neel, if you like. Take your clothes off."

He dropped his pants and stepped out of them, then lay back on the towel that covered her bedspread.

She sat beside him and tried rolling a prophylactic onto his limp penis.

"You had too much to drink, I think," she said, with a half smile.

"I had nothing to drink."

She finally got it on and began working him up and down with her hand. "You let me know when you're ready." Her back was to him and she had three moles as big as her nipples along her spine.

She pumped him harder. "Okay," he said.

She lay back and he rolled on top of her. Her glazed brown eyes were fixed on the ceiling above him. She guided his penis inside her and started bouncing in some rhythm that was different from his, a rhythm as mechanical as a long boring stroll through the park. He bowed his back and kissed her little tits. These nipples have suckled a child, he thought. They were unusually dark and distended and had been worked by some little toothless mouth as surely as Neel's had been. *Where is your kid now, whore?* He took one nipple in his mouth and bit it.

She pushed him off her angrily. "Don't do that again," she snarled. A fire lit her expressionless eyes. "If you do that again," she said, "I'll throw you out."

He stared down at her, suspended from his locked elbows, and pounded his hips into her as furiously as he could. *That doesn't sound like you, Neel.* She turned her face away from him now.

64

He dipped to her other nipple and started playing over it with his tongue. *Bite me,* it said. *Gently. I love it, you know that.* "Ouch!" she cried.

She pushed him out of her, her eyes twisted with fire, and reached for a small white buzzer at the head of her bed.

Behind him the wall parted, and a huge black man, her eunuch, stood with massive arms folded over his bulging chest. "What's the problem in here?" he grumbled. One of his front teeth was capped with glinting yellow gold.

"Get him out of here," she said. "He hurt me."

"Put your pants on and beat it," the black man said, taking a couple of steps toward the bed. "We don't like men hurting our girls."

"She said she liked it," van Rijks said. "She said—"

"I said nothing of the sort!"

"I'll count to three, and if you're not dressed and walking . . ."

"All right. All right," van Rijks said. He rolled from the bed and pulled on his pants. He stopped for a moment to look at her. She had wrapped herself in the bath towel to cover her nakedness. She did not look like Neel at all, and he was sick with himself for what he had done. How could he have stuck himself inside her? The smell of her putrid sex and the rubber that had pinched his penis filled the room. Shuddering, he rolled the prophylactic off and dropped it at his feet on the rug.

The black man shoved him out the door, and he turned suddenly, swinging a wild fist at that obscene gold tooth. A black hand pummeled into his chest, sending him reeling, breathless, into the perfectly still, dark street. He listened, as he caught his breath, for the sound of his pursuers' feet pounding along the alley, but all he heard was the faint rising whine of a police siren and the slam of the whore's door.

Molen was waiting for him at the Café Zwart. He told van Rijks he had business to attend to and couldn't go back to his place for the portfolio and paint box. Van Rijks made him write down his address and told him he would be at his apartment at three o'clock tomorrow afternoon to collect his things. "If you are not there," he had said, "I am going to find you and kill you." Then he asked Molen for some more of the drug he had given him the night before, but Molen said he would have to buy it. It was too expensive to give away. Van Rijks gave him a hundred guilders.

On his walk back to the Hotel Kap, he kept to the shadowed sides of the streets, wishing desperately with each step for somewhere else to go. He did not want to be alone. He was afraid, after all that had happened, to enter that small close room, to hear no sounds other than his own breathing and the random monologues that would start the recriminations in his head.

He stopped to buy a bottle of cheap wine and a bottle of jenever and drank half of each before he reached the hotel. Then he sneaked past Mrs. Kolb, who lay snoring on the zebra-skin couch while the television blared.

6

Sunday morning, Pieter Beckum ate a light breakfast of coffee and rolls. Then he went straight down the rickety wooden stairs, down the steep sides of the high dunes, to the beach. He rented a lounge chair and a canvas windscreen and coated himself with lemon oil. The wind blew cold off the ocean, and the waves, even as they broke against the shore, were brown in the early-morning light. Occasionally a warm gust, a promise of summer smelling heavily of salt and drying fishnets, wafted to him. It would be nice to be lying on an Italian beach now, where it was warm already. He hadn't gone on a holiday in quite some time, and for the life of him, he could not figure out why. Even old Henk, the busboy who made a point of chatting with him whenever he ate in the museum cafeteria, went on holidays more frequently than he. Sunbathers were beginning to move toward him, staking out their patches of sand for the day. In the near distance, wind surfers battled fiercely with their full-blown, brightly colored sails.

The Queen would probably be at the museum by now. He was pleased with himself for resisting Jan's pressure to be there with him, to help him arrange things. A year ago he would have given in, but he felt stronger than that now. The more time passed, the more he was able to limit his job to the most rudimentary responsibilities. He had decided that since the appropriations committee had cut his funding, he would cut his commitment to the museum. Almost all he did now was supervise Demmie's apprenticeship, instructing her on varnish applications, simple relinings, and retouching. Once a week, he lectured visiting groups of art students during his morning rounds to inspect the condition of his paintings He did not particularly like it, but he imagined his job to be somewhat like a tenured university professor's—stable to the point of boredom. What frightened him was this vague apprehension that, should he have to work again, he would not be able to pull himself around.

While lying in the chair, accumulating the heat of the sun until a fine sweat beaded the lemon oil, he thought too of Demmie. She was leading him somewhere, though only he knew that.

It was her influence that had him at the beach today, suntanning. Ordinarily, he would not even have considered it. But she had opened so many possibilities for him that he found himself pursuing ideas and desires, from the simple to the obscure, that he had never known, or never would have admitted, existed within him. Once, after they had started having their lunches together, he had spotted her sitting alone at the café in front of the Americain Hotel as he walked to the museum. Her head was tilted back and the tender line of her long throat was offered up to the rays of the sun. Her eyes were pinched shut, and he was struck with the desire to sneak up and passionately kiss her neck.

It was then he had realized that he was feeling something more than a minor infatuation. He thought of love, though he could not assign to his feelings so strong a word. Yet something inside him failed him in that moment so suddenly that not only did he not kiss her, he continued walking as if he had not seen her at all. And all the way back to the museum he thought about her, with her head held back in such a carefree attitude, with nothing more serious than the idea of a tan playing through her mind, and it occurred to him then that she was right, that life offered more, life *had* to offer more, than simply a single-minded devotion to work. His lifelong failure to understand that, to seek that indefinable *more,* was what caused the malaise that now pervaded him so entirely.

Last night, though, before he had fallen asleep, he indulged himself by imagining he was lying in bed with her. The windows

68

were wide open, and the cool, wet-heavy North Atlantic air whipped into the room, snapping the gauze curtains. They had just finished making love; her blue eyes sparkled with mischief. They lay there—the flat smell of musk mixing with the salty air —talking of trips south, to the beaches of the Mediterranean.

Now, as he drifted into sleep on the chaise longue, sweat streamed in rivulets from his chest, down his sides. He could smell the herring man's truck parked in the sand behind him. Salt air and herring and Demmie's sweet fragrance of lovemaking were fresh in his nose. The herring man began clanging his bell, and Pieter lifted his head to watch the people rise from their blankets and lumber through the thick sand to his truck. He almost got up himself. Then he did get up, but not for herring. He rose to move his screen upwind of the truck and to go to the solarium, where he would have a strong drink of whiskey and some idle chatter with whoever sat next to him at the bar.

7

Van Rijks woke Sunday morning with the dry taste of dirt in his mouth. He had finished the wine and jenever, and done all the white powder that he had bought from Molen, and he was still very dizzy. His head seemed extraordinarily heavy. He felt filthy, unwashed, and again he realized that he had slept in his clothes. His hands were trembling mightily and he could not figure out why. The empty bottles lay capped on the bed beside him.

Then he remembered watching the full moon through the open window for the longest time, feeling the cold depthlessness of the night. The room had seemed part of a terrifying mirage. The moon's white light rippled across the darkness to him, giving off a tangible contradictory heat. He had no recollection of closing his eyes; he had just blacked out.

And then it had not been sleep that he encountered, but an opaque blackness unconnected with anything he had ever experienced, a dimension completely lacking all breadth and depth. Across the dimension, a man dressed in glowing white robes, white as the hot light of the moon, galloped on a glowing white charger. The charger faltered, then reared in all its magnificent power, hooves flailing razor-sharp against the blackness, and tumbled, pinning its rider beneath.

Across the same dimensionless canvas, a white ambulance, devoid of markings, with shrieking siren, raced up and parked behind the fallen horse and rider. As the attendant hopped from behind the wheel and rushed to the aid of the rider, van Rijks saw it was himself in the starched whites of the attendant. He carried a large knife and wheeled a collapsible stretcher behind him. He bent to minister to the rider in white robes, but when he saw the face his heart stopped. A pressured airlessness, as if he had been holding his breath too long under water, enveloped him. "I can help you," he heard himself whispering, his words echoing till they diminished into the opaqueness. Carefully he drew the knife across the neck and severed the head with a bloodless cut. He rocked the head in the crook of his arm, as he had done with Johannes as a newborn, cooing nonsense. Then he lifted it onto the stretcher, wheeled it back to the ambulance, and sped deeper into the darkness. The whole time, the face on the stretcher behind him urged him on with its hollow eyes. He turned. It was Johannes. He mouthed words but there was no sound. He knew it was accusing him and his wife of negligence. He had cried to Neel that night, "All you had to do to know he was burning up with fever was kiss his forehead." Her voice retorted, "Your work. Too busy with your work. Murderer." They had had this argument endlessly during the following year.

He rolled out of bed and tore his clothes off. Impulsively, he felt for his beard, but of course it was gone. He washed in the sink, yet the cold water did not relieve the oppressive feeling of dirtiness. He had descended into an infernal pit of putrid smells and heart-rending visions. For a moment, he stared at his face in the mirror. The skin of his cheeks was chafed. His eyes were glassy, the edges rimmed with red. Dark crescents underneath accentuated his strange yellowish pallor. Whatever had happened last night, wherever he had been, was still with him this morning, and for the first time he felt he needed some kind of protection. The shapes of a hulking black form coupled with a white, musk-smelling softness had crawled in him last night; only with a weapon would he be able to keep them from consuming him, obliterating him. Suddenly he felt confronted with the choice of screaming or bursting.

When he came down for breakfast, Mrs. Kolb eyed him suspi-

71

ciously. "You're looking human," she finally said, noting the change in his appearance.

"Looks deceive," he said. "Breakfast, please. I am on time today."

She muttered to herself, then set a place for him at the table.

When he had finished, she came up behind him, soundless as a stalking cat, and said quickly, "You've got to be out by eleven. Or pay for another day."

He flinched with the suddenness of her words, instinctively clutching his table knife. "I'll be out," he said, without turning to look at her. At first, he had thought she was something that had gotten loose from his dreams, the frightful something that was planning to attack him. He turned the knife over in his hand, decided he would need it, and secreted it in a pocket of his trousers.

Even as he sat there, she came back and cleared his place away. He followed her to the kitchen and watched her stack the dishes, then walked out the front door. From the stoop, he could hear her running after him, her heavy feet in wooden shoes drumming the floor. He bounded down the steps, into the street.

She threw open the door and yelled to him, "Hey, painter man, where's my knife?"

Van Rijks shrugged. His left hand fingered the serrated edge of the blade in his pocket. *I need this more than you do, bag.* "What knife?"

"I put one on the table when you were eating. Come on, now, don't steal from an old lady."

"I have nothing of yours!" he cried. The rider from his dream might come around any of these corners, and where would he be without the knife? He turned away from her and walked slowly up the street.

"You won't get your suitcase till I get my knife," she threatened. "I'll call the police, you crazy bastard."

"Keep it, then."

He walked up the quay along the Keizersgracht, weaving in and out under the newly budding maple trees. He had to kill time before he sought out Molen. If every drawing wasn't in his portfolio, he would use this knife to carve on that little pimp. Carrying the knife gave him a peculiar feeling of power; he felt only half as frightened as he had been before breakfast. He looked down at the still, opaque water of the canal. All sorts of trash had accumulated there. Empty bleach bottles, prophylactics, a dead sea gull, tree branches, and the outstretched arm of a mannequin formed a collage against the piles of the footbridge. For a while he stared blankly at this mess, then turned his head away; the severed arm, the dead gull, the rubber: again last night came back to him, as if this canal collage provided missing parts of a puzzle. But it was a puzzle he did not want to solve. He made a conscious effort to force air through his lungs. His heart was trilling.

He found himself running, but the faster his legs propelled him, the more intensely his chest vibrated, as though his heart were a tuning fork and each jarring stride set all his organs oscillating. Then he heard the bell, the clear resonance of clapper and iron, in the towering steeple of Westerkirk, and he stopped. The gold of the crowned steeple shone against the pale blue morning sky. Whatever it was that was after him, that refused to let his mind rest, would never dare to follow him in there.

The bells were announcing the commencement of services. Families dressed in their bright spring finery were crowding in through the massive front doors. A young boy in a somber suit handed out pamphlets. Van Rijks stood in the back, watching people file into the seats around the pulpit. The choir members, at the far end of the church, were dressed in green jackets and black slacks. They whispered and pointed to their sheet music. The orchestra, directly behind the choir and a tier higher, tuned their instruments—cellos, violins, basses. He heard the French horn clearly over the drone of the congregation.

Above his head, music boomed from an elaborate Renaissance carillon. An immense brass and crystal chandelier, flickering with dim light, hung from the high ceiling.

He strolled up the outer aisle, pausing at each pillar to study the prints of Rembrandt's religious drawings. It occurred to him then that this was the church where Rembrandt was buried, and he felt as comfortable as if he were in his own classroom. The drawings portrayed all sorts of religious agony and ecstasy. He traced his fingers over *The Good Samaritan*. It was one of his favorites because of its marvelous irreverence. Who else could get away with a dog shitting in the foreground, while one of the Bible's principal parables occupied the background? Van Rijks could feel the electricity in the sure, perfect lines come alive under his fingers, travel up his arm, enter his chest, then spill out in a wellspring of emotion. *Like this. To draw like this.* He was crying.

He cowered behind a pillar, wiping his face on his sleeve. Paint was chipping from the concrete walls and from the tops of the columns where they joined the vaulted ceiling. There was magic here; he could sense it. For all the decay—the years-worn maple benches and the broken stained-glass windows—here the forces of light were triumphant over the darkness; here an artist could be valued.

Van Rijks pulled a cigarette from his pocket and lit it. How grand it would be to live here. *I will check in after I get my things from that witch at the hotel. I'll hang my drawings here.* The thought buoyed him.

He went around the back of the church, then up the center aisle. A droning intensified like a mounting wind; he turned to make sure the minister had not entered. *Why the noise?* He stubbed out his cigarette on the floor, and a palpable roar seemed to rise to the rafters.

He looked around for a seat, and hundreds of faces, unconnected to their torsos, glared. Their eyes shot at him like lasers —full of heat and concentrated light. Their mouths pumped furiously, but, as in his dream, he could distinguish no articulate sound.

The pulpit was built around one of the middle columns of the church and the pews were clustered around it. He ascended the steps quickly, fully determined to confront them all. Once up there, his mind emptied. There was a stool in the corner and he pulled it up to the open book of Scripture, sat, and looked out at the sea of dumbfounded faces. Say what you must, he thought; but what is it I want to say?

In the parapet above the pulpit, a light with a heart-shaped covering shone down on him and the book of Scripture before him. The light bathed him, made him feel clean, righteous. His hands gripped the pulpit; he hadn't felt this good since before he had stopped teaching. They had all been such marvelous children, until they had turned to death for him. All he had ever wanted to do was teach them; now it was all queered.

He began to speak in a loud voice. "I stand here among you, sent by a power far greater than any of ours here, greater still than all our power together." The light from the parapet warmed his face. *Where were the children? This was for them.* He did not know where the words came from, or where they went; he opened his mouth to shout.

"I am from Him who watches over us, and I am eternally an example to you all of His divine wrath. . . ."

Something tugged at his jacket sleeve.

He looked down and saw an old man in a gray suit standing on the steps of the pulpit. "Please," the old man said, "you must come down from there. Services are about to begin."

"I know," van Rijks said. "I am beginning them." He looked out on his class once again and was shocked to see not a child's face in the audience.

The tug at his sleeve again. "Please come down. You are troubled. I will talk with you. Perhaps there is another way to impart your message. I am an elder of this church."

"I want to tell them about my son."

"That's blasphemy." The elder's face was soft with age, but there was a smoldering fire in his eyes.

"Not *His* son. My son." Van Rijks corrected him.

"Come," the elder entreated him, the fire dying in two transparent pools.

Van Rijks took his hand, allowing himself to be lured down.

As he descended the stairs, several young boys appeared from underneath the pulpit. Each grabbed him somewhere—an arm, a leg, his belt. He was being pulled down the aisle and through a sea of converging faces, as though he were being tossed on the crest of a wave. The whispers sounded like jeers now from the very people who had so compliantly allowed him to ascend. "Hypocrites!" he cried out. If he could only free his arm, reach the knife in his pocket, he would cut these tentacles away.

They threw him outside, and a handful of teenage boys rushed to block the doorway. The elder pushed through the boys. "I'm sorry, but you cannot stay in our church," he said.

Van Rijks looked baffled. "It's not your church," he said softly.

One of the young boys stepped out, fists balled on his hips. He said, "Beat it, man. Go home and sleep it off."

Van Rijks fingered the knife in his pocket. He could see his arm snake out, a sharp silver flicker at its tip, to carve the boy's face. He had done neat work last night on the white horseman. *Home, you little snip?* He still had several hours before he met Molen, and he had no home to go to. He did not even feel as if he had a home in Leiden any more. He had whimsically tried to convince that arrogant guard yesterday in the museum that the National Gallery was his home. The home of all artists. He had the hotel receipt that confirmed it in his pocket. "Thanks, kid," he said, winking. "I think I will."

A great procession of police cars and long black limousines was leaving the front of the Rijksmuseum. A crowd of people lined the Stadhouderskade, waving miniature red, white, and blue flags. He saw Juliana's sagging, grandmotherly face at one of the limousine's windows. She waved absently, and almost as soon as the car disappeared around the corner, the crowd began to dissipate.

What's she doing here? Anger rocked inside him as he remembered his humiliation at being dragged out of the Dam, then booted out of the National Gallery, on *her* birthday, by *her* hired goons. What did she have against him? He had never met her, or said an unkind thing about her.

He walked up the steps of the west wing entrance, through the revolving doors, and up the great marble stairway. He ambled down hall after hall, not knowing or caring where he was going, looking for someone important. He did not ever want her here again; he did not care if she was the Queen. Finally, he found himself in a dead end after a maze of smaller galleries, standing in the center of a large, high-ceilinged room.

One each of the four walls hung a huge group portrait. The center of the room, where he stood, was somewhat darkened, but the muted natural skylight from above accented the paintings with an eerie amber haze.

Suddenly he was tossed back into the madness of the Dam yesterday. Someone struck the tines of the tuning fork, sounding the vibrations of panic in his chest. A chill climbed his spine. It seemed as though he had stepped inside the confusion in his own head by entering this room, and though his instinct was to run, his feet would not budge. Slowly he rotated, eyeing the paintings, and each of them held more people than he could count.

In all but one, men lounged about long tables, tearing great hunks of meat from the bones of slaughtered and cooked animals, showing their teeth, revealing themselves to be no less animal. Others drank wine from gold goblets till the blood-red fluid over-flowed their mouths and streamed down their necks. All of them were laughing, jubilant, and he could hear their revelry pitch about the walls of the room, rising steadily, loudly, as surely as he could hear the ragged panting of his own breathing. Some of them carried rifles and aimed them carelessly. Between two of the walls, he found himself in a crossfire, and he froze to the floor like a rabbit caught in the blinding headlights of a speeding automobile.

This is not fair. You cannot turn art against me, into a trap.

Then he remembered the boys in the church who had sent him here. They were conspirators. He wanted to strangle them. He wanted to yell for the lights to be turned on, but he found himself voiceless with the weight of the darkness pressing down on him. Again, no air. The top of his head was going to disintegrate in some violent eruption. He jammed his fist into his coat pocket and felt for the knife. It was warm from his body heat.

A young man and his girl friend huddled motionless on a couch in the shadows. He could not figure out why they did not see what he was seeing, feel the horror he was feeling, unless, of course, they too were a part of this. A single guard, dressed in a black uniform, stood near the door with his hands clutched behind his back, blocking the exit. Any moment, he knew the guard would raise his hand to signal the figures, and they would descend upon him, guns and bones and goblets and bared teeth, and rend the insubstantial flesh from his bones.

To one painting, on the far wall, he drew close. His shoes creaked on the parquet floor. Though there were as many figures in this painting as in the others, it lacked the chaos. It seemed somber, supremely ordered, and it calmed him. Then he recognized it, as he might recognize a familiar face in a tremendous crowd, and did not feel so utterly disoriented. It was Rembrandt's *The Night Watch.* The naming of it calmed him more. He was with a friend; he would be all right.

He stepped closer still, drawn by the absolute sincerity that emanated like a distinct and cosmic light from the eyes of the central character, Banning Cocq. Rembrandt knew about painting what he himself knew, and could execute what he had always failed to execute. It was the true inner self that was captured here in the details of his figures—the stupidity in the cowlike face of one character, the drunkenness in the wine-colored nose of another, the vanity of station in the ornamentation of still another's clothes—but more, he had set some part of the human spirit free in the combination of light and eyes and soul. He wanted to shout, Yes, yes, I know! . . . He moved in, breaching the tapestry rug before the painting, and a shrill buzzer shot off like an air-raid siren, deafening him. He could feel his heart shudder, and blood began pounding through his convulsing vessels as if it were being driven by the steadily powerful hammering of mallet against anvil. His ears throbbed, burned. The guard raced from the door, toward him, as though he were about to pull out a weapon and attack.

"Step back," the guard ordered. "Off the rug." His jet-black uniform made him suddenly look as though he had escaped from the painting. And as van Rijks retreated, he felt his entire body cringe. The buzzer died away.

When he looked back toward the painting, it no longer appeared the solace it once was. It seemed that the yowling buzzer had started a muted yet sinister riot before him. The dozens of armed figures now moved frantically out of the dimensionless darkness, marshaling behind the black-clad figure of Banning Cocq, who seemed to be stepping out entirely into the third dimension, his dimension. In a moment, he would find Banning standing on the floor beside him, like the guard, and it would all be too late.

Then Banning's outstretched hand began extending through the varnish layer itself—pink and fleshy and of the same substance as his own hands; as if by magic it had come alive and was going to grab him by the throat and drag him in among them. Still, he could not move, and he knew that if he touched it, transcended whatever ungodly realm it was in which his seeing such things was possible, the hand would be warm with the blood that pulsed within it.

"Oh, no," he said aloud, "not you too."

All the subjects behind Banning were staring at him now, urging him with their eyes to take the step forward, to clasp the hand, to enter the painting and obliterate all that he had ever been. And if he did, he knew he would join their own particular type of hell, frozen in time and circumstance so that all their sins and vanities were displayed in a single petrified moment, eternally scrutinized by anyone who had the two guilders it required to walk through the doors of the museum.

"No," he said again, but he felt his right hand reaching away from his body. He belonged with them.

The drummer boy, off to the right, began a roll with his sticks across the head of his drum; van Rijks heard it as clearly as he heard the tentative shuffle of boots on cobblestone beneath their feet.

Then, above Banning Cocq, he saw that the militiaman looking

79

away from the drama, seeming to ignore them all, had Molen's gaunt weasel face, and his fear turned to an all-consuming rage.

The boy with the powder horn, heading into the darkness at a dead run, became Johannes. Why hadn't he seen this before? Why did they want to trap him, break him down into nothingness? And Neel, foreshortened to the size of a child, yet still wearing her own old haggard ruddy look, a chicken tied to her belt, floated in the center of the composition in a glowing dress like some disembodied spirit. And Stolk was there. The headmaster too. He needed a handrail to grasp for support but there was nothing. His knees felt jellied, and the floor began to swirl beneath him.

He smelled sulfur too, acrid in his nose yet sweet in the back of his throat, as the men filled the muzzles of their muskets. He squeezed on the blade in his pocket till he could feel the bite of the serrated edge in his palm.

And suddenly, rising out of the painting like some devilish apotheosis, looming above the shoulder of the soldier wearing the bronze helmet, the one who had looked so much like Molen, there was the eye, the part of the nose, the shadowed diagonal of face. It was the eye which he had drawn in every face, drawn days ago on the child on the train, drawn to exorcise from himself a guilt that was ultimate, perpetually haunting. It was like seeing his own soul rise up and accuse him of some unpardonable sin. He could feel the dry pressure of Johannes's eyes on the tips of his trembling fingers as if he were touching them all over again. And every figure in the painting seemed to join in a taunting chorus—*Your fault,* they sang. *Your fault.*

He pulled the knife from his pocket. "You're wrong!" he screamed, running forward, leaping to reach the eye, to jab it out and grind it to pulp beneath his heel.

The buzzer exploded as the knife fell short, ripping the flesh of Banning Cocq's hand. The canvas was heavy, thick, like the dried hide of a dead animal. His blade caught for an instant; he was certain that he had hit bone and it had felt so good. He drew the knife out again, plunged ferociously, and the tearing of the canvas sounded like painful anguished groaning. "You're wrong!" he kept yelling as he thrust into flesh and bone, cut away sinew.

The guard jumped him from behind, locking a stout forearm tightly about his neck, but he kept slashing. His air stopped; he felt his throat being crushed, and he tried stabbing over his head at the guard, twirling like a dervish to get at him. He would kill them all.

More hands clutched at him now, pulling him away and down to his knees. The young girl screamed from the couch; echoes reverberated hollowly from all the walls.

As he lost consciousness, he noticed only that the loudest scream did not come from the buzzer or the girl, but from the combined cacophony of all the figures in the painting as pieces of canvas fell to the floor and great bloodless gashes rent the torsos and legs of the men marching out of the darkness.

8

When Pieter Beckum got home, he showered and changed into a robe. He thought of calling Demmie and asking her to the cinema. He was tired of being alone. But he didn't want to appear adolescent, dogging her because of some silly infatuation. Their relationship was new, and he did not want her to get fed up with it. She required, as she told him emphatically, a certain freedom to move about.

He fixed himself a light supper of salad and cheese and ate it at the table on his balcony. He finished a carafe of wine, becoming light-headed in the process. He watched the traffic stream underneath him, the cool evening air filled with the dissonance of sounding horns and the metallic clanging of tram bells. From where he sat, he could see the twin spires of the Rijksmuseum beyond the high full oak trees in the traffic circle. The sun was setting behind his studio in the east tower, washing the sky with pastel hues of pink and purple. He made a mental note to cancel his apartment and move farther from the museum.

The phone rang but he did not answer it. Then it stopped. It rang again, this time continuing longer, its bell insistent. He went inside, to the mantel, and picked up the receiver.

"Pieter Beckum," he said.

"We've had a catastrophe," a voice said. It was frightened, high-pitched.

"Who is this?"

"Jan." There was a lot of commotion at Jan's end. "It's terrible."

Pieter had to contain the laugh that rose in his throat. He knew Jan was high-strung, his public-relations job had made him so, but he had never heard him so distraught. He sounded a bit comical. Pieter expected to hear that someone had fouled up the Queen's visit.

"Slow down, Jan. And tell me exactly what you're talking about."

"Pieter, *The Night Watch* has been destroyed."

"Very funny. Who did it? Juliana?"

"I'm serious," Jan said. A sobering silence swelled the line. "The museum's premier piece has been destroyed by a madman, and you're cracking jokes."

"You are serious, aren't you?"

"You must come at once. I've tried to reach you all day. Why didn't you come to the museum as I asked?"

"I couldn't," Pieter said. "I was feeling rather bad and I had to get out of town. Who did it?"

"I don't know. Some fucking lunatic. The police came and carted him away."

He had never heard Jan curse before, and it brought a smile to his lips. Crises, he thought, bring out the best in people.

"I didn't hear about it. I was at Zandvoort. It's not on the news yet, is it?"

"Not yet. But it will be all over the papers in the morning. The press is here already, howling like a pack of starving dogs. How long will it take you to get here?"

"A few minutes, I suppose. I have to get dressed."

On his way to the museum, Pieter felt an absolutely euphoric delight. He knew, somewhere inside, that he ought to have been horrified, but damn it, he wasn't. Instead of driving straight there, a trip that would have taken him five minutes, he drove up the Vijzelstraat, the long way around, speeding, weaving in and out of traffic. He had to calm himself down. He could not show his excitement to Jan, the Director General, the police, the press. His mind raced no longer with possibilities of what should be, but with an anticipation that made him hum the same ditty Demmie had been humming in the studio two days ago. He was going to have his masterwork after all; he was going to labor, as he had been trained to do, on the single most priceless—and, to his mind, most beautiful—painting in the whole museum. The whole country, for that matter. It seemed as if some beneficent angel had seen his predicament and thrown a little grease into the dwindling fire of his life.

Part II

THE RESTORATION

9

On his way out the door, Pieter had grabbed his camera, quickly checking it to make sure he still had some film in it. He was standing in front of *The Night Watch* half an hour after Jan had hung up the phone. He and Jan and the Director General were alone in the gallery. The police had cordoned off all the entrances to keep the press at bay.

There were great arching slashes in the wall-sized canvas, and one piece, a long dark triangle, had fallen from Banning Cocq's crotch and lay at Pieter's feet on the floor. He snapped several pictures of the damage from different angles. The slashes began at the center of the painting and moved to the right in a series of violent rips. None of the faces were damaged, but the guard had told them before he was dismissed that the man had been jumping at something, trying to strike something out as he howled.

"Was the man left-handed?" Pieter asked, slinging the camera over his shoulder.

"My God, what a catastrophe," Jan kept saying. Since Pieter had received his call, Jan's voice had risen an octave, and now it seemed stuck that high.

Pieter picked up the triangle of canvas from the floor; then, matching it to the hole, he noted how brittle strips of the original canvas were peeling away from the old relining canvas.

"The guard told the police the man was left-handed," the Director General said. "How did you know?"

"Just a guess. The way the slashes enter, their direction from left to right, moving away." Pieter imitated the slashing motion with his hand.

There was a moment's silence; then the Director General asked, "Can you fix it?"

Fix it? Pieter said to himself, a sudden anger closing his throat. This is not a broken car; it's *The Night Watch*. He had to throttle his dislike. Now you need me, he thought. He stared at the Director General, a thin, mannered man, who cleaned his eyeglasses on his opened vest. He looked exceedingly bored with having to waste his Sunday evening here, instead of carousing at one of his clubs. He wore expensive suits and tailor-made shirts and spent more time making speeches at civic functions than administering his museum. At least Jan, twitching and rubbing at his bulging belly, appeared disturbed.

"I can fix it," Pieter finally said, hoping his tone conveyed the surge of contempt. He approached the painting, took out his pen, and probed the slashes. At once, the painting ceased to be the awesome masterpiece everyone knew. It was now merely a damaged work of art, and it would be his job to make it whole again. Some of the slashes were deep, penetrating all the way through the heavy relining layers. Some went clean through to the wall. He remembered his father explaining to him that canvases were alive; when he was younger, working in his father's studio, he had imagined them crying when he cut into them. "They breathe," his father had told him, "so treat them as you would a living thing. They stretch and sag with age, as people do. And some of them, in a very real sense, die, regardless of their master's technique or the quality of our restorative work." And here he was now, standing in front of *The Night Watch*, which was alive in so many more ways than the purely technical, bursting with a perverse exhilaration at the sight of the grave wounds before him.

Then the first problem occurred to him. With so many slashes in the canvas, it would be impossible to remove *The Night Watch* to the studio. The entire original canvas might peel away from its support. He checked himself against telling the Director General. He did not trust the man with this piece of information.

"I have to go to my office to think," Pieter said. "I want to be alone when I make the assessment."

"Fine," the Director General said, slipping into his coat and smoothing his dark hair back with both hands, "but put your thoughts in writing for me."

"What about me? What shall I tell them?" Jan pointed to the gallery door, behind which the press waited.

"Tell them we'll have a conference in the morning," the Director General said. "In the meantime, let them in for a short picture-taking session. Tell them they'll have to get their information from the police for now, but we'll issue the first of a series of releases after Mr. Beckum makes his assessment."

Pieter started out of the gallery, then turned back to Jan. "Who did this?"

"I don't know."

"It took phenomenal strength to go through all that canvas and varnish," he said. He took a last glance at the wounded painting. "There was a guard on his back while he did this?"

"He was crazy," Jan said. "You know what crazy people are capable of."

"I have an idea now."

He took the private locked elevator to his studio in the east tower. When the door opened, he used another key to unlock the barred gate that let him out of the elevator. Then he passed through three double-bolted doors—all part of the tower security system. Only he and his restoration staff were ever allowed up here.

The last hallway he walked down had narrow stone walls and a high, dimly lit ceiling. Dozens of empty, dusty frames hung in an orderly fashion; they smelled of centuries of musty halls as cold and close as these. The sound of his heels rapping the stone floor echoed hollowly. This hallway, when he walked it alone, always made him uneasy. It reminded him of childhood visions of dungeons, places where soldiers took children they caught and did unspeakable things to them.

89

When he opened the door to his office, he was startled to see a shapeless form hunched over his desk.

He reached out and flicked on the overhead fluorescent light. It sputtered like ill-defined lightning, then burst into brightness. Demmie was dozing in his chair.

"What are you doing here?" he asked. "And in the dark."

She jumped out of the chair. "Jan called me when he couldn't find you. Anyway, it's not dark," she said.

She had on a bright turtleneck sweater and wore dancer's striped woolen leg-warmers over her jeans and boots. Outside, the sky was a dismal, drizzly gray. Its pale light filled the large windows, competing subtly with the artificial light.

"Besides," she said, "I'm here to help if you need it. Is there anything I can do? You want me to turn on some heat?"

"No." He put the triangle of canvas on his desk and slumped into the chair. He felt exhausted. He had not known how to interpret the Director General's attitude downstairs, but he was just beginning to understand the nature of his own uneasiness. He was terribly understaffed. That was the key. He had said as much to the Director General two months ago, and the man would not have forgotten. He needed at least two more sets of competent hands to keep the job. The Director General might, at this very moment, be on the phone to Brussels for outside help. Damn it, he needed a plan, something to outsmart that mannered fox.

Demmie sat on the corner of his desk and picked up the canvas, examining it carefully. She looked as excited as he had been. "This is part of it?" she asked. Her eyes suddenly darkened with seriousness. She nudged Pieter with her boot. "Is there anything I can do?" she asked again.

"I haven't had a death in the family," he snapped. "I just need to be alone so I can think."

Without saying a word, she dropped the canvas on his desk and stalked to the door. He wanted to ask her please to understand, he was troubled right now, confused; but he could see by her pained look that the damage had already been done. She whirled toward him, the tight rings of her hair bouncing like little blond

90

springs around her face, her eyes narrowed with incomprehension against the gray light. It was not the soft face he had kissed in the apprentices' studio, and that made him feel as bad as his paranoia about the Director General. She opened her mouth to say something, then spun around theatrically and walked out, closing the door quietly behind her.

He found himself staring at the triangle of canvas on his desk. The wine had worn thin, and so had his exhilaration. What sort of person would do this? Vandalism of this sort, so senseless in its nature, had always baffled him. It hadn't been a year since some other lunatic had smashed Michelangelo's *Pietà* with a ball peen hammer. Art was supposed to offer solace to the disturbed, not provocation.

And *The Night Watch*. Regardless of any skill he brought to this masterwork, any sure-handed technique, painstakingly learned, it could never be the same again. He could minimize the scars, but he could not efface them entirely, as if they had never existed. That was the ultimate, sobering reality of his work. Just as he believed he could never have taken back the words that had so scarred his father, even if, at the time, he had wanted to.

He had been sixteen, working in the two small rooms on the first floor of their house in Rotterdam. The solvents—alcohol, varnishes, resin mixtures—permeated the studio with their pungent smells, and on humid, rainy days the smells seeped into the living room above the studio. He had come to hate those smells, the closeness of the room, the unending debt to his father for becoming his father. He felt like a slave, tied by obligations, not chains, to the work this man did while other children kicked footballs in the school yard. During a routine cleaning, he had discovered that one of his father's wealthy clients had bought a fake Corot. His father was ecstatic with his discovery and was rewarded handsomely by his client. Later, his father came to Pieter, large dark eyes moist with pride, his face flushed with emotion, and said, "Anything I can do for you. Name it." And Pieter had hesitated, seeing his chance to escape, then blurted, "Get me an apprenticeship in a museum. A real museum." His father had been stunned, but he agreed. Pieter knew he had wounded the man irreparably; until the day he died, the closeness of their relationship had never been restored. Now he wished his father were alive so he might understand that his son could have worked in that little studio all his life and never had this chance at *The Night Watch.*

Down in the gallery, he had known immediately that the painting would require a complete relining. The cuts that had gone all the way through necessitated that. And the canvas would never be able to withstand the rolling it would take to bring it up here, because the suture, which held the relining canvases to the original, would be weakened beyond repair. Even when *The Night Watch* had fallen under a vandal's knife in 1911, it had never been damaged through the heavy varnish to the paint layer, the very heart of the work.

The problem he felt worst about, though, was his understaffing. He could pull Stan Martins, the frame-maker, off his projects. Stan had had a little restoration training in Brussels. But he still needed one more person.

Theillen's folder sat on the desk top in front of him. He racked his brain for someone else, anyone else, who might be competent enough, but it all came back to Theillen. He had the background; he was in town, anxious to work, and would take whatever orders he was given. All it would require was an apology. He pictured himself arguing technique with some learned consultant and knew what he would have to do.

In the bottom drawer of his desk he found the report he had prepared a year before at the request of the Amsterdam Town Council, proposing a complete restoration of *The Night Watch.* They had rejected the idea immediately. He believed then that the Director General had had something to do with it, though now it was all a dim puzzle in his mind. Jan had explained afterward that the rejection had political overtones, but that had never made sense to him. In fact, Jan had confided, the Director General had received his appointment as a political favor and was merely biding time until the government changed hands again so that he could move on to something more fulfilling. Perhaps, Jan had speculated, he simply did not want to chance losing revenue while any work was done on the museum's star attraction.

Pieter finally buried the triangle of canvas inside his report to keep the edges from curling, and put it away. He could no longer concentrate on all the thoughts that raced through his mind. And now the terribly upset look with which Demmie had left him began to intrude upon his reflections. They would begin first aid on *The Night Watch* in the morning, but for now, rest.

When he finally came downstairs, he noticed the muted evening sun reflected through the stained-glass windows. Hours had elapsed, but it did not feel that way. It was staying light till nearly ten o'clock, signifying the onset of summer and the heavy influx of tourists who would fill the city. This would be a mad time for a restoration; the museum would be filled with three times as many visitors as during the winter. On his way to the front door, he passed the cafeteria; the sight of Demmie, sitting alone at a table, caught the corner of his vision. This time, however, she was bent over a cup of coffee.

"You look introspective," he said as he approached. "Did you come straight here from the dance studio?"

"Yes," she said. "And I talked the guards into letting me stay."

"Why did you wait?"

"I don't know. You should have seen your face. I made some coffee." She pointed beyond the railings to the steam tables where there was a half-filled pot at one of the machines. "Want some?"

"Sure."

First she chose a coffee cup, then rejected it for a large hot-chocolate cup. "Want some whiskey in it? I put some in mine and it makes a wonderful difference."

"All right," he said. "I'm really sorry for taking your head off upstairs."

"Forget it," she said. "But I have to admit, I wanted to yell right back at you. Then I realized where I was. Besides, you had a right to your mood and I didn't. You've had an awful lot of pressure thrust on you suddenly." Next to the cash register there was a row of upturned whiskey bottles with mechanical throttles at their necks. She pumped two shots into his cup.

"Take it easy."

"Have you decided what you're going to do?" she asked, handing him the cup.

"Tentatively." He sipped the cup. The whiskey made him wince as it burned down his throat.

"Will you take me to see it? The Director General and Jan wouldn't let me in." A note of expectancy filled her voice. She turned her chair toward him and put her arm around the back of his chair.

"No," he said, swallowing a healthy slug of her concoction. "I can't stand another look at it right now, and I don't want to think about it, either. You'll see it first thing in the morning."

"You had a desperate look on your face upstairs."

"Did I really?"

"You looked crazed."

He laughed. "The man who did it looked crazed. I looked thoughtful. There's a distinction." He still felt uneasy about something, though he could not name it. "Can I tell you something? When I first heard the news, I was elated, and I noticed the same thing on your face upstairs. But by then, my feelings had worn thin. I guess that's why I snapped at you."

"Do you feel guilty about being happy for the chance to work on something important?" she asked. "Because I don't."

"When you put it that way, no, I don't feel guilty, but I did." He finished his coffee; then, pointing to her cup, he said, "Hurry up, now. We're going to be spending enough time in this place. Let's get out of here. Do you have your motorcycle?"

"I took a tram from the studio."

"I'll give you a lift."

Her coat hung on the rack by the door. He got it for her and she threw it around her shoulders like a cape. One of the guards let them out. Pieter said to him, "Make sure Mr. Hansson knows he is to meet me early tomorrow. There's going to be quite a lot of commotion here."

94

"Good night, sir," the guard said. "I'll see that he gets the message."

Pieter had jammed his Mini-Cooper in among some of the reporters' cars and the police cars. They had filled the drive where the buses ordinarily lined up, but now there was only Jan's car left, parked beside his.

"What's going on in the morning?" Demmie asked as she got in.

"Meetings. A press conference. We must all be on our best behavior. I would appreciate it if tomorrow you dressed a little more sedately."

She began to protest.

"Just for appearance's sake. In case some reporter should want to get your face on camera. You know, the best thing for the museum and all that."

They drove east on the Weteringschans. He zipped around the traffic circle, cutting off a tram. Its bell trilled a reprimand at him. A frail bearded organ grinder shook his brass cup full of coins at tourists as they exited the brilliantly lit poffertjes stand.

"Are you going to call in help from outside?"

Pieter sounded his horn at a bicyclist who wobbled into the road in front of him. "I don't want to."

He drove the rest of the way in silence. With the windows rolled up against the harsh night air, he could smell the faintly acrid smell of Demmie's sweat. He had come to her studio, watched her conduct class, seen the glistening of sweat run down her neck, but he had never assigned it a precise smell. And now it seemed as pleasantly aromatic as his fantasy of musk and ocean breeze in the hotel at Zandvoort.

She had a small flat overlooking the Dapperstraat. The street was still now, except for a few small children kicking a football along the sidewalk. All he knew about the neighborhood was that it had one of the best markets in Amsterdam. In the morning, and for the rest of the week, the whole street would be packed for blocks in both directions with throngs of shoppers and with merchants selling fresh fruits, vegetables, meat, fish, and dry goods.

When they got to her apartment, she asked, "Do you want to come up for a drink?"

Demmie's apartment was a large single room which she had partitioned in half with a Plexiglas wall. All her furniture rested low on the floor—a sofa, a small table, a legless chair. Huge brightly colored pillows were thrown everywhere; lush green plants hung from hooks in the ceiling. There was a small wood-burning stove in the center of the living room. From where he stood, he could see through the glass, into the bedroom. The mattress was on the floor too. The walls were covered with silver reflective wallpaper and cheap poster reproductions of the paintings that the tourists bought at the sales desk in the museum. Had he ever given it any thought, he would never have imagined her home to look quite like this, but, he reasoned, her bizarre taste in decorating simply matched her outrageous taste in clothes.

"Have a seat," she said, pointing to the floor. "I'll fix something to drink. Is jenever all right? Somebody left it, and it's all I have."

"Can I have some spa with it?"

She brought the drinks and folded into the sofa beside him. Her dance shoes, stiffened into the shape of her feet, lay in the corner where she had tossed them. Dance magazines were strewn on the table, and pictures of dancers in various poses hung on one of the walls.

"Can't you decide whether you want to be a dancer or a restorer?"

She got up and turned on the stereo. Soft jazz filled the room from hidden speakers. "Can't I do both?"

"I didn't think so," he said. "But I'm changing a lot of my ideas lately."

"Well, I have to dance right now," she said. "As long as I'm in shape and training, Marie will let me teach at the studio. But I'm too old to make anything out of myself as a dancer. I'm just using it to support myself during my apprenticeship."

"Twenty-five is too old?"

"When you're competing with sixteen-year-olds, twenty-five is ancient."

"Thanks."

"Oh, I didn't mean anything by that, and you know it." She clasped his hand reassuringly.

He held up the glass of oily-looking jenever to the light, then brought it to his lips. "Well, today is going to change a lot of things. For one thing, I'd like you to compile your recommendations for work on *The Night Watch.* And for another, I'm going to get you a salary, beginning tomorrow." The third thing he was afraid to tell her, afraid she might sense the cruelty in it and shame him. He almost said it: no dancing. But he cut himself short and sipped the jenever again.

"Does that mean just you and I are going to restore it?" Her eyes widened with incredulity.

"No. We'll need others."

"Who?"

"I don't know yet. But mainly it will be you and me."

"All right!" she shouted as if he had just given her a present. Leaning across, she popped a kiss on his cheek. He felt his arm go out, circle her back, and press her chest to him. Her face was only inches away; her breath carried the heavy liquor smell of jenever. In the movies, he thought, this is where it happens. They kissed.

He backed away and held up his glass. "To Rembrandt."

"To success," she countered, clicking his glass.

Then it was Demmie, pressing into him, and he felt the delightful hunger of all her youth in the softness of her lips. When he had kissed her in the studio, she had shown reserve, or shock, at the way he had surprised her. Now no one would walk in on them, surprise them, and the notion of their own untouchable freedom had him embracing her so tightly that he could feel the childlike brittleness of her ribs beneath the tautness of her flesh. He stopped then, though he hated himself for doing so. *Twenty-five is ancient.* He thought of kissing a child, passionately, and he was overwhelmed with a sense of his age. She was fifteen years younger than he, not a child and yet too fresh for him, too lovely and young. Propriety was killing him after all. The last woman he

had been with—a teacher he had met at the Concert Gebouw—
was born in the same year as he; she had tasted this passion so
often, he had guessed, that her vitality in bed was diminished to
rote movement and muffled whispers. He could tell by the rave-
nousness of her embrace that Demmie was anything but sexually
jaded. He lay beside her, tracing designs on her leotard, outlining
the strictured globes of her breasts, the two darkened ellipses of
her nipples, and thinking of a way to get out of her apartment
before they had gone too far, as far as he dreamed they could.

10

Pieter woke early and stopped to check the newspapers on his way to the studio. *De Telegraaf* had its usual sensational headline, with a grainy close-up of the slashed masterpiece: NIGHT WATCH DESTROYED BY MAD ARTIST. *Het Parool* and the other papers carried headlines on their front pages too. Even the *International Herald Tribune* carried it. This insensible act had clearly shocked the entire world. Better yet, Jan was doing his public-relations job excellently, no doubt with proper supervision from the Director General himself.

Pieter had had trouble falling asleep, because he had angered Demmie before he left by telling her that she would have to stop dancing during the restoration. "I will need your total concentration. It will be the masterwork of your career." Later, in bed alone, he'd tried to rationalize his demand by telling himself that any apprentice would give his or her soul to be participating in the *Night Watch* restoration, and it was a small sacrifice for Demmie. But the question kept coming back to him: Did he need to make her stop, or was it a subtle attempt to control her when he knew that controlling her was impossible? He felt guilty for exercising his arbitrary power over her. But she had given in. She had thrown her gnarled pink dance shoes at him and said "All right." Then he had called Theillen.

While he had not wanted Theillen as an apprentice, he knew now that Theillen's presence would be critical to the Town Council's letting him keep the project. He began his conversation with an apology for rejecting him the day before. He took great pains to explain that his colleague at the university, under whom Theillen had studied, had attitudes concerning restoration which were antiquated and diametrically opposed to his, and that this had unreasonably prejudiced him.

Theillen eagerly accepted his apology and promised to be the first one at the museum in the morning. That done, Pieter was able to push aside what he had said to Demmie and sink into deep sleep.

Theillen was sitting on the steps outside the west wing entrance when Pieter arrived. In his olive T-shirt and jeans, he looked like one of the hippies who sat around the Dam, not like the crucial link in this project. Pieter took in his ample forearms as they shook hands, happy at their size. They would need his strength for manipulating that huge canvas. Theillen's sandy-colored hair was thinning, and he wore thick, round gold-framed eyeglasses.

In the elevator Pieter told him, "I'll have a set of keys made for you as soon as the Director General releases the new funds."

Theillen beamed, speechless. He shifted his shoulders, and Pieter thought, Stop fidgeting, damn it. Christ! Four months of fidgeting.

Pieter showed Theillen his office, then opened the door which led into the apprentices' studio. He told him to take a seat at one of the empty easels. The others would join him soon.

Pieter was at his desk flipping through the old proposal for cleaning *The Night Watch* when Stan Martins came in. Until he began specializing in the restoration of frames, Stan had been trained at the very institute in Brussels from which Pieter suspected any *outside* help might come, the Institut Royal du Patrimoine Artistique.

Stan was the same height as Theillen, but of a much slighter build. He had a thick dark bush of oily hair, close dark eyes, and a long fleshy nose. He wore the same type of navy-blue tunic the cafeteria help wore. Stan brought three men from the maintenance department as Pieter had instructed him. Pieter told Stan to join Theillen, then explained to the maintenance crew that they would be constantly on call, and that they would have to keep him informed of their whereabouts at all times when they weren't working directly under him. Then he dismissed them.

Finally, Demmie strutted in. From the moment she stepped off the elevator, he could hear her heels echoing solidly through the hall. He suddenly knew he should not have told her how to dress. When he had told her she would have to stop dancing, she had said she hated ultimatums.

She pushed open the door, and he nearly shouted at her to go home and change. She wore a long white mandarin jacket, a bit threadbare at the cuffs. Her hair was covered with a flowered Tartar wrap, and she wore pegged black pants over her high-heeled boots. She posed in the doorway for an instant, catching his eyes with a defiant, childish glint; then she undid the wrap from her head, shook out her curls, and took off the coat. Underneath, she wore a very demure tailored shirt which made her look almost restrained.

"Is that part of your theatrical costume?" he asked.

"No," she said. "It's part of my disguise. I love disguises, and I thought we'd be mobbed by press. In there?" She pointed to the apprentices' studio. He waited a moment, composing himself, then followed and introduced Theillen to the others.

Each of them now sat at an empty easel. Rows of solvents in amber bottles lined the shelves behind them. Porcelain dishes, mortars and pestles, dental and surgical instruments, paint, mahlsticks, and giant rolls of canvas were scattered about the room, making it look as if more work had been going on than actually was. Macrophotographs of his last restoration hung on the walls. Some of Stan's partially restored frames occupied a large table in the corner. Bags of plaster—some ripped at the seams and spilling their white powder in precise little islands—sat on the floor. His first thought was of *The Night Watch;* it came with the delicious edge of panic.

"Demmie, I want you to do something," he said quickly. "Find some envelopes, small ones, and take a fine brush, some tweezers, a palette knife."

She made notes of the tools as he called them out.

"And get down to the gallery. I want you very carefully to scrape the paint dust that got caught in the frame ledge during the slashing. Scrape up all the chips that fell to the floor too. Put it all in the envelopes. Label everything."

"Now?" she asked.

"Yes, before too many people are allowed in there and they track it away on their shoes."

As she headed out the door, he called her back. "Take Theillen with you."

He would send these paint samples to the Art Institute for analysis. The dust would contain varnish and ground as well as paint samples, and their composition might be important later. But the main thing was that the people at the institute would feel as if they were going to get a share of the action.

When Demmie and Theillen returned, she told him there was a police inspector waiting at the elevator downstairs. "Would you bring him up here?" he asked.

She took off down the hall. Theillen waited till he was told to join the others.

Demmie, returning shortly, introduced the policeman to Pieter. "Inspector van Velde," she said; then, "Did you know that they can't charge the man who did it?"

"That's not exactly accurate, Miss de Graaf," the inspector interrupted.

"That will be all, Demmie," Pieter said.

After she closed the door, Pieter asked, "Now, what was she talking about?"

Van Velde sat in the desk chair, leaving Pieter to sit on a corner of his desk. The inspector was an older man, much older than Pieter. A bristle of salt-and-pepper hair on the top of his head looked like an upturned shoe brush. Pieter watched the man's eyes taking in the accouterments of his office. He had a thick, athletic body that bulged at the shoulders, arms, and thighs of his cheap brown suit. When he crossed his legs, white socks showed at his ankles. "I am assigned liaison duty between the museum and the police department. I am not here to answer to you or to that woman who brought me up here," van Velde said. "I am merely going to give you a briefing before your press conference."

"What press conference?"

"Mr. Hansson told me you were scheduled to give one at ten o'clock this morning."

"I didn't know it would be so early."

"At any rate, this case will be kept confidential for a number of reasons. The man's name is Menk. He was an unemployed artist from Rotterdam. We contacted the man's wife. She said he'd been going to a psychologist for months. The psychologist claimed he came for one visit and that he was on the verge of a nervous breakdown. Schizophrenia of some sort, maybe. The doctor would not commit himself. I think the wife is a bit off too. Anyway, what your assistant was referring to was our inability to prosecute Menk under criminal statutes. You see, Beckum, there is no statute in Dutch law covering the vandalizing of works of art, per se."

"Oh, come on. . . ."

"It is true. We are holding him under Article Thirty-five B— a vague statute covering willful destruction—and of course he is charged with concealing a weapon, but he could be out soon enough. We can hold him for no more than twenty-four hours under Thirty-five B."

"But this man destroyed *The Night Watch!*"

"I don't have a lot of time and I don't want to argue the merits or deficiencies of our legal system. I have to be at a Town Council meeting with a complete report in an hour. They own *The Night Watch,* and they pay my salary. What we are trying to do quickly is get the man committed to the State Psychiatric Institute. Of course, there will be no trial, and the writ is before a judge this very minute. You may tell the press that the man has been committed. He is safely out of the way."

"Why no trial? He must be punished for what he did," Pieter protested. "It's only right." He knew it was not van Velde's province to decide these legal issues, but he felt like railing against someone. The man should have his hands cut off.

"Beckum," the inspector said dryly, "the man is obviously insane. What good would it do to try him, punish him?"

With that, van Velde pushed himself out of the chair and walked to the barred gate in front of the elevator.

"I will be at your disposal, should you need me," he said, handing Pieter a card with his phone number on it.

"Thank you." Pieter shook the man's puffy hand, feeling irritated by his gruffness. He had never had much experience with the police; everything was either black or white to these people. As the elevator door opened, Jan was standing inside, combing his hair into place. He looked startled to see them.

"Oh, good," Jan said, "I see you two have met already. Then I guess you know, Pieter, you have a press conference at ten. I was just on my way to tell you."

Van Velde got in the elevator and rode it back down with Jan, leaving Pieter standing in the hall with a lot of unanswered questions.

"That bastard," he said aloud, not knowing whom he meant the expletive for. He looked at his watch. He had a half hour.

He spent the time left before the press conference in the gallery of *The Night Watch*, further surveying the damage and jotting notes. He had wanted to give his staff a pep talk, impress upon them the gravity as well as the precariousness of their positions, but the way van Velde had acted toward him, as though he were simply a nuisance to be quickly dispensed with, put him off, and he was in no mood for pep talks.

A few minutes before ten, Jan entered the gallery. "They're outside waiting," he said, motioning over his shoulder. "Did you think I'd abandoned you, Pieter?"

"That thought had crossed my mind."

"Nonsense. Anyway, answer their questions and don't worry about a thing. You'll have to get used to this sort of exposure."

"What do you mean? What are you committing me to?"

A guard opened the gallery doors. Jan checked his watch. "It's time."

Two guards had come in through the back entrance to the

gallery and now took up positions in front of the painting. The journalists crowded in, forming a semicircle around Pieter and Jan. A rising din of voices filled the room. Flashbulbs began popping off, one after another, their bright explosions causing Pieter to wince. It's too much, he thought. The extreme flashing is going to traumatize the painting. "Tell them to stop the pictures," he ordered Jan.

"A few more?"

"No," Pieter insisted. "Later."

Jan raised his hands above his head, ordering the photographers to stop. Several more flashes went off, then things settled down. Snatches of English, French, and even Japanese wafted to him. Jan had been a newspaperman in a small town before he had come to the museum. By himself, he would not have had the kinds of connections necessary for the orchestration of this spectacle.

Jan quickly introduced himself and Pieter. The questions started at once, in a confusion of language and dialect so thorough that Pieter wanted to escape. Translators, sent from embassies in The Hague, asked questions about the man who did it. Pieter said that he had been an artist, was insane, and had been committed to an institution. Jan interrupted to explain the nuances of Article 35B.

A Dutch reporter asked Pieter what the final condition of the painting would be. He was tempted to say, Good, we begin with the stupid questions first, but he restrained himself. Be diplomatic, he kept telling himself; this has nothing to do with the work you have at hand. He explained that it was his job to see that *The Night Watch* looked as if it had just come from the Master's palette. Then he began reading from his notes. "The painting was cut a dozen times with a knife, the cuts varying in length from thirty-nine to a hundred centimeters. In some places, the knife went completely through the paint layer and the original canvas, which had become frayed by the speed at which the blows were inflicted, as well as by the bending of the knife blade. There is considerable paint loss. The area that fell out of Banning Cocq's breeches indicates that the canvas had not been properly affixed to the relining canvas. Also, there is a break in the canvas, three centimeters wide, where long strips of the original canvas are peeling away from the relining canvas. This afternoon, we will apply the appropriate first-aid measures to inhibit further breaking away. The entire canvas will have to be relined. Since the knife attack scraped the varnish down to the paint layers in several spots, all the varnish will have to be removed. And the missing paint, of course, will have to be reapplied."

An English journalist asked, "Who will paint over the damaged areas?"

"I will," Pieter said.

A reporter from *Het Parool* wanted to know if the solvent they would use for scraping away the hardened varnish would damage the paint layer.

"Tests have already begun, and we will inform the Town Council of the results when they are ready." Pieter could hear the faintest quaver of his voice, but he was sure no one else detected it. He was nervous as hell. Jan was right to have called them a pack of dogs. This was not like lecturing his art students once a week. What underscored all their questions was the intimation that he was not providing the whole story. Well, he could not say what his plan was till the Council approved it. But he felt like a liar for assuring them that this was a routine restoration, because it was not. When they began asking Jan leading questions about the madman—whether Menk had terrorist connections, and was it true he was really a Moluccan—Pieter decided to slip out. He whispered to Jan that they could each have one photograph, and no more, and left through the gallery's back door.

Pieter called the Director General and asked him to stall the Town Council meeting for a couple of days so that he and his staff could administer the first aid. The Director General was altogether too obliging. "Whatever you need, Pieter. It's your business. . . . One other thing," he said before Pieter hung up. "We've come up with an acceptable alternative to moving *The Night Watch* to your studio."

11

Pieter entered the *Night Watch* gallery to begin the first aid with a distinct feeling of nervousness. He had not had the courage to ask the Director General what he had meant about his "acceptable alternative" to moving the painting. He wondered how many other people had plans to interfere with his work, and to what degree. He felt as though he was waiting for an axe to fall without knowing around which corner it was poised. The newspapers had continued their front-page coverage, though the column space became considerably smaller each day. He and Demmie shot two rolls of film on the painting, while Theillen and Stan manipulated the spotlights, holding them at oblique angles so that the raking light exposed the surface irregularities in the varnish layers.

As they disassembled their equipment, Pieter explained how the attack in 1911 by a mad pastry baker had been inadvertently thwarted.

"Rembrandt's style was such that he thought his paintings ought to be viewed from a distance. His heavy use of impasto, for example, where he built up the paint, then used the butt end of his brush or a palette knife to score in detail, only becomes coherent if you step back from the painting. But more, it creates a certain three-dimensional thickness. When past restorers used liberal applications of golden glow and toner to protect the irregular surface of the painting from dirt, they created a layered coating as defiant as tempered glass, and the attacker was unable to cut through it with his knife. Today, we have such thorough damage because, during the 1947 restoration, this glasslike coating was stripped away in favor of varnishes that wouldn't distort the colors."

"In other words, it was a trade-off," Demmie said.

"Exactly. And I expect we shall all be surprised at the resonance of color when we strip the varnish down to Rembrandt's paint level."

They covered the large slashes on the back of the canvas with strips of transparent tape to keep the painting from further stretching apart. On the front side, Pieter used cellotape to replace the triangular piece that had fallen away from Banning Cocq's breeches. Each of them worked in an almost reverential silence that Pieter interpreted as apprehension until Demmie said, "Do you think the fellow was a pervert or something? I mean, he cut the vitals from between old Banning's legs."

Theillen didn't know how to react, and he began snorting to hold back his laughter. When Pieter started, everyone joined in.

He had Demmie and Stan cut patches of mulberry paper to fit over the slashes on the front, while Theillen mixed paste. Then Pieter stretched the sheets of mulberry paper over the damaged areas and secured them to the canvas with the paste.

On the second day, they degreased the entire painting with xylene and flannel cloth, rubbing in overlapping circles, then covered the rest of the face with mulberry paper. Pieter's original plan had been to outfit the large apprentices' studio with equipment that would control temperature and humidity, but with the Director General's call he felt as if he were in limbo. Where would they restore it, if not in the studio? The gallery was not equipped to handle the work. There weren't even any extractor fans to remove the noxious vapors from the solvents they would use, much less the equipment to create a delicate, constant balance between temperature and humidity. He wanted some answers and he wanted them soon. They simply could not waste time playing politics while the well-being of *The Night Watch* was at stake.

12

It was a few minutes before two o'clock, and Pieter watched a long single-file line of grim-faced spectators shuffle past the roped-off painting. Extra guards had been assigned to the gallery until a wall sealing off the painting could be completed. It was the Council's intention not to lose a single guilder on the painting, even while it was being brought back to life.

Pieter had been stunned into silence the day before when Simons, the Minister of Cultural Affairs, a bone-thin man with short dark hair and large ears, told him that the Council had unanimously agreed to have the restoration carried on in full public view. The other members of the Council—mostly businessmen—were conspiring to control the exposure of the destruction so the museum would receive maximum revenue. It was not a selfish motivation on the part of the Council, Pieter thought, but it was a careless decision that could jeopardize the painting.

Pieter had ignored all the other people sitting around the long table that had been moved into the Director General's office. "Mr. Simons," he had said, "that would be a mistake. We're not talking about some minor artist's work. There must be sufficient privacy for complete concentration. My staff will be under great psychic pressure while restoring this painting. Quick decisions have to be made, delicate acts carried out."

Only then had Pieter looked around for some sort of agreement, but all the faces of the Council—even the Director General's face—were averted. Simons laughed. "How about semiprivacy?" Everyone laughed with him except Pieter. "We have been in touch with the staffs of other museums, and they have supplied us with ideas about how this can be accomplished. We'll cut windows into the partitioned walls. You'll have curtains to close when you need privacy."

"It sounds like a circus," Pieter said. He knew precisely where his anger came from. They were going to transform this restoration into one of those "media events." The words tasted foul in his mouth. These men had no sensitivity to the mystery and drama of fine arts; it was all paint and canvas and wood to them, materials only, devoid of artistic spirit. They had already played down the slasher to the point where he was given only a line or two in each publication. It seemed to Pieter that he knew less about him now than he had immediately after the destruction. And they would now highlight the restoration as a special attraction to draw crowds from the Holland Festival, who would be just curious enough to pay two guilders to see a wounded masterpiece.

"I'm afraid we're quite determined to have this done," Simons said. His elbows rested on the table, pushing up his shoulders; Pieter felt like snapping them as he might a chicken's wings. Simons continued, his voice droning, "We can't deny the public access to *The Night Watch*. A lot of people come *only* to see that painting. The museum cannot afford to have it removed for the months you say it will take to restore it."

"You do this at the jeopardy of the painting, sir," Pieter said.

Simons winced, but Pieter did not care. It needed to be said. The extra pressure of a public restoration was something he hadn't planned on.

Simons stood, aggravation shaking his skinny frame. "The restoration staffs of the museums that have already contacted us are willing to do the job we want if you are unwilling to; it would be no rough matter to—"

"All right," Pieter said, knowing all along he would capitulate, but wanting to push the responsibility square into their faces. "Explain your plan to me."

"I'm not finished," Simons blurted. "We also shall hire the film crew of our choice to make a documentary to show in the museum's theater, as well as on the Eurovision channels, on the day the restoration is completed. We shall want to be active participants in this restoration; it is *our* painting." Simons sat down, his face a deep shade of crimson. The air seemed to throb with tension.

Pieter leaned back in his chair. Of course he would work in whatever way they wanted him to. He had no other choice. But he took some small consolation in upsetting them by letting them know that they would be culpable if something went wrong with their plan; it seemed, by the tension in the room, that culpability was something they had never considered.

And now, at precisely two o'clock, he ordered the guards to chase the last of the mourners from the gallery. Stan Martins brought in his maintenance crew to build a joist system for lowering *The Night Watch* out of its frame. They constructed a platform that looked like a small stage, then covered it with a heavy layer of cork so the painting could be laid face down. Finally, they built an oblong wooden dais, slightly larger than the work platform, and attached wheels to each end so they could slide the dais the length of the painting to allow Pieter to kneel and work above it without touching the surface.

Pieter had to admit the plans for the workroom were good. The gallery would be cut in half by a huge wall. It would be hermetically sealed and temperature-controlled—a constant 20 degrees Celsius to ensure against blooming when the layers of varnish were stripped away. Five large windows would be cut into the walls. He would have his curtains to shut out all those baleful faces too.

That night, he called Demmie to tell her he was taking a holiday during the week the work crew would be building the studio and to invite her along. Then he called Theillen and told him to study in detail the reports of *The Night Watch*'s past restorations and to take a couple of days off, because they were all going to have a long sustained stretch of it.

Demmie was waiting for him on the sidewalk in front of her

111

apartment, sitting on her suitcase. When she saw him coming, she stood up and waved. He seemed to see the shimmer of expectation in her eyes from half a block away. He had not told her where they were going, only to pack for a week. "You've been dying to get me off alone," she had said over the phone to him the night before, her voice dropping to studied sultriness. And he had admitted, for the first time out loud, that she was right.

It was the first warm day of spring, and the market in front of her apartment was packed as usual with shoppers. Booths stretched for blocks in each direction. The merchants alternately sang and bitched at the shoppers as they weighed out fresh vegetables, fish, meat, and fruit. Under canvas awnings, people were trying new clothes on top of the ones they were already wearing. Patate frites stands coughed plumes of oily-smelling gray smoke.

They hugged and she offered her cheek for a kiss. "How do you stand this madness six days a week?" he asked, motioning to the surrounding confusion.

"I look at it a different way. I can just walk downstairs and buy anything I want. Fresh. I don't have to travel across the city as you do." Her hair was pulled back. She wore a green-visored, duck-billed cap and no makeup except for the thick gloss of pink on her lips. She had on a tight pink T-shirt; her baggy denims were rolled to mid-calf.

"You don't look as if you're ready to travel too far," he said. "Did you bring your passport?"

"Passport? Where are you taking me?"

"Just run upstairs and get it."

"Pieter . . ." She started to ask him again where he was taking her, but he put his fingers to her lips.

"You've told me to practice being impulsive," he said, "so don't muck it up. Go." He had to smile at the words that came from his mouth. She was making him feel her age, not his, and he loved her for it. As she ran back up the stairs, he licked his finger clean of her lipstick.

He drove straight to Schiphol Airport, where they took a KLM flight. In a couple of hours, they were in Milan. From the airport they caught a taxi to the train station and pulled into Florence early that evening. "This is the final destination," he told her. "I've made arrangements to stay here for a week, with a couple of days on the Italian Riviera in between."

They carried their luggage several blocks, dodging drunk khaki-clad soldiers who careened from the bars along the narrow sidewalks, to a small pensione on the Via Fiume. He stopped at the corner, trying to see the block as he had seen it fifteen years before, but it was not the same. Movie companies filled the basements and first-floor apartments, where artists had lived. Carts full of tin movie cans lined the sidewalks. To conceal his disappointment, he put his arm around Demmie and squeezed her to him.

"You like markets?" He pointed to the Via Nazionale. "Two blocks from here is the San Lorenzo market. The Medici chapels too. When I was an apprentice, I lived here for a year."

She leaned her head to his shoulder. "Do we have to walk much farther?" she asked. "I'm exhausted."

"Half a block. Come on."

"Oh, Pieter, I love it, I don't mean to complain."

They rode the elevator to the top floor, and he explained that this had been his pensione. When a short, balding man greeted them at the door, Pieter asked, "Does Paolo still run this place?" He spoke slowly, conscious of how little he had used his Italian.

"He is my father," the man said equally slowly. They followed him down a dark hall lined with mirrors in carved gold frames and antique cabinets. "He retired some years ago, to the country. Around Pisa. I keep the pensione now with my family. Here is your room." He pushed open the double doors, revealing a spacious, high-ceilinged room. A burgundy tapestry rug covered the waxed parquet floor.

Demmie immediately crossed the room and threw open the French doors to give them better light. "Ooh, Pieter, come here," she called. A garden, directly below them, was in full flower; they looked out over the city, over the uniform red-tiled roofs to the panorama of the distant, rolling green hills beyond the Arno River.

"This is beautiful." Demmie squeezed Pieter's arm.

In the center of the room, a long, narrow table was covered with a white linen tablecloth. To the side there was an antique double bed, with an inlaid red brocade headboard and matching silk spread. All the wood in the room was a dark, richly stained rosewood, like the chests in the hall.

"Things have certainly improved since I was here last," Pieter said.

"They have," the proprietor said. "My name is Vincenze." He was smiling broadly now, a jolly-looking man, with a long full Roman nose and black eyebrows that joined in a V above his nose. He seemed pleased that his guests liked the accomodations. He disappeared from the room and returned an instant later with a full bowl of fruit. A knife was sticking out of a polished apple. "You will find it the cleanest pensione in Firenze," he said.

He stood by the table, drumming his fingers.

"Of course," Pieter finally agreed.

Demmie sat at the table and cut into an apple. Of course," she said in French, "prices have gone up too."

Vincenze turned suddenly vicious. "I speak all languages, dearie. Of course they have gone up. Everything in Italy has gone up." On his way out of the room, he stopped to close the double doors. "I will wake you for breakfast so you don't have to share the table with others, and I change the sheets daily."

"I'm so embarrassed," Demmie said, dropping her head into her hands. "Did I embarrass you?"

"No."

"Do you want some fruit?"

"No. It's late and I'd rather eat dinner."

They had to eat at a trattoria. The meal was stale, and Demmie teased him about trying to save a few lire. Afterward they walked up the Via Nazionale to the Piazza dell' Indipendenza and sat in the park. A warm evening breeze rustled the leaves above them while they ate cold watermelon by the light of the melon stand.

Children rode other children on their bicycles along the sidewalks of the piazza; their parents clustered on cement benches to argue and shout about each other's politics. The expectation of Demmie's touching him, running her fingers through the hair on his chest as they lay on the pensione's goose-down mattress, played through Pieter's mind as he watched young lovers, their Vespas leaning against trees, languishing in the shadows. They drank more wine, walked down more amber-gold streets, and by the time they got back to the pensione, they were so tired they fell straight to sleep.

In the morning, Vincenze's light tapping at the door woke them. Pieter lay in bed and watched Demmie pad across the room to open the French doors. The strong morning light diffused his vision. It was moment or two before he realized that, except for a small triangle of silk panties, she was naked as she stood there with her back to him.

She turned and fluffed out her hair. The front of her body was cast in shadow. A thin cord of crackling gold fire seemed to burn down her armpit and along the hourglass curve of her breast and hip to the floor. He felt like pardoning himself for staring at her, but she was so naturally unashamed of her nudity that he admired her openly. He felt himself getting hard under the covers.

"What did you do to me last night?" she asked.

"We went right to sleep," he said in a fatherly tone he did not understand. "Come here." He wanted to caress her now, in the full yellow light, because he had not even remembered the feel of silken warmth as her skin brushed his through the night.

Vincenze tapped again on the door. "Breakfast," he called.

She took a robe from her bag, threw it around her shoulders, and traipsed down the hall to the bathroom. Pieter lay there wondering what would happen if they never went back to Amsterdam. No one knew where they were.

Vincenze poked his bald head through the opened door. He raised his eyebrows knowingly and made a clacking sound with his lips. "Breakfast in half an hour, signore."

"I get the point," Pieter muttered.

Vincenze prepared fresh espresso and rolls. He sputtered about the kitchen, complaining about some Frenchmen who had left one of his rooms a mess. "Are you going to be out this afternoon?" he asked them. "I want to wax the floors." Then he proceeded to itemize aloud the shopping list he intended to fill as soon as they finished their breakfast. Demmie kept looking at Vincenze, then at Pieter, and rolling her eyes.

They spent the blistering hot morning shopping along the San Lorenzo market. Pieter bought her a new scarf and a small cameo ring that looked ridiculously minuscule on her large hand. He could not remember ever seeing her wear the same scarf twice. He asked her how many she owned, but she said she never counted them.

Before lunch, they walked to the Duomo to admire Michelangelo's unfinished *Pietà* and to climb to the top of the cathedral's tower, where they tried to pick out Vincenze's pensione in the terra-cotta blur of roofs. They hired a carriage for a ride through the city and up along the banks of the muddy Arno. As they passed the Uffizi Gallery, Demmie made him promise to take her there, and to the Accademia before they left.

That night, Vincenze gave them directions to a small restaurant close to the pensione. Pieter had cornered him in the kitchen. "Tell me a nice place to take my friend," he said. "Not a tourist place. I want to eat where you eat when you go out to dinner."

The restaurant was like no other he had ever seen; the kitchen was out in the open, among the tables. The cooks prepared the spaghetti *al dente* while they argued freely with each other, oblivious of their hungry audience. Pieter expected pots of boiling water to fly from one of the stoves at any moment.

They ordered octopus and squid with linguine and drank two bottles of wine. A squat, wine-dark man in an orange T-shirt, with loose false teeth, played a guitar and sang romantic Italian songs at each table.

By the time they got back, Vincenze had turned off all the

lights. They let themselves in with a key and staggered down the hall, trying to keep from laughing. They sat on their balcony for a while, passing back and forth the bottle of Chianti that Demmie had insisted they buy. Finally, she went inside and turned on a small brass lamp with a lead shade that cast the room in a red glow.

"You know what?" Pieter asked.

"What?"

"That red bulb wasn't in here yesterday."

They both laughed. Demmie said, "Vincenze probably has a peephole cut in one of the walls."

Pieter considered that possibility, considered shutting off the light, but he had waited so long for Demmie that he wanted to see what her face looked like when she was making love; to see if her nostrils flared, if her eyes fluttered. He wanted nothing to escape any of his senses.

"This reminds me of the red-light district," she said. "It really feels illicit." She pushed Pieter back on the soft bed and fell on top of him.

"I think that's what Vincenze had in mind." They kissed and he began opening her blouse. His stomach was trembling with anticipation, as though he'd suddenly caught the chills. He wondered if she could feel his nervous shaking and simply had the grace to accept it without comment. "I feel I should tell you something," he said.

"That wouldn't make it any less illicit. Besides, you're so provincial. Just tell me you like me."

"I like you," Pieter said, cupping his palm over her breast. He kissed each nipple, feeling them distend against his tongue.

"Let me undress you," she said. She rolled him off her and unzipped his trousers.

For an hour, they caressed each other in the shifting softness of the down mattress, as if its softness were an extension of their tender affection for each other. The smell of flowering gardenias in the yard below filled the room through the open French doors.

Wherever his tongue touched her skin, he could taste velvet, fragrant satiny velvet, as if velvet could have a taste. He became drunk with the sight of her too—the slick sheen of beads of perspiration in the hollow of her stomach; the supple dancer's arch to her strong back.

There had been other times, after much wining and dining and promises of things he never believed, that he had taken women to bed with him. But they were infrequent occurrences, and they had always seemed fraught with lies—both his and theirs.

Those women required him to coax them through whatever pleasure they derived. And often he knew their thrashings were as false as his own; it seemed to be the duty of women his age to let the man feel there was something in what he was doing that was irresistibly pleasurable. He always came away feeling somewhat soiled, as though he had lied his way to pleasure, or at least allowed their lies to find fruition in the dark with him—nearly all of them had mistaken his disinterest for stamina.

But with Demmie the mystery he so desperately sought took shape in her movement. She had experience beyond his wildest imaginings. And he felt completely comfortable—even grateful— as she guided him, sometimes with her hands, through the sensations she wanted to feel. Once, she even placed his hand on her sex and told him, "Here, this is where it feels best." And she giggled as he stroked her. He did not feel demeaned by her instructions, and by the time they had finished, he wanted to tell her that he loved her.

Their holiday seemed to gather a momentum of its own too. In the morning, they walked to the market and bought fruit, cheese, and bread, stuffed it into a carrying net, and caught a train to the beach at Viareggio.

They took a room on the strand, where the hotels were jammed together, wall against wall. Each was allotted a small portion of beach for canvas chairs and umbrellas facing the ocean. But for two days he and Demmie seldom left the room. Pieter sent out for breakfast; in the afternoon, they would lie in the sun for an hour while the maids put fresh linen on the bed. When Demmie brought up some aspect of work, Pieter silenced her. He felt too good about their hiatus, as if they had been shipwrecked and the project they faced upon their return was oceans away from them now. He knew how much time the restoration would consume—both actual and emotional—and there would be few days like these back in Amsterdam.

When they returned from Viareggio, Pieter took her to the Uffizi, as he had promised, and to the Accademia where he had studied when he was Demmie's age. Many of the sculptures that crowded the halls had been vandalized by radical students; male figures had had their penises whacked away, the vacant spaces sprayed with red, green, and black paint. Political slogans were written across their chests and thighs. Demmie laughed over Pieter's horror at this graffiti. He claimed it denigrated the sacredness of all art. "Bull," she whispered to him as they stood behind a tour group. "You're just filled with the fear that fills all men—that someone might cut your . . ."

Pieter nudged her with his elbow. "Quiet."

". . . balls off," she said.

Pieter brought his camera along and took several rolls of pictures—all of Demmie. She even allowed him to photograph her nude one afternoon as she stood on the balcony. "You paid for it," she said, leaning against the railing, turning slowly in the resplendent sunlight. A crowd of men gathered on the street below. They shouted, *"Che bella!"* and made lewd gestures. Pieter climbed on the table, trying for a shot of Demmie leaning over the rail, with the howling, gesturing men in the background. "Blow them kisses," Pieter urged her. "Incite them."

Two of the men tried to force their way into the pensione, but Vincenze turned them away at the door. Then he ran down the hall and scolded Pieter for such a foolish, immoral display. Pieter held back his laughter at Vincenze's irritation and apologized convincingly. As Vincenze walked out of the room, he made the same obscene clacking sound with his mouth he had made that first morning, after watching Demmie walk down the hall in her bathrobe.

119

They left Florence the following day. After they picked up Pieter's car at the airport and were on their way home, he asked her to move in with him.

"I couldn't," she said, slouched in the seat with her visored cap pulled low over her eyes.

"But what about what we did at Vincenze's? And at the beach?" He cursed the urgency in his words; he had expected that answer the moment he thought of asking her, but now he did not want to hear it.

"That's what I mean about your being so provincial. You shouldn't attach so much meaning to what we do in bed. I care for you," she said, her voice softening, "very much. So I sleep with you."

The sky was getting dark; the air cooled with the threat of a shower. The reality of being back, of having to face everything at the museum, descended upon him. A longing swelled in his throat for Florence, where everything, like the warm weather, seemed to stay constant, where his and her passion were one. As a restorer, hadn't he been taught that his life's work was to keep things as they were? Hadn't it been his father's words to him, when he was a teenager, that had formed the chief tenet of his life? "Restoration is an art, but it is not like the other arts," his father had told him. "It is not our job as restorers to advance, to evolve, like the schools of painting. People bring us their paintings, and we must maintain them in a fixed state; we must keep them exactly as they are, as they were always meant to be."

He found himself asking her, "Wasn't it good?"

She straightened in her seat and pushed her cap back. "Sure. And it will be again. Often. I like older men." She laughed at her own joke. "Oh, Pieter, don't be so serious. I don't want to give up my life and assume yours."

He glanced at her face as he drove. Droplets of rain spattered the windshield, and colors from the traffic's lights dotted her cheeks and forehead with red and green. The wiper's shadows swept rhythmically across her face. Instinctively, he knew she was right. Especially now, with the restoration in progress. How would it be working all day together, then seeing each other all night? It would ruin everything. She held her pale eyes straight ahead, as if mesmerized by the ripping sound of the wet tires against the road. He felt as though his holiday had been one rare dessert in his life, and now he was left only with its aftertaste.

"Will you come home with me tonight?"

"Only if you promise not to pressure me to move in. My freedom is important," she said, closing her eyes again and leaving him to fight the traffic by himself.

13

Jan had seen to it that the Town Council's plans for the restoration studio were executed perfectly. When Pieter came into the museum, not only was the gallery ready but the items on his list for the first phase of the project were already laid out on worktables. He wrote a quick memorandum to the Director General, with copies for the Town Council, commending Jan for the timeliness of his work and advising them that the restoration of *The Night Watch* would commence immediately.

The painting was still in its frame, which was fastened to the gallery wall. The top of the frame remained open so the painting, attached to a stretcher, could easily be slipped in or taken out. Pieter climbed the scaffolding and attached the blocks and tackles to the stretcher. From the floor Theillen and Stan Martins slowly hoisted *The Night Watch* out of its frame while Demmie, standing on the other scaffold, pushed the stretcher back to keep the face of the painting from scraping against the inside edge of the frame. Then Theillen and Stan held the painting aloft, and Pieter and Demmie climbed down to guide it, face up, onto the small padded work stage.

Aside from the slasher, no one had touched *The Night Watch* in nearly thirty years. Pieter rolled the movable dais over the painting, knelt down in the center with a flannel cloth, and began dusting away the bloom, a cloudy film that had been caused by the moisture in the breath of spectators who had come to admire it. Somehow he had expected the painting to feel different, perhaps alive to his first touch, as if the communion he sought with it would come that easily. It was covered with hardened varnish, not resilient skin; the flannel rag snagged in the heavy impasto of van Ruytenburch's coat. Then he heard his staff clapping and looked up at their faces, all smiling excitedly with their own eagerness to lay hands on the painting.

Demmie pointed behind him. The gallery curtains had been left open, and the spectators on the other side were silently applauding. Pieter let each of them—Demmie, Theillen, and Stan—climb the dais and dust a portion of the painting. He found himself smiling and, when he looked toward the windows, nodding with an imbecilic grin on his face.

After lunch, they turned the painting back over to remove the stretcher. The film crew arrived and began setting up their lights. At first, only a few people peeked through the window, but as the commotion with the cameras and lights got under way, the gallery filled entirely. The pressure of all the staring eyes made Pieter uncomfortable. They had not seen the morning's first bit of work, he thought, but had gathered for the spectacle of the filming, like the curious at the scene of a terrible accident, and a proprietary jealousy took him over.

"Close the curtains," he told Demmie.

He drew chalk lines around the old relining canvas, twenty-five centimeters from the edge. They would remove all the inside area, but for now they would need that twenty-five centimeters in place, to turn the painting over.

He did not notice the temperature change in the room till he saw rings of perspiration on Theillen's T-shirt. Demmie had an almost imperceptible mustache of sweat on her upper lip. "Damn it!" he shouted. "Someone check the temperature."

"Twenty-four," Demmie said.

"Shut off those lights," Pieter ordered.

The film crew's director, a goateed Dutchman with wiry hair, a pale complexion, and nearly purple lips, told his cameraman to keep shooting. "A few more feet," he pleaded with Pieter.

"Shut them off now."

Pieter called the director off to a corner of the workroom. "We're going to have to work something out. The days you want to shoot, you'll have to let me know in advance, so I can regulate the temperature to compensate for the heat of the lights. The canvas will stretch and sag if we fluctuate too much."

"That's impossible," the director said. "We are shooting two films simultaneously. . . ."

A light tapping at the gallery door distracted Pieter's sudden anger. He was about to send the film crew back to the Town Council: no cooperation, no documentary.

Demmie drew back the curtain, then let Jan in. There was too much commotion in the workroom now. They would never get anything done at this rate. Jan hurried over to Pieter. "This is wonderful," he said. "There are so many people out there. Open those curtains, Pieter, please. It will do well for the museum if the public can see." Guilder signs danced in Jan's quick dark eyes. He looked as though he had dropped a few pounds from his paunch too.

"This is not a performance, Jan. There's only so much I can put up with. In fact, I'm about to throw your film crew out of here."

"But why? Have they disturbed you?"

"They're creating too much heat."

After Pieter explained the danger, Jan called the film crew into a huddle. There was a brief, muffled argument. Then the director had them gather their gear, and they left.

When Jan came back over to Pieter, he said, "There, you see. It's all simple if we work together. They will notify you twenty-four hours before they come. Anything else you want, don't hesitate to ask."

"Thank you," Pieter said.

"Now a favor for me," Jan said. "Give the afternoon crowd a bit of a peep, will you?"

"They can watch the documentary, like everyone else," Pieter snapped.

124

"Now, Pieter," Jan said, "don't be so tense. Just try to be fair. They have a right to see what's going on too."

Before they finished for the day, Pieter and Demmie and two of the men from the maintenance crew brought down some extractor fans from the tower. "One of these fans must be kept on at all times to remove noxious vapors," Pieter cautioned the others, "or we'll all get very sick." Then he instructed the guards on how to check the temperature, and they left.

He and Demmie walked to a small restaurant on the Leidseplein, where they ate dinner. He ordered steak and salad; she had trout, broiled in butter. He asked her why she never ordered steak.

"Don't you think I can afford it?"

"I don't eat meat," she said.

"Since when?" He couldn't remember for certain, but he felt sure she had ordered a meat dish in Italy.

"Since ever. My parents couldn't get any during the war, so they just stopped eating it. Then I came along, and they didn't bother feeding it to me either. So here I am, a freak. A vegetarian from the days before it became chic. Can we change the subject?"

"Why?"

"Because they're dead."

He waited for her to break into one of her impish grins, but she didn't. She pushed a piece of fish around on her plate; her eyes suddenly dulled with pensiveness. Finally, he said, "I'm sorry."

They ate in silence for a while. The small orange candle set in the center of their table gave off a flickering light that made dark nets of shadows sweep her face. It looked stark, boyish. He thought of her in the pensione in Florence, with the red light casting a satin sheen over her skin. And now the change in light made a change in the way he saw her.

"How did you feel today?" she asked.

He poured himself some wine. "I don't know. All right, I guess."

"There were hundreds of people staring at you. Movie cameras. Did you feel nervous?"

"No," he lied. "I wasn't paying attention."

"Why did you snap at Jan, then?"

"I don't know why I snapped at him. Because he's an ass, I guess."

"You act as if you're made of steel, Pieter Beckum. Well, I can tell you I felt like some sort of freak on exhibition, a circus performer." She laughed.

"It wasn't all that bad. Can I have your potato?"

"I've been onstage before," she said, "and it was bad for me." She stabbed her fork into the baked potato and dropped it on his plate. "But I suspect this afternoon was a first for you. Right?"

"Right," he said. "Now can we change *this* subject?"

She winked at him. "Touché." And when she laughed this time, she threw back her head so that the shadows from the candle licked at her chin and throat, highlighting the somewhat imperfect ivory edges of her teeth. Though he had studied her mouth, kissed her lips, and examined her in different ways, somehow he had failed to notice that her front teeth were a little larger than they should be, and that they buckled slightly to the front. She was ever a mystery to him, and he delighted in the simple, slow revelation of unexpected detail.

They each had a cigarette and coffee after dinner.

"Do you want to go to the cinema tonight?"

"I already have plans," she said.

"What are you going to do?"

"Please don't ask."

They walked along the tree-shaded quay of the Stadhouderskade to the museum. He put his arm around her shoulder for the first time since their holiday, wondering what her plans might be and not really wanting to know. The sun setting behind them dappled the broad leaves of the maple trees with a high yellow light.

They crossed the bridge in front of the museum to sit on a bench. A Holland International bus pulled in front of a dock, and a group of screaming children broke from the door and ran to the waiting tour boat.

"The city's filling up too fast this year," Pieter said. "That means crowds in the museum."

"Did you look at the people who were watching us today?"

"Yes."

"I mean really look at them. Closely." She was watching the children, who had gotten completely out of control. They were crawling all over the inside of the boat, cheering. A tour guide was trying to quiet them to no avail.

"They were just a bothersome crowd to me," Pieter said.

"Some of them were magnificent." She turned to him. Their eyes were inches apart; he could see dark symmetrical lines radiating from her blue irises. Her breath still smelled faintly of fish, and he suddenly wanted to kiss her more than anything in the world.

"Magnificent?"

"Those people. The spectators. Something in why they were there made them look so tragic to me. That's why I acted so strangely at dinner; I think the whole day unnerved me, and yet I loved it."

"They're just curious," Pieter said. "We have become the summer attraction, and they are the watchers of catastrophe. Even the Tourist Information Office is recommending a stop at the museum."

"Why are you being so cynical?"

"I'm sorry," he said. "But everything seems on the verge of going out of control. As you said, it's a circus."

"One woman really dazzled me," Demmie said, looking back to the children on the boat. Two of them were outside on the roof now, and the tour guide was chasing them. "She could have stepped right out of *The Night Watch*. You know the little girl with the chicken tied to her belt?"

"Yes."

"Except for a difference in age, this woman could have been her. They had the same ghostly pale face, the same pursed red lips. God, I saw for the first time why Rembrandt was so great. It made me shudder. I mean, the people he painted are still alive and walking the streets of this city today. It took kneeling over that face with a dustcloth in my hand to realize what I should have known all along."

The boat finally chugged away from the dock and passed under the bridge. The children were all sitting in orderly rows. "I bet we could find your face in there if we looked real hard," she said. "Walk me to my bike, all right?"

They crossed the Stadhouderskade and ambled through the giant archway that cut through the museum. Her voice took on a hollow, artificial deepness, as if the vaulted stone ceiling's amplification had removed its vibrancy.

"She had these gloves on, this woman. They were sheer nylon, like stockings, except the fingers had been cut out. Her fingers were pressed to the glass. I can't explain it exactly, but that one detail I remembered made me feel the whole of her life and it depressed me. As if we weren't on stage; she was. Do you think that's screwy?"

"Not at all," Pieter said, thinking, Yes, it's mildly screwy.

"You're just patronizing me, Pieter. Please don't do that."

"I'm not," he protested. "I've had those feelings before." He wondered, just then, how she saw him, whether she wasn't jamming him back into the very box he was struggling to get out of, the one of the all too serious restorer who could neither feel nor enjoy the most insignificant detail of life. He made a mental note to show her the pictures from the Queen's birthday as soon as they were developed.

Her motorcycle was parked behind a fence by the maintenance building at the back of the museum. It was a white 750 BMW. He could not imagine how she could handle such a heavy machine. She threw her leg over the seat and tucked her long skirt into her crotch, then pressed the electric starter and the cycle hummed to life. "You have to let me take you for a ride someday. To the beach, perhaps." She unfastened her helmet from the handlebar and put it on, stuffing in her blond ringlets.

"Perhaps," he said.

"Perhaps," she said, mimicking him, her eyes coming alive like two tiny bolts of lightning, her lips spreading in a mischievous smile. "Perhaps. Pieter, dear, you make me scream. If you don't loosen up, you'll pop." She kicked the engine into gear, jumped the curb, and braked. "You're not getting any younger."

"That was unfair," he shouted as she drove away. He watched her thread confidently through the traffic, then disappear around a corner. He thought she, of all people, would have appreciated the change he was trying to make in his life. He thought of her little old lady at the gallery window with the sheer nylon gloves. The truth, of course, was that the spectators had made him tense. He had failed to share that moment of honesty with her because he believed it would have revealed some weakness or incompetence on his part, and now he wished he had, so that she could have driven away knowing he was, in some ways, just as vulnerable as she.

14

From the sidewalk across the street from the fish shop, van Rijks watched Stolk saw the head off a large salmon. His white coat was smeared with pink streaks of blood; a small paper cap covered his head. From nowhere, a large tabby cat sprang onto his cutting table, and Stolk lurched backward, startled. He threw down his knife and wiped his bloody hands on his sides. The cat sniffed at the fish while Stolk's mouth pumped furiously. Then he picked the cat up by the scruff of its neck, struck it, and dropped it out of sight behind him.

Van Rijks pulled the visor of his sailor cap low on his forehead, quickly crossed the street, and let himself in the door that led to his room. He waited at the base of the stairs in the darkness, listening for Stolk, hoping he had not made too much noise.

Everything was as he had left it. Drawings of anguished faces on the walls, an empty easel, the single rumpled bed in the corner, red and black chalk dust smeared on the floor by the window. That fish-killing bastard hadn't been up here since he had gone. He became suddenly frightened. Had he ever left this room and gone to Amsterdam? Or had his imagination played him some elaborate hoax? And if he had left, how long had it taken for all this to have happened? A month? A week? A day?

Go to the mirror, asshole. Take a look. You can't grow a beard like that in a day or a week. He looked in the mirror, and his face confirmed his absence from the room. His eyes were glazed over from the pills they had given him; the beard was almost full again. He cocked the cap, and a little hair touched the top of his ears. *An admirable disguise.* He started laughing. *One more to try it out on, though. Neel.* He felt in his pocket for one of the vials, uncapped it, and popped a pill into his mouth.

He found the books he had stacked on the floor of the closet. He'd hidden hundred-guilder notes, the remainder of his savings, in the pages of six of them. *Smart as a fox,* he said to himself. *Stick with me and I'll teach you a trick or two. Now move. A little rest will do you good, but not here, not now.*

As he opened the door that led to the street, he almost stepped on the cat, blocking his exit. It stopped pawing at the salmon head that Stolk had neatly severed, hunched its shoulders, and looked up to him. *Please,* he said, averting his head, *don't do this.* The cat gave a throaty possessive hiss. *You have to look. At your feet.* The cat had torn away the perfectly round yellow and black eye and was batting it against the door, trying to pin it with a paw. He jumped over the cat and bounded down the street, leaving the door wide open.

He stole the first unlocked bicycle he found—it was leaning against the side of a café—and pedaled ten kilometers to his house. By the time he got there, it was nearly dark. He knocked, and there was no answer. He knocked again, louder.

"Who is it?" Her voice.

He stepped back from the landing so she could see him from the window on the floor above. "Me," he said.

"Who is it?" she called again.

He could see the outline of her body behind the closed lace curtain. He removed his cap and looked up at her puffy oval face. "Me, damn it!" he yelled.

"I didn't recognize you," she said as she let him in. She ran her hands through her unkempt red hair, smoothing it. "They said you might come."

"Who?"

"Don't be ridiculous. Who? The people from the Psychiatric

Institute. They're looking for you, you know. The police. What have you done? They wouldn't tell me."

One of her eyes was a little larger than the other, giving her face a slightly unbalanced look. "Why are you looking at me like that?" he said.

"I was just looking at the beard."

He followed her up the steep, narrow stairs to the living room. He couldn't control his giggling; everything here was the same too. The television was blaring. He could smell food cooking in the kitchen; it filled the house with a flat potato smell. He wondered, again, if he had ever left *this* place. Time seemed to be drawing him backward. The next place he would show up in would be his classroom; no doubt he would be bawling his eyes out. And he would forever be drawn backward by these funny pills, these funny thoughts that tickled his mind, forever backward with the tremendous pull of a vortex, swirling him down into some bottomless black hole until he was completely obliterated at the moment of his inverted conception.

"Where's Johannes?" he demanded.

"You're not going to start that again," she said. "Don't come back and start tormenting me." Her eyes were filling up.

"I'm not joking, Neel. Where's Johannes?" He turned down the hall to his room.

"He's dead!" she cried. "Now, stop it. Go away, like you did before." She slumped into an armchair. "Just go away."

He stopped himself at Johannes's door. *Go in.* "Like the fish eye, you devil," he said aloud, "I can't."

"What did you say?"

You have to. Go on.

"No!" he yelled. But he went in anyway, against the grip of his hands on the doorjamb, against his will. There was nothing of Johannes left, as if Johannes himself had never existed, and he wanted to scream out against it all. A sewing machine sat on a table in the center of the room where Johannes's bed had been. He had wept there. Or had he? A broken mannequin, nude, had been shoved into a corner. Tissue and bolts of colorful material cluttered the floor.

"Let me call the hospital." She was standing in the doorway, wringing her hands.

"Where are his things?"

"It's been a year," she said. "I moved them into the attic. I needed the room for work. I can't keep a shrine here. Not forever."

"Bitch," he snarled. Some voice chimed in: *Unrepentant, insensitive whore,* it said. "It was your fault." He pushed past her, and she followed.

"It was not my fault." She was sobbing again. "Nothing could have been done."

He swung around, his face pulsing with red-hot rage. He had formed one sentence that summed it up. "All you had to do was kiss him on the forehead to know his brain was burning up with fever," he said. It was the only truth that had come from his mourning. "All you had to do was pay attention to your child and it could have been prevented, instead of—"

She struck his face, sending a line of white froth flying from his mouth. "Stop it," she commanded. "Stop it now."

He dropped to the couch, stunned. "I'm leaving the country," he said, calm now. "Give me some money."

"What have you done?"

"Leave me alone, damn it. I haven't done anything."

"Then why are you leaving?"

"Just give me money and I'll leave."

"I don't have any to give."

Why was she doing this to him? Why was she looking at him this way? She had the same crooked eyes as Johannes, and they were filling up with loathsome pity now till they overflowed with tears. "Stop crying, please. Stop crying. I'll go away, Johannes. I love you." He reached for her hand, to feel whatever tenderness shivered in that flesh, but she shoved a crisp hundred-guilder note into his palm.

133

"My savings," she was saying; her hands shook as she counted out four more notes. "It's all I have. You're crazy, you know. You need help." Her lips were taut, stretched white with anger. "I'm going to call them when you leave. Tell them you've been here."

15

The work floor was covered with cork, layers of felt, and a thin transparent plastic called Melinex. *The Night Watch* lay face down. Theillen and Demmie removed the tacks that held the relining canvas to the stretcher; then Pieter and Stan Martins lifted the stretcher away and set it against the wall of the workroom.

Next, they moved the dais over the painting to begin the grueling work of cutting away the old relining canvas. Starting in the area marked with chalk where the largest cut was, Pieter peeled back a small strip of wax-impregnated canvas, then cut it away with a small razor-sharp knife. The canvas underneath, Rembrandt's canvas, was a darkened mottled brown with a relief of wax and resin almost three millimeters thick which would have to be scraped away before the new canvas could be applied. He proceeded quite slowly, cutting away canvas around the slashes in ten-centimeter strips. Then he rolled up the strips and handed them to Theillen, who stacked them on a small table in the corner.

Demmie was kneeling beside Pieter on the dais. After each initial cut, he pulled with both hands in even jerking motions, the canvas curling stiffly, strands of thread standing out like thin white wires.

He could feel the sound of tearing in his hands as tiny vibrations, and it exhilarated him. He knew the greatest danger now was that he might inadvertently rip some of the Rembrandt canvas around the slashes. He asked for silence so he could listen closely to the sound, holding his breath against the subtle change in tone that would indicate he had made a mistake.

After lunch, he told Theillen to draw back the curtains so the people in the gallery could watch, and he continued removing the most difficult pieces from around the slashes. That whole first afternoon, he worked bent over on the dais. Demmie and Theillen flanked him, watching silently. In the morning, he would turn the work over to them and they would strip the canvas out to the chalked border. This tedious task would test their mettle as much as anything. After the exhilaration of the first few cuts, it became slow, boring work.

Jan called him that evening to let him know the film crew would return to shoot some more footage. Though Pieter could not figure out why, Jan had asked him to save the strips of canvas for collection at the end of each day.

For two days, Pieter left the gallery curtains closed while Theillen and Demmie worked. Theillen did well. It wasn't long before he had figured out the precise angle of cocking his wrist to cut the maximum canvas in one motion. He seemed to have established a peculiar rhythm too—a slice, two tugs, and another slice —that enabled him to come away with almost exactly ten centimeters each time.

Demmie cut quite slowly. At first awkward, with a strange backhanded movement, she did half the work of Theillen, though it was no less precise.

By the third day, Pieter decided to open the curtains. He was curious to see if Theillen and Demmie were affected, as he had been, by the tension of watchful eyes. Theillen seemed to slow down, taking less away, his rhythm suddenly disjointed; whereas Demmie grew bolder. He didn't see her turn to look at the crowd who pressed up to the glass, but he had the extraordinary feeling that had he asked her to describe one person, someone she thought might have been out there, she could easily have done so.

Jan came down from his office and collected the steadily building pile of old canvas in a brown paper sack. Pieter cornered him by the door as he tried to leave.

"What are you going to do with that canvas, Jan?"

"Nothing that I know of," he said. "The Director General's orders. See you." He slipped out the door, and Pieter drew the curtains.

Pieter and Demmie had lunch twice that week, and she teased him with descriptions of people who had been watching them.

"It's really quite entertaining." She was eating a cheese sandwich and sipping beer with him on the crowded plaza of the Leidseplein. The azure sky was flecked with wisps of pearly cirrus clouds. Demmie hiked her skirt to tan her legs.

A young, long-haired boy strolled among the tables, strumming a battered guitar, and with a raspy voice sang old Beatles songs. He stopped at their table, eyeing Demmie playfully as he sang, and she handed him a couple of guilders. As Pieter watched the exchange, he felt a stir of jealousy.

"One guy with a big bristly handlebar mustache," she said, turning her attention back to him, "looked like that jolly man in *The Night Watch* with the top hat. I think I've seen him before, selling oranges and doing bird whistles at the Albert Cuypstraat market. I'm toying with this theory that I shall see every character in the painting out in the gallery before we're through. Anyway, I imagined him caught in the middle of the painting, as incongruous as my little girl with the chicken, jostled by the fuseliers and spear carriers and totally amused by it all."

"You have to stop this fantasizing," Pieter said. "This is precisely the effect that I didn't want the open curtains to have on you. It's going to impede your work."

"It doesn't really hurt," she said, "because I don't have these fantasies while I'm working. They just sort of come to me later because these people impress me."

"Just the same, I think I'll leave the curtains closed more than I leave them open. We're not a spectacle, you know."

"I know. But they are," Demmie said, a crumb sticking in the corner of her mouth.

"How do you like working with Theillen?"

"All right, I guess. He seems proficient, but he's very somber."

"I know. You haven't made up any stories about him, have you?"

"No," she said. "Would you like me to?"

"Very funny."

A blue police van stopped at the edge of the plaza. Two officers got out and, after a brief argument, chased the strolling minstrel away.

"Why don't you leave him alone," Demmie called out.

"Will you simmer down?" Pieter said.

"It's an outrage. He wasn't hurting anyone."

"It's against the law," Pieter countered. Then, "Would you like to come over tonight?"

"So what if it's against the law, and I'd like to but I can't. I'm tied up all this week."

He drove by her apartment twice that week. Her lights were out and her motorcycle was gone. He wanted to be puzzled by her avoidance of him, but he knew she was probably seeing someone else. Perhaps the plaza minstrel, or Theillen. That would have been a fitting irony. He was sickened by thoughts of the terrible, sweaty couplings she might be having. He had noticed one pleasant-looking young man watching the restoration, and it occurred to him that if she was capable of making up stories about the people who watched, she was just as capable of tracking one of them down. There were no bounds of propriety for her. He would have given his soul to be younger, so that he might understand her; or for her to be older so that she could understand him. There seemed such a chasm between them. He lay in bed those nights and imagined her wrapped in some boy's arms, doing those things he wanted to believe she reserved for him. Before he finally fell off to sleep, he realized that her fantasy-making could indeed be quite interesting, if it weren't, at the same time, so painful.

After the relining canvas had been cut away, Pieter surveyed the cuts with a 40x microscope. Most of the threads in the original canvas had been pulled straight by the moist adhesive of the mulberry paper that he had pasted over the cuts on the front. With tweezers dipped in diluted epoxy, he carefully aligned the warp and woof of the remaining threads, sticking them temporarily to the mulberry paper. It would be impossible simply to reline the canvas, as was customarily done, because the original canvas would eventually lift along the tears where the continuity of thread was broken. These cuts would have to be bonded and the relining canvas laid over them.

Jan, with his perennial nervous pacing and his ever-thinning paunch, brought news that the Town Council wanted the work stopped. They wanted to film a staged presentation by Pieter in which he detailed the work already done on *The Night Watch*, as well as how he intended to handle the bonding of the cuts. The film director had convinced Simons, Pieter was told, that this material should be edited in to give a sense of drama to their narrative on the restoration.

"How did they know we were coming to the bonding stage, Jan?" Pieter was exasperated with their flair for theatrics.

"I don't know," Jan said. "They just did. They're keeping a close eye on this project."

"They're not omniscient, Jan. Are you their watchdog?"

"Come on, Pieter, don't insult me. I have to prepare the weekly press releases and they get one. They always know what you're doing."

16

From Centraal Station, van Rijks walked straight up the Damrak to the Café Zwart. The street was crowded, and there were more policemen than he had anticipated. But he had fooled Neel; she hadn't recognized him with the beard, hat, and dark glasses, and now he would fool all the others. This muggy evening, he felt as though he were invisible, and he had to resist the impulse to ask a policeman for directions just to taunt the fates that had conspired to free him.

First he searched the bar for Molen's face, then spotted him at a corner table talking to an elderly lady wearing a velour dress; her hair was piled on top of her head and long earrings dangled from her lobes. He looked around, too, for the man whose face resembled a bulldog—he remembered sketching him here—but he was nowhere in sight. Van Rijks sat at a table beside Molen's, with a young American couple, and ordered a pils.

Molen was telling the lady that he was a diamond cutter and that he had never seen quite such an exquisite jewel as the one she wore on her ring finger. Van Rijks watched Molen's thin neck twitch as he talked. He could see a tiny network of purple veins on Molen's ears, which stood out too far, and he had to fight back the sudden temptation to pummel the back of his head.

"Excuse me," van Rijks said. "Could I trouble you for a match?"

Molen gave him an aggravated sideways glance and lit van Rijks's cigarette.

After van Rijks finished his beer, he interrupted Molen again. "Terribly sorry. But do you have the time?"

"What's with you?" Molen growled. "Can't you see I'm occupied?" He turned back to his woman. She peeked over Molen's shoulder at van Rijks, her face reddening a little; then she shifted her chair around the table.

Van Rijks took off his sunglasses and tapped Molen again.

"What is it now?" Molen asked, desperation tinging his voice.

"Don't you recognize me?"

"Never seen you. So leave me and the missus alone, will you?"

Molen shifted his chair around the table too, closer to the woman. *Missus;* van Rijks laughed to himself. *You whoremonger.* Then, as if struck by the blow van Rijks had contemplated delivering to the back of his head, Molen shot straight up out of his chair, his face pale with fear.

Van Rijks jumped up at the same moment, caught Molen by the collar, and shoved him toward the door. He called to the woman, "He won't be back."

"What do you want?" Molen asked, once they were on the sidewalk. "I tried finding you, but you disappeared like. All of a sudden. Where have you been?"

Van Rijks guided him along the sidewalk and across the street. "Never you mind where I've been, weasel. You've got something that belongs to me, and I want it now."

They caught a taxi to Molen's apartment, three dingy rooms above a sex shop in the red-light district. Dirty sheets covered the windows; crates doubling for tables were scattered about the place with unshaded, dimly glowing lamps on them. Three small mattresses were strewn about the living-room floor.

"So this is where the distinguished diamond cutter lives, huh?" He pushed Molen onto one of the mattresses.

"I was just trying to make a guilder," Molen said. "She'd have popped for plenty too, but you had to muck it up for me. Couldn't wait."

"Get my drawings."

Molen scrambled to his feet and disappeared into the other

room. He returned moments later with the black leather portfolio and dropped it at van Rijks's feet.

"Here."

Van Rijks opened it and spread his drawings around the floor. The sight of them caused his lungs to tighten, and his pulse quickened, pounding wildly in his temples. He knew he was due for another pill, but he had so much to look at, so much to remember. There was the wash drawing of the mother and child —the child with the death mask sucking his mother's teat. He could not recall his hands drawing those gruesome lines, but his initials were scribbled in the corner. His hands were shaking now; an electric tingling of energy mounted in steady beats inside his veins. He needed to remember these drawings to convince himself that he had not done what everyone had claimed. But the drawings were as vague as apparitions, as if they had been part of some disturbing dream he could not piece together.

And then he saw his rough sketches of the Queen's birthday. The gypsies, jugglers, the Moluccan whore, the acrobats, the witch-faced old hags in the gull-winged bonnets. He realized in the juxtaposing of all these subjects on a single sheet that he was a member of a race of lunatics. Of course he had done what they said. The ironies of his drawings on that page thoroughly frightened him, not because they offered any threat against him but because he was the only one who could see it all. Before, he had trained his eye to pick out unusual detail in all that was commonplace and to find beauty in it—like the veins in Molen's ears or the armless mannequin in Johannes's room. Now those details became the maddening flaws of unredeemable people. The veins in Molen's big ears made him want to strike him; the armless mannequin made him want to torture Neel with grief.

"Hey, you bastard, some drawings are missing," he snarled.

Molen broke for the door, and van Rijks brought him down by the ankles. "Let go of me!" Molen shouted, trying to kick free. Van Rijks was on his chest, his hands tightening on his neck; he could feel Molen's brittle Adam's apple giving way to his thumbs.

Then he stopped.

Molen's face had turned crimson, comically crimson. His eye-glasses had come off and his dark eyes swelled and pulsed with the same weakening beat van Rijks felt in his scrawny throat.

Molen scooted across the floor on his back, rubbing his neck with both hands and wheezing as if he had tuberculosis.

"Where are the other drawings?" van Rijks asked, his voice as calm as if nothing had happened between them.

After a moment, Molen said, "I sold some. I figured you were never coming back for them, so I took them to the flea market at the Waterlooplein."

"Where's the money? I want the money."

"I spent it."

"Then you owe me."

"I don't have any money," Molen whined. "I can't pay you."

"But you can work for me. You can sell the rest of them, and you can bring me the money."

"These drawings don't fetch much. A few guilders."

"Sell them anyway. I'll make more." He liked the idea of having an agent, even if Molen was a greedy pimp. He took a vial of pills from his pocket, opened it, and popped one into his mouth. It tasted bitter, and he had to swallow hard to get it down.

"What have you got there?" Molen asked. "Share it with me, will you? You hurt me."

Van Rijks tossed him a pill. *Guard those friggin' pills, damn it. That's all you've got. The weasel will suck you dry, that's his game, and then where will you be?* "Get up," van Rijks ordered. "I want you to find me a safe place to hide."

17

Pieter ordered the gallery closed for a week so he could work on the Town Council's newest demand. He sent his staff home for the time being, fighting the urge to call Demmie at every dead spot in his routine. She had phoned him once, but he had cut the conversation short with the excuse that he had more work than he could hope to complete in a week and needed his every instant. In his pining over her, he had lost sight of just how damaging the Town Council's idiotic demands could be. Of course they would demand he do more than simply work in their windowed studio. This should not have come as a surprise, but it had. And Demmie was distracting him to the point of making him dull-minded. Damn it, if she wanted to carry on with other men, so be it. He did not have the time, or the energy, to be enticed into distraction on her account. He would immerse himself, as he had always done, in the project at hand. He did not understand her, and he decided not to try any longer. Jealousy, at his age, was ludicrous. He had done well throughout his life without enduring relationships. What kind of desperation was it that now demanded he hold on to *her?*

That week, Pieter worked in his studio like a man possessed. He had heard that restorers at the Institut Royal du Patrimoine Artistique had been using Araldite, an epoxy resin thinned with acetone, as an adhesive in their relining for some time. He had been waiting for the opportunity to try this new technique. Since *The Night Watch* was heavily impregnated with resin, he knew he would not be able to use animal glue. It would cause the canvas to shrink.

He pulled some linen threads out of a piece of slashed test canvas, passed them through his Araldite solution, then laid them, from one frayed end to the other, across the cut he had made. As the canvas dried, he watched it under the microscope until his eyes ached. What he discovered astounded him. Since the canvas was woven linen, containing a high percentage of cellulose, he expected his test piece to tighten, form folds. But the Araldite had not penetrated the linen threads; it enveloped them. Future restorers would be able to reverse his work if they found a better bonding agent. Who on the Council could find fault with that? He twisted the patched canvas, folded it, pulled against it with all his strength, and still the Araldite held firm. The only problem —the one to which he had no immediate answer—was how he would keep the network of threads from forming bulges on the paint side of the canvas.

He checked the reports from previous restorations of *The Night Watch* to see how the remaining wax-resin adhesive from the relining canvas had been removed.

Both in 1851 and 1947, a knife had been used, which meant that further scraping by his staff would cause irreparable deformations to the canvas. He brought bottles of ethyl acetate, ethylbenzene, and xylene down to the workroom. He applied each in small swatches to the back of the canvas. Xylene proved the best solvent, since none of it penetrated the front of the painting and it evaporated immediately.

He ironed small pieces of canvas, of varying thickness, to the back of the original canvas with a wax-resin mixture to test adhesion. The thick canvas used in the 1947 relining had absorbed all the adhesive in the center of the painting, causing Rembrandt's canvas to separate from its backing. The triangle fell away from Banning's breeches because of this poor work. By the way the canvas had curled around the slashes before he had applied the mulberry paper, he knew it would simply have been a matter of time before the entire canvas came unglued. However, with a canvas too thin, the adhesive would penetrate completely to the original canvas and mar the paint surface.

The last thing he did before the Town Council meeting was phone Theillen and ask him to stop by the studio. Pieter gathered the reports on *The Night Watch*'s restorations, his scope of work, and all his notes and photographs of what had already been accomplished—everything except his presentation for the Council—and gave them to Theillen.

"Take this box to your apartment," he told Theillen, "and keep it there till I tell you otherwise."

"What's in it?" Theillen asked.

"Our future," Pieter said. "I feel as if I'm going to walk into a den of lions tomorrow. I don't trust those people, any of them, and I want to be prepared to hold out against any more of their unreasonableness."

"Good luck," Theillen said. He hoisted the large box on his shoulder and started for the door.

"I would appreciate it," Pieter said, stopping him, "if you would keep this to yourself. No one else need know."

He had chosen Theillen for this task because Demmie had been so impressed by his reserve. He had come to like Theillen, liked him even more for not acting as if Pieter were crazy in his paranoia about the Council, and for not pressing him about the box's contents. When he had interviewed Theillen, he had misjudged him, seeing his own prejudice instead of the boy's potential. "I am a good worker," Theillen had told him, and he was turning out to be as capable—with his incongruous body-builder muscles, his tattoo, and his T-shirts—as anyone he had ever taught.

The Town Council gathered in the private film theater on the first floor of the Rijksmuseum. Simons had brought guests, consultants from the Institut Royal du Patrimoine Artistique. It was no secret that Pieter had been understaffed from the inception of the restoration, and these others, Pieter knew, instead of offering encouragement, were waiting for him to make a mistake.

A dozen people filled the front row of the auditorium, while

146

Pieter's staff sat in the back. He stood at a podium on the empty stage, reading his report into a microphone. The film crew's lights were sizzling from the third row; he could feel their heat drying the skin of his face, stretching it tight across his brow, just as canvas tightened from prolonged exposure to heat.

Demmie passed out photocopied sheets with the results of his tests and the chemical compositions of the hydrocarbon solutions he had tried. He had the film crew extinguish their lights while he used a slide projector to flash photos of the damaged *Night Watch* on the screen behind him.

When he reached the slide illustrating his tests with Araldite, he became nervous. The very people who had used this technique for years, who knew so much more about it than he, were beginning to shift in their seats. The man sitting next to Simons began whispering in his ear. Then he raised his hand to ask, in a nasal, patronizing voice, if the fibers would show when they turned the canvas back over.

"No," Pieter answered, "because we will shave the threads with scalpels to their thinnest possible dimension." The answer had been so simple that it had completely eluded him while he was performing the tests. Of course it would work. And he could see it had been precisely the right answer by the way the man shrugged and sat back in his seat, looking at Simons with an embarrassed grin.

Another man asked what type of canvas thread they would use to repair the cuts, and Pieter told him they would remove the threads they needed from the old relining canvas. When there were no more questions, the Council applauded his presentation. The consultants from Brussels were the first to shake his hand when he stepped down from the stage. He could feel the strength returning to his voice as he thanked them for coming.

Simons clambered up on the stage and took the microphone. He announced that everyone would be the guest of the Town Council the following night at the Municipal Theater. He handed out envelopes which contained engraved invitations to the ballet. He called Pieter off to the side and said, "There is always time for relaxation, eh? Something to relieve the pressure you must be under." He handed Pieter his invitation and shook his hand.

Pieter wanted to tell him that it was the goddamned Town Council that was creating the pressure with their meddling in his work. If they would all leap off a pier . . . "Thank you," he said graciously.

Pieter met Demmie at the back of the auditorium. She gave him a peck on the cheek.

"Not here."

"You were wonderful," she said. "Did you hear me giggle when your voice cracked?"

"I didn't ever hear it crack. You're coming tomorrow night?" he asked.

She put her hand on his arm. "I can't."

Why not? He began to ask, but remembered his resolve. No silly adolescent scenes. He really hadn't any idea how to react any more; he did not any longer know whether to pursue her or give her up. He wondered if he had offended her, somehow dissatisfied her. When he noticed Theillen leaving the theater, he abruptly broke away from her and stopped the younger man.

"You can bring that box back to the museum tomorrow," he said.

Then he followed Theillen out of the theater, conscious of one thought—he had failed to say goodbye to her.

18

Friday, the day of the ballet, they had already begun removing the superfluous wax resin from the back of the painting with xylene so they could apply the mending strips across the slashes. The workroom was filled with the pungent smell of tar and evergreen; the extractor fans created a monotonous, irritating hum. Pieter had Demmie and Theillen working from the dais, sponging on the xylene, then swabbing away the pasty residue.

The curtains were open and Pieter found himself completely fascinated by the face of a man peering over the shoulder of an old woman. All he could see were the man's eyes, a diagonal of face. Something was inexplicably familiar about him. He searched his memory for the face in the painting which, as Demmie had said, would be the man's counterpart, but he came up with nothing. The man wore a navy-blue seaman's hat; he had wide-set, puffy eyes, and when he shifted, Pieter noticed his splotchy brown beard. He felt that tingle of knowing something intimate about the man's life, as if he, Pieter, had left the workroom suddenly and settled, specter-like, in the man's shoes, sharing the same pulse.

This man—in the frozen attitude of looking over a shoulder, completely absorbed in watching their work, with his watery eyes and pallid complexion—could have been a subject who had escaped from Rembrandt's palette. A single moment of pure unselfconscious human longing was so perfectly clear to him in the man's face that Pieter wanted to go out and say something to him.

Then something tipped inside his head and his breath snagged in his throat. Theillen straightened at the same moment; their eyes met.

"I think you better come look at this, Mr. Beckum," Theillen said.

Pieter climbed on the dais, exchanging positions with Theillen. Demmie knelt next to him, shaking her head. Rembrandt had sewn three horizontal bands of canvas together to give *The Night Watch* its monstrous size. Along the seams, the thread was splitting and the xylene was penetrating to the paint layer. "Shit," Pieter said. It would have been better to chance scraping here. "Demmie, run upstairs and bring down the file from the last relining."

She leaped to the floor without making a sound, and in spite of his annoyance he found himself admiring her gracefulness. "Bring some thread down too," he called after her.

He told Theillen to close the curtains, saying a quick goodbye to *his* spectator. By watching that man, he had been guilty of the same distraction for which he had reprimanded Demmie, and yet he had known, even before Theillen straightened, that something had gone wrong. He was connected with the painting now, had heard it call to him, as a mother might hear her child crying even while she slept.

The report showed that *The Night Watch,* during its last relining, had had these seams shaved so that when they were ironed flat no impressions would show on the paint surface. "The shaving," Pieter told them, "caused the seams to weaken and split." He reinforced them by stitching them with the thread Demmie had brought him. Then, with an erasing knife, he scraped very slowly and carefully till he was satisfied that most of the resin was removed.

"That's it for today," he finally told them. "We'll begin grafting the cuts after the weekend."

That evening, the Leidseplein seemed in the throes of a wild carnival mood. Loud music blared from the cafés surrounding the plaza while couples crowded together at the tables, drinking. Cabs

150

deposited people in front of the clubs and jockeyed for position at the tram stop; minstrels strolled the plaza. Banners proclaiming HOLLAND FESTIVAL hung from the balcony of the Municipal Theater. The spectators in the gallery had nearly tripled since the month-long festival began; it seemed to Pieter that the city could not possibly accommodate the influx. Brightly colored lights strung overhead in the dwarf maple trees of the plaza lent an artificial gaiety to the night. A group of lavishly dressed people milled in the portico of the theater. Some of them sifted across the street, deciding, like him, to have a glass of wine before the performance.

He thought briefly of the man he had seen watching Demmie and Theillen work, and marveled at how his instincts had clicked on. He wished Demmie had consented to come with him, though he knew he would have gotten sidelong glances from Jan and the Director General if he had shown up with her as his date. He could not free his mind of the image of her leaping from the dais. The absence of sound as she hit the floor had been what so impressed him.

He finished his wine and entered the theater. Jan and some of the members of the Town Council were clustered around a central marble pillar in the lobby, smoking cigarettes and laughing too loudly. Theillen stood off to the side by himself. Pieter shook hands with everyone in turn. Theillen nodded but did not come over.

An usher wearing a black theater uniform greeted them and showed them upstairs. Simons had reserved the most perfect seats in the house for them—first balcony center. Their view of the stage was higher than the orchestra level of the small theater so they could see the dancers' footwork, but lower than the other balconies so their perception of depth and the dancers' form would not be distorted.

The first number was a pas de deux from *Romeo and Juliet*, performed competently by two very handsome dancers. The stage was bare of even the simplest scenery; the dancers moved among perfect islands of yellow light with a fluid, unaffected grace. But

Pieter could not concentrate. His mind drifted to *The Night Watch* lying on the gallery work floor. He thought of these dancers, moving from light to darkness, lingering sometimes in the penumbra between perfect shadow and full light, as characters who had escaped the Master's canvas. And it seemed to him in that moment that whoever had choreographed this piece knew, too, that the skillful use of light was more than a technique used to reveal certain aspects of character: it revealed, through simple contrasts, incontrovertible truths.

It was all as elementary as the way most people looked at Rembrandt's work. They celebrated him for the light pouring subtly over his canvas, illuminating in the boundless darkness the truth that his use of detail yielded. But Rembrandt knew that light did not work that way. Light came from a single source and suffused over distance. His light did not shine on the forehead of Jeremiah as he lamented the destruction of Jerusalem; it emanated from it. The ornamentation of Lieutenant van Ruytenburch's brilliant yellow coat in *The Night Watch* was its own source of pure light, as each subject Rembrandt painted was its own source of luminance. That was why his paintings were so true.

And he thought, too, of his own relationship to Rembrandt, now as he sat there in the dark, in the theater's plush red velvet seat, arm against arm with these people who were all connected to what he found significant in his life. He was repairing the masterpiece, so he was the source of *their* light. It would be *his* name that would forever be linked with Rembrandt's. He wondered if there wasn't something in the eternal scheme of things that had always linked him with Rembrandt, if he wasn't somehow made up of some of the molecules from the dead painter that had floated unassociated through the universe until his birth.

And something else became abundantly clear to him: The man who had slashed *The Night Watch* would likewise not only be associated with Rembrandt and, through him, the painting, but also with Pieter himself, even if he was only referred to as "the lunatic, the madman, the slasher."

152

Pieter knew this as surely as he knew that every painting had two surfaces—its paint side and its canvas side. And if he was the painting side, glowing with all the positive energy that made art endure, then the madman was the canvas side, obscure, never seen, existing as mysteriously as the dark side of the moon.

It was that madman's power to destroy art, perhaps more vulnerable than anything else, that enhanced art's value. This destruction—and he hated himself for thinking it, though he knew it was true—had given the painting new life, new meaning, and extended the very time of Rembrandt, insured it for another small eternity. He and the madman were catalysts for the continuation of art.

He wanted to shake the councilman who sat beside him by the shoulders, tell him why they were all sitting together tonight. He felt like the chandelier hanging from the ceiling above him, which earlier had been bursting with brilliantly contained light. He had to tell someone about these thoughts as they rushed in on him; but there wasn't one among them who would not have looked at him with blank, uncomprehending eyes.

The dance lasted longer than it should have. The performers were giving in to their tiredness. Sweat flew like glass slivers from them as they pirouetted. He wanted to stand up and applaud them for spurring his imagination. In a way, he could understand that the mad artist had attempted something greater than the sum of himself, though he knew, as soon as that thought had formed, that he had simplified everything far too much, and had made it also a little perverse.

The lights came up, and the dancers received ovation after ovation. They pranced out from behind the parted curtains and bowed, smiling the same transfixed smiles with which they had danced. The only thing that betrayed their tiredness was the rapid rise and fall of their rib cages as they sucked air through clenched teeth. A bouquet of flowers arced over the orchestra pit and landed at their feet.

During intermission, everyone retired to a large room with a terrace overlooking the Leidseplein, where a long table had been set up. Two young men in black waistcoats mixed and served drinks. Pieter asked for a brandy, then went through the doors behind the table and out onto the terrace. Some of the more outrageous clubs were opening their doors. The people in the plaza below were Demmie's age, and each dressed more outlandishly than the next. Jan came out after him and was talking gibberish about the dance. Pieter tried to listen, but he quickly lost his tolerance for Jan's public-relations sense of things and excused himself to talk with Theillen, who had bought a beer and stood under a lamp drinking out of the bottle. There was something nice about Theillen's not using a glass when everyone else was posturing like celebrities at a gala opening.

"What did you think?" Pieter asked. He hung over the side and watched a tram rumbling beneath them.

"Nothing," Theillen said. He was looking over the side too. "I liked it."

"Do you come to the ballet often?" God, he sounded like Jan then, making noise with words and saying nothing. The silence of the workroom was one thing, but the threatening silence between two people in a social situation was quite another. Jan probably understood that better than most people, and his prattle, though usually inconsequential, had some purpose.

"This is my first ballet," Theillen said. "And it bored me to tears." He took a healthy slug from his bottle, then shrugged his shoulders.

Pieter laughed. It was the perfect answer, and he had deserved it. "I think you'll do fine at the museum," he said. "I like the way you work."

The bell chimed for the second dance, and the lights on the terrace blinked twice. They went back to their seats. When the curtains parted, the stage had been transformed completely. A huge piece of polyurethane covered the stage floor and stretched back up and out of sight. The effect was such that there appeared to be a huge mirror in front of the audience. Where it curved up toward the lights, there was no crease in the material, completely destroying the audience's depth perception.

The music commenced and a dozen dancers sprang from the wings. Each wore the sheerest of leotards; each line of their muscled bodies was defined by shadow. And the dozen dancers gave a dozen reflections as they slid across the stage in comic parodies of classic poses—arabesque, relevé, effacé. It was a contemporary ballet such as he had never seen before, and the audience began laughing heartily.

Two pairs of dancers, the principals, seemed to fight among themselves as changing hues of amber, the color of aged varnish, played over them. More dancers came out, chose sides. Pieter watched the crowded stage, still amused with Theillen's straightforward answer, and wondered if this wasn't more to the boy's liking. And then, among the seeming chaos of dancers and their amber reflections, with the music rising in volume to an almost violent din, he saw Demmie.

It was like seeing a face in the gallery window, then recognizing that same face in the painting. A burst of excitement released inside him. Her partner pushed her across the slick vinyl stage; her back arched in a perfect bow, her leg extended in arabesque. Then she broke free with a series of pirouettes in a wide circle around two of the battling dancers, tantalizing them with her inaccessible grace. It was a perfect solo for her, and Pieter's lips stretched in a wide smile, as proud as he could be of her and of what she could do. Everything, all her evasions, flitted through his mind.

Theillen, sitting behind him, was tapping on his shoulder. "I didn't know . . ." he whispered.

"Neither did I."

Pieter waited till everyone left the theater. He sat on a plush red couch that circled one of the columns in the center of the lobby. The chandeliers were dimmed. He had begged off the rest of the evening with the Town Council. Jan was peeved at him, but he didn't care. He didn't care about anything.

Slowly the dancers began to trickle out. Without the stage and the flattering lights, they lost their mystique. They walked heavily on their turned-out feet, their shoulders rounded with exhaustion.

Finally, Demmie came out. She still wore her leotard; it was coral-colored and he could see the flattened roundness of her breasts and the darker circles of her nipples. She wore baggy white pants, cinched at her waist and ankles, and a long flowered scarf.

She ran up and gave him a firm kiss on the lips.

"You're not angry with me?" Her face was still greasy with makeup.

"No," he said. "You were marvelous."

She hugged him tightly, then hooked her arm in his, and they turned toward the door. "I wanted it to be a surprise."

"It was. Are you hungry?"

"Famished," she said. "But I'd like to go home and shower first."

"Let's run across the street and have a quick bite."

They sat out on the patio of the Americain Hotel. The umbrellas were folded and the sky above them was star-flecked, cloudless. Some people from the theater audience who were eating there glanced fleetingly at him and Demmie. The night air was a bit cool, and he draped his jacket over her shoulders. Cars shot around the curve between the theater and the hotel, bathing them briefly in the yellow beam of their lights. She ordered fried trout with almonds, and he had an omelet. Afterward they drank Courvoisier to warm themselves.

"Will you have time for me now?" he asked, a deliberate whine coloring his voice.

"Yes," she said. "I'm sorry about deceiving you, Pieter, but you really ought not give someone like me an ultimatum. I have to dance because I love it, just as you love—"

"Stop," he said. "Don't explain anything. You were marvelous." His happiness at recognizing her on stage had been tinged with guilt at being such an ass about her dancing. He had tried to control her—something he had no earthly right to do—and he had paid for it with several nights of anxious jealousy. "Do you want to go away for the weekend?"

"Okay," she said. "Where?"

"Volendam."

156

"I have an idea." She leaned forward and took his hand. "Since it's so close, I want you to ride with me."

"On the motorcycle?"

"Yes."

"I couldn't."

"Yes, you could," she insisted. "It will be great fun, and it's only fifteen kilometers." She added, "Nobody will see you."

"That was cheap."

When they left the Americain Hotel, they drove straight back to Pieter's apartment. She told him she wanted to soak in his tub. It was a luxury to her, since she had only a shower in her apartment, and tonight her legs were very sore. The bathroom itself was half the size of her apartment. A double marble sink stretched the length of one wall. A deep porcelain tub was set on four claw feet along the opposite wall. The floor was carpeted, and two large windows opened out to the canal below.

She lay in the tub for a long time with the steaming water as high as her shoulders. When he knocked on the door to ask what was taking so long, she invited him to get in.

"Are you serious?"

"I'm giddy and half drunk," she said. "Not serious. But you can come in anyway if you like."

"I like." He brought a bottle of brandy with him, and two glasses, and when he got in, the water he displaced nearly overflowed the tub. They soaped each other for a while, then he toasted her performance.

"I nearly left my seat," he said. "I wanted to join you up there onstage."

"They all say that." She flashed him a grin. "But it was nice of you anyway."

"It's true, even if they all say it. Who's *they?*"

"I was just kidding."

He sipped his brandy, then let the snifter bob in the water beside him. She was smiling. He came forward and kissed her. He began touching her under the water, and he got hard.

"Let's go into the room," she said.

She went in first, and by the time he joined her, she was wearing the pink leotard again. The flowered silk scarf was wrapped around her neck. She had draped her white pants over the lampshade to obscure the light. When he rolled her back on the bed, he asked, "What's the leotard on for?"

"You wanted the dancer you saw on stage tonight?"

His heart surged with joy. Yes, he had wanted the dancer, as if she were a different person altogether, as much as he wanted her.

"And I want to be made love to as a dancer," she said.

He kissed her gently, feeling the pressure of her teeth behind her full lips. He squeezed her breasts through the silky material. Finally, he said, "Please take it off."

"No." Her sultry voice carried the sweet smell of brandy. "Tear it," she said, offering up her hips.

He stretched the material, twisted it, then tore it at the seam and slowly entered her.

Afterward she lay with her head in the pit of his arm. The room smelled of their drenched bodies and the sweat-soaked leotard she had worn onstage. She had opened the big windows so the cool breeze from the canal could drift in.

"I learned something about myself tonight," he said. "And you were the only one I could think of sharing it with."

"Mmmm?" she purred. She seemed to be drifting off to sleep. "Was it related to us?"

"Sort of." He hugged her to him. At that moment, he wanted to tell her everything about himself, everything he had learned, not *from* her but just by being with her. He wanted to tell her each thought and feeling he had had these last days, all in the same instant, to have them all flash before her as they had flashed before him, but he knew that he could not, through words, convey the vital chemistry of such an avalanching set of insights.

All he could say was "I thought about the restoration while I was watching you dance."

"That's not very complimentary."

"It is," he said. "In a way. I mean, that dancing I watched

tonight excited my imagination. Isn't it supposed to do that?"

"And so I excited thoughts of your work, and an erection tonight."

"You also excited thoughts of immortality in me." There, he'd said it. And he knew then that what he'd just said contradicted all that his father had taught him. Restoration *was* like the other arts. It did evolve. It could elevate the man, the imagination; it could affect time.

"Do you understand that we will be *forever linked* with the name of Rembrandt? Forever?"

She rolled on top of him and very tenderly kissed the top of his nose. "Pretty lofty," she said. He wanted to take her leotard off now so he could feel the silkiness of her luminous flesh. She drew circles on his chest with the tasseled end of her scarf.

"I'm serious, you know." He lit two cigarettes and gave her one. "There is a drawback, though. The man who slashed the painting will be in that same company. He is the dark side of our moon. Without him, we might still be trying to find ways to keep ourselves busy in the studio."

"Go on."

So he told her what he could tell no one who sat with him at the ballet—about the subtle interplay between light and darkness, about the penumbra that lies somewhere between creation and destruction, and about whatever it is that exists within that penumbra that makes truth and beauty more than simple abstractions.

When he finished, he felt drained. She lay there as though she expected him to continue, but he couldn't. He did not know if she had understood him. He felt more than abstract then; he felt feeble, as though language ultimately had failed him.

But she sat up, straddling him, casting him in sudden shadow. "Pieter," she said, "it's beautiful."

The lamp shone behind her; it outlined her silhouette with a dim thread of unfocused light, the same amber light that had made her glow so gloriously on stage.

"I'm not sure it's beautiful," he said, "but it strikes me as true."

159

"But it *is* beautiful," she protested. "In a weird kind of way, it's a complementary dimension. What do you know about this man?"

"The same as you know. He's been committed to some institution."

"Can we find out about him? I mean, if he's our counterpart, we should know something about him."

"Are you crazy?"

"But you said it yourself. He is our other side."

"It wouldn't serve anything."

"It would serve to help us find out about ourselves," she said, quite solemnly. "Promise me, Pieter."

"Promise what?"

"That we'll find out about him."

"No," he said.

"He's an unconnected character, a man the press has called a lunatic, but that doesn't make him so. We need to know about him if what we are doing is to have any meaning. Trust me."

"No," he repeated emphatically, but he knew that something in her mind had set. She would put herself on that course, with or without him. And that would mean more time spent without her. What the hell was going on? His relationship with her was beginning to smack of the bizarre.

He rolled the leotard over her head and shut out the light. Before he fell asleep, he told her about the spectator he had noticed in the gallery earlier that day, hoping, halfheartedly, that she would forget whatever new scheme was stirring in her brain. "I can't really describe it, but the look on his face really captured me. Much the same as that little old lady's nylon mitts must have captured you. And I don't know whether I picked him out or he picked me. Our eyes just sort of met and my heart went out to him."

Then he found himself asking her the same question she had asked him.

"Do you find that a little screwy?"

"Certainly," she said. "You ought to be committed."

19

Saturday morning, they went for crêpes and coffee at a small upstairs pancake house near the Rokin, then walked three blocks to the Press Institute. When he had finally agreed to this expedition, after she woke him up in the middle of the night, he felt that he had not conceded to Demmie, but rather that he had made his own decision to satisfy his curiosity.

The Press Institute occupied an old warehouse next to the University of Amsterdam. Pieter explained to the receptionist, a dark-haired, soft-spoken woman, what his position at the museum was and what he was looking for. The woman led him and Demmie down steep stone stairs to the basement of the building. She flicked on a set of fluorescent lights. Rows of wooden shelves held countless newspapers, stacked flat and arranged in chronological order.

"You'll find the papers you're looking for along the last row. The international papers are in the room adjoining this one," the woman said.

"Thank you," Demmie whispered.

As the woman left, Pieter asked Demmie why she was whispering.

"I don't know. I just kind of picked it up from her."

They began sifting through a month's worth of daily Amsterdam papers—*Het Parool, de Telegraaf,* and others. They went through the papers from Rotterdam, The Hague, Utrecht. In the other room, they scanned the international papers.

A curious pattern emerged. There was not a single picture in any of the papers of the man who had done it. They found a partial one in *de Telegraaf*. Through the foggy window of a police van, one ear showed, and a portion of a right profile of the man's head. Almost all his face was obscured by the half-closed curtain covering the window. The picture was buried in the second section. All the other pictures had been of *The Night Watch* or of the Director General with one of the Town Council members, usually Simons. There was also no consistent mention of the man's name, nor where he was from. One placed him from Haarlem, another from Maastricht, still another from Eindhoven. He was called "the madman," "the lunatic," "the slasher." His name surfaced as Vermeulen, Menk, and Stolwijk.

"What's going on here?" Demmie asked.

"I haven't the faintest notion," Pieter said. "But the police have deliberately fed a lot of wrong information to the public."

"Can't we call that detective? What's his name?"

"Van Velde."

"Can't we call van Velde and find out about the man? Or at least why everything's mixed up about him?"

"We'll see," Pieter said. He did not like what this pointed to. It just didn't seem as though newspapers were so careless with that kind of detail. A calculated misrepresentation was going on, and he and his staff—even the museum—had been used to mislead an awful lot of people.

Sunday, they motored up to Volendam, on the IJsselmeer, on Demmie's BMW. The cobblestone streets of the little fishing village were lined with small brick homes; their red-tiled gabled roofs angled sharply. She parked by the docks. A few fishing boats had just come in with their catch; others were on their way out. Nets hung in the sun to dry, and men were washing and scaling tubs of fish. They walked among the tourist shops: the proprietors were dressed in baggy black pantaloons and wooden shoes; the women wore gull-wing lace bonnets and black skirts. Pieter took pictures of Demmie as she mugged with some of the locals in front of their shops.

They bought cheese and bread from a grocer on one of the side streets, then walked to Volendam's park for lunch. They sat near an oak footbridge; under it, a quick-moving crystal stream ran. Mallards splashed in the water. Flowers bloomed all around them, and they leaned against a buckeye tree and spread out their food.

Demmie looked wonderful—all windblown—lying back under the tree. She had worn white straight-legged jeans and a baggy pink paratrooper's coat. Her helmet was white, and she had painted her lips with a faint white lip gloss.

"Why do you dress so outrageously?" Pieter asked.

"Why not?" she said simply. Then, as if she were talking about her dancing or her work at the museum, she said, "Sometimes, when I'm doing it well—dressing, I mean—it can put me in a mood. Bright colors, bright mood." She furrowed her brow. "Dark colors . . ."

This morning, he had brought her coffee and rolls in bed. She had looked up at him and said, "Tracking him will help you." She had not even wished him good morning.

"How will tracking him help me?" he had asked. He was still tired, and he didn't mean to ask her that. He meant to dismiss her question.

"He is the yin to our yang. As you said, he is the destruction to our creation."

Finally, he said, "I'll make some discreet inquiries." But her talking had helped him realize one thing about himself, that this was not the first act of vandalism he had had to deal with, and that each act had puzzled him in its own way. Now the time had simply come to find one of these vandals and ask him why he had done it.

On the way up to Volendam, he thought about it. He wondered if in some outlandish way she was right about tracking this man. Maybe it would add another level of understanding to the restorer's work, much as adding a layer of a certain toner brings out the resilience of muted colors. She was more worldly than he had ever been at her age, and many of the things she said struck him as prescient, though he was never sure if she even recognized it.

His love for her was somehow connected with her unique way of seeing the world. At the same time, her vision suggested a danger, a recklessness that made him feel he ought to be constantly looking over his shoulder whenever he was with her. Like the stark darkness and light contrast of early chiaroscuro, or his creation and destruction thesis, he was afraid to find out that the fulfillment of his love for her had another side too—a similarly quite dangerous antithesis.

When they finished their lunch, Demmie asked him if he had ever been married.

"No," he said. "Why have you waited until now to ask me?"

"I don't know. I don't like to pry into people's lives. I was curious, that's all."

"But you've been sleeping with me," he protested.

She laughed. "Is that how it goes? A roll in the sack and no more privacy?"

"No, that's not how it goes, though that is the predominant pattern. I've never asked about you, either."

"You didn't have to. You had everything in front of you from the time you interviewed me. Name, place of birth, parents, schooling, all that bunk. But you've not told me a single thing about yourself. It's a big secret with you. Like the way you worry about people seeing when I touch you in public." She reached out and grabbed his thigh, high near his crotch, and he started. "See?" she said, laughing. "That's the reaction of a married man."

"You've slept with a lot of married men?"

"My share. Enough to recognize that."

"Well, no, as I said, I've never been married. I'm just very"—he paused for a moment—"circumspect. And I don't like being surprised." He lowered his voice dramatically.

She moved closer to him, facing the wooden footbridge. "Sounds boring," she said. "Tell me a story about yourself."

He thought for a moment about what she might like to hear,

164

then realized that that was ridiculous. "I have no parents," he said.

"That needs a bit of clarifying, wouldn't you say? Pasteur did away with spontaneous generation."

"You sure you want to hear this?"

"Yes." She stuck her hand inside his shirt and made circles in the hair of his belly with her fingernails. "After all," she said, "we *are* sleeping together."

"Well, I was separated from my natural parents during the war. Actually, during a bombing raid. We ended up in different shelters. The one they had been in got destroyed and I had no way of finding out whether they survived or not. I was eight then, and a Jewish couple found me wandering the streets like a waif. Tattered clothes and all.

"They took care of me. But the thing about it was, they were constantly trying to avoid being captured by the Nazis and so they kept moving around. And I kept getting farther and farther away from any hope of finding my parents.

"We were almost caught once, hiding in a barge near Rotterdam with a fisherman. The three of us slept on the floor, and late one night a Nazi officer came by to take some fish from our bargeman. When he saw us sleeping there, he asked the man who we were. The man told him we were his relatives, from The Hague, on our way to Amsterdam.

"As soon as the soldier left, the man hurried us outside and hid us in his dinghy, tied up under the gangplank. No sooner had we covered ourselves with a tarp and fishnets than the bastards returned. They screamed at the man. We heard them ransacking his boat. Then guns started going off, machine guns. They peppered the boat and the bushes on the bank. I heard the man cry out once. Then I saw him hit the water in front of me."

"Dead?"

"Yes. I remember seeing the blood spread like an oil slick against the dark water. Then he went under like a sack of stones. I started whimpering when I saw that. Loudly. But they were still firing off their guns at the bushes on the bank. My father—I've

165

always called him that—ripped a sock off my foot and jammed it in my mouth to muffle me. I nearly choked to death.

"We spent years on the run. It really did strange things to all of us. I used to have dreams, until I was a teenager, about being in that dinghy, and I'd wake up whimpering, with the strangling feeling of the sock clogging my throat."

Demmie was silent; she laid her head on Pieter's lap and closed her eyes. He ran his fingers through her curly hair, releasing a clean floral fragrance from her scalp. He had never spoken of this incident to anyone. It had remained buried inside him, for him alone to meditate upon.

"After the war," he went on, "they tried for months to find some other relatives of mine, but they failed. We never talked about it again, as though shifting families at the age of eight was the perfectly normal thing to do.

"We were, in a classic casebook sense, a group of paranoids too. My mother would always lock up the house by eight o'clock, just as if a curfew still existed. She listened to sounds on the street so intently that she would often open the door for guests before they knocked. We didn't own a radio; they refused to buy one, so we spent our evenings reading books. My father lavished art books on me. He was an independent restorer." He stroked her hair, and it seemed as though she had suddenly come awake. He realized that his voice had been droning, that he was reciting his past as unemotionally as if it were a history lesson.

"But that was then," he said, "and this is now."

Demmie said, "You're sweet. Kiss me."

He did, and after that she said, "You didn't have to tell me something that important to you. Especially if it hurt. I'm sorry for prying."

"That's all right." He stood up and pulled her to her feet. "All that was my way of telling you how I came to work at the museum. Even I didn't realize I was going so far back."

She held his elbow as they walked back. They stopped to browse in shopwindows along the narrow streets, and he told her about his father's restoration studio in the front apartment of their house, and how they spent their days removing fly marks from paintings with chamois cloths, or cleaning and relining landscapes and portraits, barely earning enough money to support the family.

As they were getting on the bike for the ride back to Amsterdam, Pieter said, "Do you want to hear a curious piece of family coincidence?" He was surprised at how much he was talking about his early life. "While I was studying in Italy, I got a letter from my father, who told me his brother was one of several people charged with spiriting *The Night Watch* and other treasures out of the Rijksmuseum. They hid them in the mazelike caves of Mount St. Peter in Maastricht so the Nazis couldn't confiscate them."

"That's no coincidence," Demmie said as they rode away from the docks, "it's irony."

20

Pieter knelt on a foam-rubber mat on the dais directly above the longest V-shaped slash. Around each of the cuts, the back of the relining canvas had been scraped away, down to Rembrandt's original canvas. He checked the realigned warp and woof through his binocular microscope to make sure the mulberry paper was still holding tightly, then placed the first thread, from end to end, across the top left arm of the V. On the stainless-steel surgical tray beside him there were hundreds of single threads laid out side by side. Demmie picked up each thread with a pair of tweezers, flattened the ends with a hemostat so the thread frayed, dipped it in the thinned Araldite solution, and handed it to Pieter, who placed it a few centimeters from the last. Then he examined the placement under the microscope. If the threads were spaced too closely together, their sheer bulk would show as ridges on the paint side. On the other hand, he knew that spacing them too far apart would give him a weaker mend that could give way when they restretched the canvas. He had nightmares of coming down to inspect *The Night Watch* one morning, after the restoration was complete, only to find the painting bursting along the mends from too much pressure, like some cartoon fat man splitting his britches. There was no way to tell how weak the canvas had become with their scraping and their application of cleaning solvents to the back. Only when it was finally hung would he have any real indication.

Theillen flanked him too. He cleaned the Araldite from the

tweezers with a dry cloth, then handed them back to Demmie. It went on like that for hours, Pieter placing the threads Demmie handed him and applying gentle pressure across the cut with a palette knife to flatten the thread, then handing the tools to Theillen to be cleaned, while Demmie prepared another thread. The fraying of each thread end was done so it would form a fanlike web, increasing the surface area of the bond. When Pieter checked the span of each thread across the cut with the microscope, he sometimes adjusted a crooked placement or removed a thread altogether. The more fibers he laid across the cuts, the more the back of the canvas gave the impression of being surgically stitched.

The documentary crew came back and shot two days' footage. The heat from their lights became intolerable, and Pieter had to halt the work several times to check the temperature in the studio. Even with one of the extractor fans going, the vapors from the Araldite solution mixed with the heat had made everyone dizzy.

During the filming, Jan came down to ensure that the gallery curtains would be open. "When the cameras are here," Jan told Pieter, "more people show up at the gallery." Then he went outside to lecture the spectators on just what was being done to the painting. Pieter believed Jan rather enjoyed his share of the limelight. Jan had been working all week in the anteroom to the gallery, supervising the construction of a display—pictures of the slashed masterpiece, a narrative on the work that was being done to it, as well as a brief history of *The Night Watch.* For the first time since he had known him, Jan was filled with boundless energy. He was preparing press releases, lecturing the spectators, speaking to civic groups to raise money for new security for the museum. And he was losing weight with each passing week. He had trimmed off a good ten pounds, stopped complaining about his stomach, and even begun writing some free-lance articles about the restoration for the newspaper he had formerly worked for.

After four days, Pieter's back ached so badly from kneeling that he let Theillen and Demmie place the threads across the two smaller slashes. He allowed them to check their own work under the microscope; then he double-checked it. He was surprised at how few mistakes they had made—a thread overlapping another, one of the fan-shaped frayed ends not pressed flat enough to bind. He had not needed Stan, so he sent him to the studio upstairs to begin designing a new frame for *The Night Watch,* a temporary one that they would utilize after they had finished varnishing the front.

When all the cuts had been satisfactorily bridged and the Araldite had completely dried, they spent a week shaving down each of the threads to its thinnest possible dimension with surgical knives. They wore magnifying eyeglasses so that, as they shaved, they would not accidentally sever any of the threads. They could only work for a few minutes at a time because, as Pieter explained, the glasses would eventually give them headaches. "And that would mean unsteady hands, right?"

Pieter took one afternoon off, without telling Demmie where he was going. He called Inspector van Velde, whose office was on the Spui, and asked for an appointment. He told van Velde that he had some questions about the man who had slashed the painting.

"You'll have to speak with the arresting officer," van Velde said. "It wasn't handled through this station house. I don't think you'll have much luck there, though."

"Why not?"

"Because the man was committed to the State Psychiatric Institute. The files are closed on him by court order. You know that. It's the law."

"I want to talk with them anyway," Pieter said.

He drove to the detectives' headquarters in Bijlmeer, a suburb of the city. He did not understand why the detectives had been called in from so far away. There were several stations closer.

The building which housed their offices was part of the modern modular architecture of the whole neighborhood, and Pieter passed it twice before he realized it was a police headquarters. Prefabricated high-rise apartments were everywhere, like so many dun-colored boxes balanced on top of each other, abutting the dreary gray sky. All this squareness attested to the growth of the city; the suburb was not close or charming or warm like the blocks in the old city, and he felt as though he had driven to a foreign place.

The police officer at the front desk directed him upstairs to the detectives' offices. As he walked the halls, he became aware that the entire building was constructed of concrete and metal. In spite of the warm summer air outside, a cold, almost mechanical breath circulated the halls. He knocked on the appropriate door, and when he heard a grunt he entered.

A young man with a very straight back sat at a desk in the center of the room. His nameplate read SCHIPPER. Off to one side, another detective, with thick gray hair and an unhealthy belly spreading his sport coat, pored over some papers. He must have made the grunt, Pieter told himself; he did not even look up to acknowledge Pieter's entrance.

One of the walls of the office was made of heavy, tempered glass from three feet above the floor. It opened onto a gigantic room filled with desks and police officers. Victims or suspects— he had no way of telling—sat across from the officers at many of the desks.

He explained his position at the museum, then said, "I am here to find out something about the man who destroyed *The Night Watch*. I understand the investigation was handled through this office."

"You are correct about that, Mr. Beckum," Schipper said. "However, there is not much I can tell you." He shifted his broad shoulders. His complexion was as pink as Demmie's; his dark hair was beginning to grow over his ears. He could not be more than twenty-eight, Pieter thought.

"Can we start with a name?"

"That information is in the papers," Schipper said.

"There are three different names in the papers. Which is the correct one?" Pieter's voice had assumed a strained edge.

The older detective got up from his desk and ordered Schipper

171

to follow him. They met a short stodgy man in shirt sleeves behind the glass wall, and Pieter watched what appeared to be a rather animated argument. Then Schipper returned, a shade pinker.

"There is no information I can release to you, Mr. Beckum. I'm sorry. You will have to consult the paper for anything on this man. You see, there are very strict laws protecting citizens committed to psychiatric institutes. And since he has—" Schipper stopped himself.

"Since he has what?" Pieter glanced quickly through the glass to make sure the other officer was not coming back. "Come on. Tell me."

"The man committed suicide."

"What?"

"I will not repeat that. And I suggest that you don't either."

"Has that been in the papers?"

"I don't think so. Now you will have to leave. I have other work to do, and my boss there"—Schipper nodded quickly toward the man in the shirt sleeves—"said we're not allowed to discuss the case."

Schipper walked with Pieter to the door. "There are no pictures of this man. Why not?" Pieter asked.

"I don't know. That's all."

Pieter shook the detective's hand. "Tell me his name." He looked him squarely in the eyes, but Schipper pulled his hand away and closed the door.

As Pieter walked down the hall, he heard the detectives' door open behind him. He spun quickly. Schipper popped his head out. "Van Rijks," he whispered. "From Leiden." The door closed slowly behind Schipper's voice with a hydraulic whisper, and Pieter walked hurriedly down the stairs.

He could not wait to tell Demmie what he had learned. A new name. A new place. Something was going on. He liked feeling the detective in himself. His father had told him it was a necessary attribute of a restorer. And he had played detective more than once in his work. When the museum purchased Terbrugghen's

Adoration of the Magi, his investigations had revealed the canvas had been terribly overpainted. He had suspected that an entire section of the canvas had been done by someone else. After taking paint samples from the seam where the disparate pieces of canvas were joined and sending the samples to the laboratory for analysis, he discovered that the paint on either side of the seam differed in age by a hundred years. When he removed the overpainting, he found the masterpiece underneath. The museum had given him a citation for his work.

He drove by Demmie's apartment first, but her motorcycle was not there. Then he thought of the dance studio, one of the converted old merchant houses that fronted the Prinsengracht. The dancers frequented a small café beneath the studio after their classes. He walked through, searching for Demmie's face. When he didn't find her, he went up the back stairway and into the studio.

She was alone in one of the dance rooms, moving beautifully to some loud African jazz music in front of a wall-length mirror. The faded pale green walls held the rank smell of a closed-up gymnasium—a sweet-sour scent of exhaustion and wet clothes. She was so immersed in her own movement that she didn't see him come in and sit down. Her spine seemed liquid as it alternately melted when the music lilted, then snapped rigid when the beat came alive. Her large hands fluttered gracefully, her fingers frozen in a doll-like attitude. When the music ended, she collapsed to the floor. He applauded.

"Bastard," she said as she came over and gave him a kiss.

"That's no way to talk to a friendly audience."

"Don't sneak up on me like that." Her soaked leotard clung to her body like a second skin.

"I went to the police this afternoon to find out about our mystery slasher," he said excitedly.

"And what did you find out?" She slumped to the floor, removed her worn pink ballet shoes, and rolled down her woolen leg warmers.

"I found out that he's dead."

"That's nice," she said, lying back.

"I thought you were interested in this?"

"I'm sorry, Pieter. I am interested. Just give me a minute to catch up to myself. I'm dying." Her ribs were heaving, and a blue vein in her neck still danced.

"I don't believe for a minute that he's dead. Something's wrong."

"That's a pretty strong accusation. A little paranoid too."

"But what about the misleading names in the newspapers?" he asked defensively.

"I don't know."

"And I found out something else. I know his real name and where he came from. It's none of the names in the papers."

She straightened her back at that, a mischievous gleam lighting her eyes. "Interesting," she said.

21

As Pieter stood on the dais looking down at the hundreds of tiny threads they had laced across the back of the canvas, it reminded him of an aerial photograph of so many railroad tracks gone berserk, crossing and recrossing on a desert-brown plain. The threads were all shaved down, and Jan had arranged for the film crew to come in to record the turning of the canvas.

Theillen and Demmie taped large sheets of the transparent plastic Melinex over the back of the canvas so that when Pieter filled in the huge slashes on the front of *The Night Watch* to the original paint level, the stopping he would use would not stick to the surface of the work floor. Next, they fastened narrow strips of soft board—two laths vertically, one horizontally, in an H pattern—to the stretcher in order to keep the center of the canvas from sagging when they turned it over. Then they placed the stretcher itself over the back of the painting, and Demmie and Theillen tacked the edges of the old relining canvas to it. As a final precautionary measure, Pieter threaded the two ropes, with their blocks and tackles, through the eyelets attached to the stretcher and had Theillen and Demmie lift the painting just enough so he could pass some narrow bands of webbing underneath. Then they lowered the painting and tacked the webbing in place. "The webbing," Pieter told them, "will keep the canvas from stretching in the middle when we finally turn it. Without it, we would place undue stress in the center of the painting, where the most serious damage is. I would hate to see those mending threads burst."

Jan came down and opened the curtains; the crowd outside was pressed shoulder against shoulder. Pieter watched Jan fight his way through the people until he was standing in front of the center pane of glass. A perfect circle of naked scalp showed on the crown of his head. His arms raised and his jaw and neck muscles corded with animated speech. Pieter saw a navy-blue sailor's cap in the back of the crowd and was about to call it to Demmie's attention when he realized she was handling one of the hoisting ropes. She and Theillen lifted slowly, while Pieter and one of the maintenance men guided the canvas upright. Then, as Theillen and Demmie paid out more rope, they lowered the painting, face up. When all four corners touched the work floor, they centered the canvas; then Pieter told Theillen to close the curtains.

"He was out there again," Pieter whispered to Demmie.

"That guy you told me about?"

"Yes," Pieter said. "The fellow with the sailor's cap. Did you see him?"

"No. Open the curtains and show him to me."

When Pieter drew the curtains apart, the man came to the front to peer through the glass. His face was clean-shaven and ruddy; his hair was strawberry-colored.

"I thought you said he had a beard," Demmie said.

"He does. That's not him. I made a mistake. I saw the cap in the back of the crowd and assumed it was my spectator."

"*Your* spectator?"

"That's right," Pieter said, his face reddening. "He's some apprentice or art student, I guess. He'll be back. I've seen him here before. He has some curiosity about what we're doing."

"But what makes him your spectator?"

"I don't know. It's something that just slipped out, though there is something naggingly familiar about his face. Potter, from the Art Institute, probably sent him here to spy on our technique."

The next day, they removed the sheets of mulberry paper which Pieter had pasted to the front of *The Night Watch* as part of the first aid the day after the slashing. The varnish underneath the mulberry paper had disintegrated, leaving two large pasty-white squares on the paint surface—one in the center, covering Banning Cocq from the waist down, the other to the right of Lieutenant van Ruytenburch.

Demmie, using a piece of rayon dampened with 96 percent alcohol, briskly cleaned away the paste. Then Pieter climbed onto the dais and ran his hands over the mended slashes to check for ridges. There were none. The face of the painting lay perfectly flat. They cut the painting away from the stretcher and removed the border they had retained from the old relining canvas.

When they had finished, Demmie pointed directly at a man through the parted curtains. He was standing in the rear of the gallery, perfectly still, as though he were a statue. "Is that him?" she asked.

It was the first unobscured look Pieter had gotten of him. The man was tall, his shoulders slightly rounded. The visor of his cocked sailor's cap cast his eyes and part of his cheeks in shadow. His shaggy hair stuck out wildly from the pressure of the cap.

"That's no apprentice," Demmie said. "Nor does he look like an art student. What do you think he wants?"

"I don't know," Pieter said. "He's just watching, I guess."

"But why?"

"A cop, maybe. Undercover."

"He gives me the creeps. How long has he been watching?"

"Since I had the curtains open."

"I don't mean today. . . ."

"I don't know," Pieter said after a moment. "A while, anyway."

22

Van Rijks wondered why he was being stared at by the man and the woman wearing white coats—he with the dark-rimmed glasses, she with the fuzzy head. She was pointing at him. He knew that certainly. He could feel the intensity of her pointing as if a beam of hot light had shot at him from her finger. He could almost hear the buzzing of their whispers penetrating the glass. Now their buzzing wafted above the heads of the people that stood around him.

He had taken the medication and there was no reason he should be hearing anything but the normal, inane conversations of the others in the gallery. But he did. He heard those two talking about him, though he could not distinguish what they were saying, and they made him nervous. Could they have recognized him? Could they, of all people, have seen through the disguise that had fooled Neel and Molen?

The crowds were everywhere in this city now. All he needed to do was take his pills and melt into one mob or another to travel safely. Faceless. He had even strolled past some museum guards and they had not looked twice at him. He was drawn back here, as surely as he was drawn back to his studio, and to his house in Leiden. But these two seemed to know who he was.

The night he had cornered Molen in the Café Zwart, he'd made the little weasel find him a place to hide. Molen took him to an old derelict house in the Jordaan. Van Rijks went out nights, rummaging through the garbage on the street two blocks over, and brought back a dilapidated bedspring, a small table, and a three-legged chair. He lit his room with candles he bought at a small grocery store in the neighborhood. He piled the debris—the broken boards, the hunks of plaster, the shattered bottles—into a corner and covered it with a sheet of cardboard.

He had tried to keep drawing, but he could no longer concentrate. He felt trapped by a colossal lonesomeness. If he betrayed himself again, as he had done with Neel, they would catch him for certain. And his loneliness caused a disorientation so complete that he felt as if he had descended from another planet, another realm. Everyone he had once cared about was gone. Molen was his only human contact, and it stretched the bounds of humanity to call him a person. Yet Molen had succeeded in doing what he had never been able to do: He sold some of his drawings.

For days he lost sleep, pacing the four-corner boundaries of his dimly lit hideout till his jangling nerves began to numb his fingertips. He'd flap his hands in front of him, like two flags snapping in a stiff wind, to bring the circulation back. Then he would sit and try to draw. But his hand shook so much that the chalk slipped from his fingers. He would put off taking a pill until his stomach felt as if it were a withered canvas sack being tugged at by thousands of tiny violent fingers. After the pill, as the heaviness worked its way into his shoulders, down his arms, and into his belly, he would sit at the table and sketch with heavy strokes until he passed out.

One night, Molen came by to bring him some money for the last of his drawings. He made such a racket, stumbling and cursing his way through the rubble of the old building, that van Rijks greeted him at the door with a candle.

"Are you cheating me?" van Rijks asked, later.

Molen was sitting at the table, counting out van Rijks's money by candlelight. "Of course not," he said. "You're not van Gogh, you know. Sometimes I give them two for the price of one if they hesitate to buy."

"There's only two hundred guilders here."

"That's all I got. Draw some more."

"I can't draw some more!" van Rijks shouted. "Those two dozen sketches took me a long time."

"Why do you live like this?" Molen asked. "Who are you hiding from?"

"Some people. Now get out."

Van Rijks knew that Molen was probably keeping as much money as he turned over. Now the little pimp was getting too curious. If there was a reward, Molen would find out about it and be the first to try to collect it. Van Rijks took his candles and searched the abandoned houses on the block for a safer place. Then he came back for his furniture, and, finally, spread out the pile of debris he had left in the corner, to make it appear as if no one had been there. When he wanted Molen, he would find him, as he had done before. All he had to do was turn over a few rocks.

Now, standing in the semidark gallery of the museum, he felt a certain calm in watching the methodical work of those people in white coats beyond the wall. They were just like doctors at the Psychiatric Institute. But he could not tolerate the whispering of that dark-haired man who seemed to be directing the operation. The night before, he had been to the university library on the Spui. He had seen the newspaper stories about the slashing. The journalists, the police officials, the psychiatrists had all claimed he was mad. *Mad.* Frothing at the teeth. A criminal of the worst sort. Not one account told the truth. Not one mentioned his Johannes. He had not been mad. He had been immeasurably depressed, and a little drugged, and he felt whatever it was snap like a brittle bone inside his head; but he was not mad. Even the courts had been unsympathetic. They refused to let him see Neel so he could explain. And when he finally escaped and came to her, she had thought he was crazy too. *I'm going to call them when you leave.* The whole world had turned against him overnight.

The man was consulting with the girl again. She was pretty enough, but neither of them had a right to talk about him. All the others in the studio were intent on their work, oblivious to the concerned eyes that watched. But everyone's focus was misplaced. He wanted to tell the people around him *his* story. *He* was more important than that goddamned painting.

He tapped the person in front of him, a short greasy-haired man with acne scars on his cheeks and small eyes. He became angry that the world was more intent on putting the painting together than they had been on putting him together. At the Institute, they had given him pills till they clogged his throat, then let him ramble about in a perpetual fog until he had outsmarted them.

"What do you think about that?" van Rijks asked indignantly.

The man said, "I think they're doing a marvelous job."

"I didn't mean that, you asshole."

"Hey," the man said, "you don't go talking to people that way." He shoved van Rijks.

Van Rijks pushed his way out of the gallery. The man was beginning to create a scene. You almost did it that time, buddy. You can't come back here, at least not for a while, not as long as you have the pills, anyway. The pills would help him stay clear; stealing them had been one of the smartest things he had ever done. He looked back to see the young, rough-looking boy close the curtains.

He had wanted to punch that man for whining so loudly, for almost getting him caught. He needed to take another pill to calm down. But the pills were beginning to disappear. Now he would have to face the problem of what to do about getting more.

23

With the backs of the slashes bridged solidly now, and the painting lying face up on the work floor, Theillen and Demmie began filling the damaged areas with stopping. For the stopping, Pieter had made up a putty of three parts chalk to one part raw umber mixed with animal glue. Then he added Venice turpentine, thinned with oil of turpentine, to give the putty sufficient flexibility. Using a palette knife, they daubed small quantities of the stopping into the slashes. Pieter explained that they needed to apply even pressure so the puttylike mixture would inundate the mending threads. "When we turn the canvas back over to apply the relining canvas, the stopping will keep air pockets from forming where there are slashes."

Demmie wanted to know if they should build the cuts up to the surrounding paint level.

"Later," Pieter said. "Even though we're working on the front, we must tend to the back first." As an afterthought, he added, "Because what we cannot see will give us the most trouble later."

While Demmie and Theillen worked the stopping, Pieter removed the insertion of canvas from the boy's drum on the extreme right edge of the painting. He called their attention to the small, dog's-head-shaped piece of canvas and the poor patchwork repair done by a previous restorer, reminding Demmie of the day she had first made her recommendation for work on *The Night Watch*. It seemed like ages ago. "Today," he told them, "no restorer in his right mind would butcher a painting like this."

He cut a piece of seventeenth-century canvas to fit the hole, knowing he was going to have to imitate Rembrandt's brushstrokes, and knowing too that some future restorer might make the same disparaging comment about his work. He did not want to be blamed for a butchered job, but there was nothing he could do about it. He had to reapply the piece of canvas and he had to paint it. At least, with the retouching around the slashes, it would be different. He used Araldite and fibers to bind the patch.

There were too many overall imbalances in *The Night Watch* that resulted from its history of well-intentioned maltreatment—from its being cut on all four sides in the late 1600s to the shoddy patchwork of unskilled contemporary restorers. And he wondered too, on a level that bordered the metaphysical, if this maltreatment was partly the cause of its current damaged state. If the center of something was changed, like a wheel whose center was thrown out of true, especially something as delicately conceived and executed as this painting, then every glinting eye, every outstretched hand, every particle of emanating light is thrown out of balance.

Stan Martins's work crew brought in lengths of 1-by-6-inch oak for the relining loom. Beside the painting, Stan laid the wood out in a rectangle, 25 centimeters wider than the canvas, then fastened the corners of the loom together with reinforcing strips of oak and two-inch screws. Stan cursed the last turns of each screw as he lost grip of the screwdriver. Demmie snickered at his cursing, but Pieter did not; he had been in the studio the day Stan sliced the thumb from his right hand on the band saw. Pieter had heard him cry out, and when he opened the door of his office, he was greeted by Stan, holding up his hand, gloved in blood, and shaking as though he had been chilled to his center. Stan was back in the studio two days later, teaching himself to hammer and screw and saw left-handed. It had seemed to Pieter that Stan accepted the slice as a matter of course, and now he understood the man's profanity, because he was cursing neither the wood nor the screws but himself.

When the loom was firm, they pasted the first wide strip of

Japanese rice paper onto the face of the painting. Pieter guided the paper over the center, patted it onto Banning Cocq's face, then brushed it flat to the ends. Demmie and Theillen carried out four more bands to Pieter, who overlapped each one until the canvas was completely covered. After the paste dried, they lifted the paper, with the paint side of the canvas stuck to it, and glued it to the loom.

Finally, they lifted the loom and lowered the painting, face downward.

They spent the rest of the week on their hands and knees degreasing the back of the canvas with xylene and cotton rags. Pieter gave the mending threads a finishing touch—shaving a few, applying a little more Araldite to a weak join. Pieter had chosen a new canvas for the relining, thinner, but with much more tensile strength, than any used before.

On the weekend, Pieter and Demmie walked to the Vondel Park for a jazz concert by the lake. A crowd had already gathered around the makeshift stage that had been erected for the performance. Bleachers were set up in the rear, and people spread out blankets on the bright summer grass in front. The sun glowed pale, losing its clear circular definition in the layers of gray haze. Clouds of sweet marijuana smoke punctuated the air.

Pieter and Demmie found room for a blanket somewhere in the center of the crowd. On stage, a mime troup performed a graceful tug-of-war. A couple sitting next to them lit up a thin marijuana cigarette and the girl handed it to Demmie, who pursed her lips, sucked loudly, then pinched off her breath. She looked at Pieter, and he could feel the muscles in his face betray his astonishment. She held out the joint to him.

"No," he said, shaking his head. He held up his hand to emphasize the point.

She blew out the smoke and coughed. "Come on, try it. It will make the music sound better."

He shook his head again. She drew in more smoke and passed it back to the couple.

Pieter leaned to her ear. "I didn't know you smoked that."

"Now you do," she said, looking pleased with herself. "It won't kill you, Pieter. In fact, it's quite pleasant."

The mime troupe collapsed in a writhing heap, to the general approval of the applauding audience. A couple of small children scampered across the stage, then ran quickly back in the other direction, chased by one of the stagehands. The crowd began laughing. They chanted, "Let the children play."

Finally the band came on. It was a trio: a tenor saxophone, a clarinet, and an upright bass. A shaggy-haired woman played the bass. The band launched into their set immediately, and it seemed as if the entire audience, except Pieter, were wired into their instruments. People alternately swayed and undulated like a grainfield under the influence of shifting winds; others sat perfectly still except for the metronomic nodding of their heads; still others staggered their body movements like seizure victims to the irregular thumping of the bass.

Demmie openly accepted more joints as they were passed around, and Pieter steadfastly refused her attempts to get him high. "I don't want to smoke it," Pieter protested.

"Promise me you'll try it—not now, but sometime later," Demmie said.

"Perhaps."

The band had come from England to perform during the Holland Festival, Demmie told him. She said they played superbly. Pieter felt as though he ought to disagree with her, but he checked himself. They were receiving a standing ovation for their first tune. Demmie had become giddy from the pot and the music, and she lay on Pieter's lap most of the time. The music was so monotonous he began looking around at the audience's faces. As he scanned the bobbing heads, he realized he might easily be the oldest one in the audience. Even Demmie showed her age compared to them. He could have been a visitor from another century for all he felt in common with these people.

His eyes still moved over the crowd. Suddenly, on the bottom row of the bleachers, spotted another displaced face. It belonged to the man from *The Night Watch* gallery.

At first, Pieter thought his eyes had played a trick on him; he stared hard at the figure sitting motionless against the rolling and swaying about him. There was no mistake. And the man was not looking at the band on the stage; he was gazing in their direction. An intense feeling of fire rose along Pieter's spine. He shook Demmie's shoulder and moved her off his lap.

The man was wearing the same cocked seaman's cap, a dark leather coat buttoned to the neck, and jeans. When their eyes finally met, the man got up, looking like a thief who'd just been found out, and stepped quickly over the people who crowded the ground in front of the bleachers. Pieter stood up too, as much from startled impulse as anything else. He did not know why, but he had to catch him. "Meet me back at the apartment," he told Demmie.

"What? Where are you going?"

"Not now," he said. "He's leaving and I have to catch him."

"Who?" she asked. She propped herself on her elbows. But Pieter was already jumping over people, spreading them apart roughly and apologizing for mashing their hands and feet in his haste. He looked back once to Demmie, who was on her feet now, and when he turned to the man again, all he could see was the disappearing leather jacket. The music broke off abruptly, and the entire audience rose up around him to applaud. He was hemmed by the crush of cheering youngsters.

He began pushing them, and they seemed to resist as a group. He dispensed with apologies and drove through them as he would toward a goal on a football field. They pushed back at him, cursing. Something compelled him, beyond all reason, to catch that man, look into his face, ask him what the hell he wanted.

Finally he broke free, but the man was nowhere in sight. He searched frantically in all directions, a slow hot fear spreading through his body. Bicyclists were pedaling down the sidewalk, weaving around the lovers who strolled arm-in-arm along the tree-shaded promenade. No man in a leather jacket. Questions backed up in his mind. Was he following him and Demmie? Or was he here to listen to the concert? What did he want? Why had

186

he run off? Damn the Town Council, and Jan, and everyone else who had something to do with all this craziness.

And damn himself too, he thought, following one of the paths that meandered through the park, around a small pond, along a shallow creek, to search for the man's face among the couples who sat drinking at the open-air café. He even scanned the playground where children played on the sliding boards and swings. For a moment, he wondered if the visits to the museum, the incident at the concert, hadn't been a hallucination, a trick his mind had played him to deal with all the pressure; but he remembered that Demmie had seen the man too and had been surprised at his sinister appearance.

He increased his speed until he found himself jogging at a good clip up one of the sidewalks that led from the park to the busy Overtoon. He caught sight of the jacket as it turned out of the park, a quick brown blur vanishing into the deepening shadows of the tree-shrouded sidewalk. When Pieter passed the clay tennis courts, he broke into an open run.

By the time he reached the Overtoon, a tram was pulling away from the island in the center of the boulevard. The man had gotten on and was seated in the rear, staring fixedly out the window at him. When their eyes met the second time, the man turned his face away and Pieter thought he detected a slight sneer.

Pieter jumped from the curb to flag a taxi. A green Fiat came to a halt in front of him. He told the driver to turn around and follow the tram that was just sliding around the corner. His voice rattled with excitement and he felt suddenly silly, like a character in a melodramatic detective movie. The driver snorted and shook his head. "Have a fight with your girl?" he asked.

"No," Pieter said.

"You a cop, then?"

Pieter grinned. "Yeah."

The driver stayed well behind the tram as Pieter had instructed him. It made several stops, and more people packed on so that Pieter completely lost sight of the seaman's cap through the back window. When he finally spotted the man pushing his way out the back door, Pieter got out of the cab and followed.

The man seemed totally unconcerned with everything about him. He stalled along the street, pausing to look in shopwindows, as though he had nowhere to go. He strolled to the corner and bought a plate of herring from a sidewalk vendor.

Pieter bought the day's *de Telegraaf* and leaned against a storefront while the man ate the herring. He felt so obvious, yet there was nothing else he could think of to use to conceal himself. He no longer had the nerve to confront the man openly; he did not feel safe with him, face to face, outside the museum. And he didn't know why, except that the man looked capable of a sudden violent outburst.

Once, the man looked in Pieter's direction, and he brought the paper up quickly to cover his face. The newspaper wavered unsteadily in his hands. When he had summoned enough nerve to look again, the man had already crossed the street and was climbing the steps of an apartment building. Pieter watched him work the door on the landing, push it open, and disappear. Pieter waited a reasonable time, then walked up to the landing and copied the names on the mailboxes. There were three buzzers; one of them was blank.

Pieter caught another taxi back to the park to check the concert site for Demmie. The crowd had departed; only a handful of people, too drunk or too stoned to get up and walk, were left.

Instead of going straight home, he stopped for a drink at the café in front of the Americain Hotel. He needed to sort things out before he saw Demmie again. He was confused, and a little agitated with himself for his cowardice. It was apparent that they were being followed, but he couldn't figure out why. Or by whom. Then it struck him that the man might be after Demmie. Given the strange, sometimes mysterious things she did, it was a more likely possibility.

When he got home, Demmie was waiting for him. She was sprawled on the couch, her long denim dress hiked above her thighs, one leg propped on the back of the couch. A glass of spa with a lemon slice floating in it sat on the coffee table; she had a burning cigarette in her hand. The television was turned on, but the volume had been completely lowered.

"You're a weird bird," he said. "Watching the TV like that."

"I can't stand it," she said flatly. "But I wanted some company."

"Are you still high?"

"No. It wears right off. I'm famished. Let's eat something."

He went to the kitchen and took a Heineken from the refrigerator. "Later," he said. "First I have to ask you something."

"Ask away." She sat up, folding her legs, lotus-style, underneath her.

He sat on the arm of the couch. "I saw the man from the gallery."

"At the concert?"

"Yes. And the strange thing about it was that he was not watching the stage; he was watching us."

"That's queer."

"I know it's queer. And *my* life has been such that there is no reason under the sun for anyone to follow me. So the question is—"

"Am I mixed up in anything?" she interrupted.

"That's the question." He felt the rising color in his cheeks.

"The answer is no."

"Are you sure?" It came out as an accusation.

"Come on, now, Pieter. I answered you." She drew on her cigarette, the glowing ash turning her high cheekbones orange. Then she tamped it out.

"I'm sorry. But I've become very nervous all of a sudden." He gulped down some beer, then said, "I'm going to call the police."

He dialed van Velde, mentioned what had happened, and asked the detective to meet him at the museum in the morning.

When he got off the phone, Demmie asked, "Aren't you getting a bit paranoid? I mean, it could all be a coincidence. Why couldn't he just be watching the restoration, like everyone else?"

189

"He's not watching the restoration," Pieter protested. "Even you knew that when you saw him."

"I know, but you can't damn somebody because they look a little strange. He's probably a very nice fellow."

"Very funny. I'll tell you something I noticed. He doesn't come at the most important times, so I'm sure he's not an apprentice or has had any professional training." He slipped into the space beside her on the couch, and she took the bottle out of his hands and drank. "I can't figure him out, and now, after running away from me today, he's really got my imagination working."

"Do you think he could be an undercover policeman?"

"Who knows? There's something familiar about him. Maybe he's an art thief"—Pieter laughed—"plotting to spirit *The Night Watch* away, and he's casing the museum. I followed him home, you know."

"You what?"

"*I* followed *him*."

"That's great, Pieter." Demmie lay back against the armrest, exhaling a heavy breath. "You've begun following a spectator from the gallery? Have you any idea how carried away that sounds?"

"Don't make fun of me," he said. "Anyway, you were the one who started me watching the spectators. I don't think I would ever have noticed him. Besides, there's something to this. I feel it. He's watching one of us. He has a reason, and I intend to figure it out."

"You think he's a friend of Theillen's?"

"Theillen wasn't at the concert today. Let's eat something."

She sprang up from the couch. "I'll fix us a salad," she said, bounding through the doorway.

"You're full of surprises," he called after her. "Everything you do, and you know how to cook."

He heard the distinct rustle of clothes, then her entreating voice. Skirt raised, she stuck her bared ass out the doorway. "Kiss it, darling, will you?"

24

Pieter was at the museum by seven-thirty the next morning. He had told Demmie not to bother coming until later, and to call Theillen and tell him the same. He wanted to add the stopping to the back of the canvas by himself, without the world looking over his shoulder, without commotion in the studio, without thinking about who was watching in the gallery. He wanted it as it used to be—a moment of privacy between him and the painting.

He entered through a private entrance at the back of the east tower and made his way through a labyrinth of dimly lit corridors. From behind a mirrored glass door that opened into the workroom, he noticed that there were no guards around. He walked through the workroom and out into the gallery. No guards again. He found four of them in *The Night Watch*'s anteroom that Jan had constructed, sitting on the vinyl couches, drinking coffee and eating croissants. Apparently they had helped themselves to the cafeteria food.

Pieter startled them when he asked in a booming voice, "Which of you is supposed to be in the gallery?"

"Me, sir." A young fair-haired guard snapped to attention. He looked frightened, like a schoolboy caught playing truant.

"Then get in there, damn it. And the rest of you get back to your posts. This is not a picnic. Have your coffee when you're off."

The guards grumbled, packed up their coffee, and walked in different directions. The museum wouldn't open for three more hours, but they all had jobs to do. Had he been a thief who had got in, he could have walked out with any number of paintings.

The empty museum, with its monstrous vaulted ceilings and long marble corridors, made him feel quite devout, as though he were walking alone through a great cathedral. He had forgotten how pleasant it was not to see crowds. The bright morning billowed through the skylights overhead; the air seemed filled with a fine gold mist, as though it had been tinted with yellow toner.

The workroom was so chilly that he put on a sweater under his white coat. He checked the temperature and the humidity. In a large porcelain bowl he mixed the stopping of chalk, umber, and animal glue. Then he thinned it with Venice turpentine, knelt over the painting, and continued with the work of packing the backs of the slashes. He felt exhilarated by the simple task of daubing the stopping in, the canvas giving with each slight pressure of his hand as though it were sighing with relief. This was as it should be—simple work done alone with the painting, not a three-ring circus of cameras, press, and spectators.

He, like everyone else, had been carried away. The pressure, the constant commotion had dredged up a lifetime of very private paranoia that had him following someone he had never seen before, that had him, too, telling Demmie things he had worked at forgetting, had built his adulthood around sublimating. He realized that he was as delicate and vulnerable and exposed as *The Night Watch* had been before it was slashed, and the queer presaging of unexpected danger seemed to be constantly roiling inside him. But that too, he told himself, was as insane as believing he was being followed. He was not a child again; there were no more soldiers who killed little children; he did not have to listen for the sound of boots on the street outside.

He had finished filling the slashes with the puttylike mixture and was cleaning his tools when he heard someone tapping on the gallery window with a ring or a piece of metal. He checked his watch, noting that the museum had just opened. Whoever it was, he did not want to see them. But the tapping started again, more insistent this time. When he pulled back the curtain, he saw Inspector van Velde.

"I'd completely forgotten you were coming this morning," Pieter said as he let him in. "I'm sorry."

Van Velde pointed to the painting. "How is it going?" His tone betrayed his boredom. His eyes wandered around the workroom. The detective wore a threadbare brown suit and a thin black tie. His graying, wiry hair was a mess.

"We're making progress," Pieter said. "Another few weeks and we'll be done."

"What's all this about being followed, Beckum?" he asked abruptly.

"Can we go up to the studio? My staff should be in soon, and I'd like to talk with you in private."

In Pieter's office, van Velde again dropped into the desk chair as if it were his own, leaving Pieter to stand. He paced behind van Velde, telling him about the man who had showed up so many times at the gallery, and had also showed up at the concert. He assured the inspector that neither he nor Demmie was mixed up in anything, and that all this cloak-and-dagger stuff was more than he could figure out. "It's starting to affect my work," Pieter said. "Is this man a policeman?"

"We have undercover men occasionally stopping in the gallery."

"Why?"

"Just to keep an eye on things."

"Come now, Inspector. Why the concert, then?"

"I don't know about that," van Velde said. "But I don't think you're being followed. Based upon what you are telling me, it sounds like an accumulation of coincidences."

"You think I'm paranoid?"

"I didn't say that. I will be happy to check this man out to see if he's one of us."

Pieter handed him a piece of paper with an address and names scribbled on it. "He lives in this building."

Van Velde eyed him suspiciously. "How did you get this?"

"I followed him."

"Leave the police work to the police, all right?" van Velde said. He got up to leave. "I'll check this out and call you back. But don't get too hopeful. With the Holland Festival going on, we're stretched about as thin as a police force could be. There are several thousand more people in the city than there normally are. It's a pickpocket's heyday. Not to mention the other less glamorous crimes. I'm afraid there's little we can do about this, unless you want to report a crime."

"But what about the incident in the park? He wasn't even paying attention to the music."

"If it was as bad as you say, who could blame him? Maybe he just recognized you from the museum, but I'll check to make you feel better."

"Call me back today, will you?"

"All right," van Velde said.

Pieter escorted him out of the studio and down the elevator.

Demmie and Theillen had come in and were melting beeswax in an iron cauldron in a corner of the workroom. The curtains had been drawn back. Demmie called him off to the side and told him that the man had been there again but had left after a few moments. Pieter felt that same sudden fire race up his spine. The man had come to watch him, he thought. He had been the only one absent. He did not know why that thought occurred to him, and he was afraid to probe it any deeper.

Pieter added two parts colophony, a resin made from pinewood, to the beeswax, and the workroom filled with the pervasive scent of wintergreen. When ironed in, the colophony would bind the wax to the relining canvas and penetrate through the relining canvas to the back of the Rembrandt canvas and harden.

It would take some time before the wax completely melted, so Pieter had Theillen tend the cauldron, keeping the temperature at a constant 67 degrees Celsius, while he and Demmie went to the cafeteria. He felt compelled to tell her of his conversation with van Velde. It was as if the detective had been humoring him, and all the while the man was watching downstairs in the gallery.

"If they won't do anything," Demmie said, sipping a cup of coffee, "why don't we continue to follow him? Three can play at his game. We won't get in any trouble. We'll confront him."

He wanted to tell her that he had already thought about that, but he could not reveal his fear of the confrontation. His leg muscles had filled with a trembling that robbed him of his strength the other day as he watched the man slide the herring down his throat and so unaffectedly go about his business. And he remembered the sinister sneer too. He would only corner him if they could do it in the museum, with the guards around.

"He could be dangerous."

"He could be, but I don't think so," Demmie said. "Besides, where's your spirit of adventure? That thing that made you pick up all of a sudden and carry me off to Italy."

"It's not the same thing," he said.

"It is," she protested. "It's the melodrama of this whole ridiculous situation. We get to take a chance." She pushed her tray away, leaving her roll untouched. "There can't be too many of those chances, you know. We could look back on this from our old age and regret the one thing we should have—"

"No," he said emphatically. "I will not follow him. We'll wait, like van Velde says. And if he does anything suspicious, we'll call—"

"You wait if you want. But I want to know what this is all about. It's become very exciting to me, and a little scary too. It's something we might talk about the rest of our lives, Pieter. Why cut it short, or cut it out altogether?"

When they came back to the workroom, the wax was ready. Stan Martins had brought down the permanent relining frame with a new seamless piece of canvas the size of *The Night Watch* fastened to two sides. They laid the frame over the back of *The Night Watch*, and Theillen and Demmie stretched the canvas, a little at a time. Pieter followed behind, tacking the canvas tightly to the stretcher with upholstery nails.

"The wax, Theillen," Pieter said. He felt so good about the

morning's work that he decided to concentrate for the next three hours and finish the relining completely. "Demmie, you stand on my right. Brush the wax on." He plugged in his electric iron and knelt on a foam pad.

It was as if they had all come to do the best work of their lives today. Theillen had simmered the wax and colophony as though it were a viscous pine-scented soup that he intended serving. He even looked cheerful as he stirred it, and he wore a lab coat over his T-shirt, something he had never done before.

Demmie, too, might have sensed the energy of the day. She had dressed in jeans and an old blouse, and there was a definite spring of enthusiasm in her gait. Pieter felt really quite fatherly, just then, or as he imagined fatherly might be, until Jan burst through the rear door trailing the film crew.

"I'm sorry," Jan blurted. "It's my fault. I neglected to notify them of the waxing today. Pieter, please be understanding. They have to get this on film."

Pieter started laughing. Jan was babbling. Cables were being plugged in everywhere. Men and women opened tripods and positioned large lights. He couldn't have objected if he had wanted to; he felt so good he couldn't even summon up indignation. It was as if this little scene caricatured the entire spectacle the restoration had become.

The cauldron of wax was set up on a table with wheels. On a shelf underneath there was a tank of liquid gas which fed a large burner under the cauldron. Pieter was still chuckling to himself when Theillen began wheeling the cauldron over to the work floor. He narrowly missed one of the film cables. As Pieter moved to warn him, the front wheel of the table snagged on a C-clamp which held the relining canvas to the loom. The cauldron tipped. Theillen's hand shot out and caught the hot lip of the cauldron; he jerked it back, and a dollop of wax spattered his hand. First he yelped; then he saw everyone staring astonishedly at him, and a sheepish look shadowed his features. The wax had hardened over the top of his hand; his fingers were curled and spread. He held up his hand, which looked like a plaster claw, and growled.

196

Suddenly everyone was around him, asking him if he was all right. Demmie went for ointment and gauze. Theillen, very casually, sat and peeled away the swatches of wax. He salved his hand in ointment, but refused the gauze and Pieter's offer to go home.

The cameras began to whir, and Demmie took the wax-sodden brush from Theillen and swirled it in a small figure eight in the center of the canvas. A vapor of pine fragrance spread through the air as Pieter, in very straight, quick strokes, brushed the iron over the wax. Almost as soon as the iron passed over the wax, it solidified into a chocolate-colored glaze, permeating the relining canvas and binding it finally to the Rembrandt canvas.

Pieter draped the cord of the iron over his neck and worked for an hour without getting up. There was something invigorating about the ironing, as though it were a sign that all was well and they were on the way to recovering the painting. The pine vapors, as they came off the canvas, were so rich he could taste them on the roof of his mouth. Then he gave Demmie and Theillen a turn at the iron so they could experience the same thrill he had gotten from this simple task.

Theillen had to use his left hand to iron, and didn't look nearly as pleased as when he was feeding chunks of wax into the cauldron. When some air bubbles formed near Banning Cocq's head, Pieter climbed back on the dais and smoothed them with a cold iron.

By four o'clock, they had finished the waxing. With a scalpel, Pieter sliced *The Night Watch* away from the loom, and they all joined in turning the painting, firmly adhered by the waxed lining to its new stretcher, onto its back. Everyone in the room applauded.

Van Velde called Pieter at home that night. He and Demmie had just finished watching the news, and she was standing on the balcony with her leg on the rail. Slowly she bent forward and wrapped her hands around her foot; then she leaned backward, and her hands traced a semicircle over her head. Van Velde told Pieter that no person living at the address Pieter had given him matched the description of the man from the gallery. The first two floors of the building were occupied by old couples, the third by a short, middle-aged pimp, named Molen.

"Did you ask him if he knew such a man?"

"I have been a policeman for twenty-five years, and I know how to do my job," van Velde snapped. "The man was nowhere around. He seldom is. But when we run across him, we'll ask."

"I apologize," Pieter said. "But I did see him go in there, and it must have taken a key."

"Not necessarily."

"What should I do now?"

"Wait, I suppose," van Velde said. "And if he shows up again . . ." His voice trailed off. After a pause, he added, "If you get a chance, you might have the museum guards detain him, then call me."

"Sure." Pieter set the receiver down. "That's a big help," he said.

"What?" Demmie asked from the balcony.

"I said van Velde was a big help."

"Does he think you're cuckoo?" She chirped the last words as she came through the door.

"Probably." After a moment, he asked, "Do you want to do that *something exciting* you were spouting off about in the cafeteria this morning?"

She chewed at her index finger as though she were weighing infinite possibilities; then a smile unfurled across her lips.

25

Pieter simply peeled the long strips of rice paper from the face of *The Night Watch*. The varnish had completely disintegrated, turning chalky from the water in the paste, and the painting looked as though it had been slathered with whitewash. Jan had come down early that afternoon to lecture the people in the gallery and cried out at the sight of the painting. He kept the film crew waiting outside the gallery because he thought there might be general panic at the sight of the ruined masterpiece.

"My God, Pieter," Jan cried. "What have you done?"

"Take it easy, Jan."

With a rag and some alcohol, Pieter knelt at the bottom of the painting and rubbed a small square around Banning Cocq's right foot. The line of Banning's calf showed clearly through the paste, as well as his entire shoe, with a tiny glinting of light on the toe. "In about three days," Pieter said, watching the panic fade from Jan's face, "we shall have the whole painting cleaned of the old coat of varnish so we can put on a new one."

"That's all there is to it?"

"A little more," Pieter answered. "We have to get the chemical composition of the alcohol and turpentine in such a state that it will remove even the oldest, crusty varnishes from the striations in the heavy brushstrokes."

"Enough of this shoptalk. I didn't come for a lesson, so don't try to teach me anything."

"I'd be a fool to."

"Was that sarcastic? Oh, never mind. I came down here with some good news for you, Pieter. So be nice."

"All right."

"You are going to be decorated."

Jan had an expectant look on his face, a tight-lipped half smile on his lips. He smoothed his hair, waiting for the significance of his message to descend upon Pieter.

"What do you mean 'decorated'?"

"You know, Royal Order of Something or Other. Juliana is going to bestow some sort of decoration on you."

"For what? This?" He let his hand sweep the workroom. It was in total chaos now, with gummy rice paper balled in a pile, bottles of alcohol and solvent crowding the worktable, a microscope in the corner, pieces of canvas scattered about the floor. "Is this a little grandstanding by the Town Council for the film documentary?" Pieter asked, suddenly becoming angry. "What's going on?"

"Not just film, but television too."

"What? What are you talking about now? More confusion here?" His voice raised unexpectedly, and he saw that Theillen and Demmie had stopped working and were watching him and Jan. They ambled over behind Pieter.

"The day this is finished," Jan started in, "the Queen is going to give you the decoration. She's also going to give one to the guard who throttled the madman. You're going to be heroes, I suppose."

"Do I have to go through this?"

"I think it's best. One shouldn't slight the Queen, even in a free society."

Demmie tugged at Pieter's work coat. He leaned back to her, and she whispered something in his ear. He broke into a broad grin. "Jan, they want to be heroes, too," he said.

"What?"

"And I agree. They should be heroes. And so should you" Pieter grabbed Jan by the shoulders.

"Cut it out, Pieter."

"All right," he said, pointing his thumb over his shoulder. "But they're going to be heroes too. They deserve it."

"I'll see what I can do," Jan said, walking out the door. "Open these curtains for a while, will you?"

Theillen drew back the curtains. Pieter went to the door and called after Jan, "If you had any sense, you'd be a hero with us." They all laughed, and Jan huffed his way through the people in the gallery. Pieter was still laughing quite hard when he saw the man at the back of the gallery. The man was staring so bewilderedly that Pieter turned away at once. He didn't know whether to run out and confront him or send Demmie out the back door for a guard to detain him. No clear decision came to him. He felt physically immobilized.

Demmie saw the man too. Her face went pale, but when she saw Pieter watching her, she giggled.

The man turned from behind a tour group and walked out of the gallery. Instinctively, Pieter realized something then about the man: he would never step to the front; he enjoyed taunting them with his evasiveness. It was queer behavior, and now it piqued Pieter's curiosity profoundly.

Seeing the man's face, partially obscured by the old couple standing in front of him, had reminded Pieter of the tour guides' standard evaluation of the utterly unattached portion of face that peers eerily over a soldier's shoulder in the back row of characters in *The Night Watch*. They all claimed it was Rembrandt's face, because it was the habit of artists of that time to hide themselves somewhere in their group portraits, and because the tourists wanted to hear interesting little tidbits of that kind. It made for better tips. But Demmie had hit upon something much more profound with her notion that the face—and it did look something like Rembrandt's—had been the center of balance in the original painting before it had been cut up.

The portion of face in the painting, it suddenly seemed to Pieter, so resembled the man's face in the crowded gallery that it was unsettling. Perhaps its wide-eyed ambiguity was what had interested him all along. Concealed in the darkness at the back of the gallery, his face captured the essence of desperate fear as well as any artist's rendering. When Pieter had turned away just now, it had been because he had glimpsed a moment of his own perplexed childhood face in that man's, a moment of being afraid and yet not knowing what he was afraid of. Perhaps an image of his face as he looked over the bow of the boat at uncomplicated horror, with a dry sock jammed in his mouth—as though he had been pitched backward in time for a glance at his secret self. All this sounded deranged in its conception, yet there was something stirring inside him, something he seldom paid attention to, which told him that what he was feeling was right. He was coming closer to knowing this man; and he knew then that there was certainly no pattern to his visits, just as there was no pattern to fear.

Theillen and Demmie spent days removing the varnish, first with rags dipped in alcohol and acetone, then with heated yellow turpentine. They started by cleaning small squares in the center of the whitened painting, then moved outward toward the edges. Each square revealed another piece of puzzle as *The Night Watch* formed itself before them. Meanwhile, Pieter worked privately in the tower, experimenting with varnishes. He needed a relatively fast-drying one to apply before he retouched the slashes, so that, as he had promised, future generations who found better methods or better paints might be able to change his work. Eventually he settled for two varnishes, both mixed from dammar, a yellowish evergreen-scented resin, and oil of turpentine. To one mixture he added poppy-seed oil; to the other, poppy-seed oil and oil of turpentine. He had only to apply them to see which dried faster.

Demmie brought news that she and Theillen had finished cleaning away the old varnish. She sat on the corner of his desk, holding up one of his beakers of varnish to the sunlight. "Looks like honey," she said. "Smells a bit like disinfectant."

Pieter was writing a progress report for Jan's press release.

"What are we going to do about that man?" Demmie asked.

"Who?" Pieter looked up. "Oh, him."

"You know, I see him out there even when he's not. Does he scare you?"

"No, but he's not helping my concentration any. Or yours. Anyway, I've decided to confront him. Ask him if he knows me."

"Very smart," she said. "And very brave. Like in the movies."

"You've got work to do," he told her.

She went down to help Theillen and Stan Martins hang *The Night Watch*. Pieter's plans called for two steel cables with counterweights to be attached to the top of the relining frame. The sides of the frame would slide up and down inside wooden guides. Stan Martins's crew built a work bridge three feet high and fifteen feet long. From it, the entire face of the painting could be easily reached by raising or lowering the relining frame. Pieter would also be able to slide the bridge back for a good vertical perspective during the retouching.

Jan came into the workroom again and patiently watched Demmie brush a light coat of varnish on the drummer in the right corner of the painting. Pieter worked behind her with a wide brush to even the varnish out. Without turning, Pieter asked, "What is it this time, Jan?"

"When I was in here the other day, you remember?" He stood below them, at the foot of the elevated work bridge; his shoulders were rounded, and he looked rather troubled. "Well, I neglected to tell you something."

"This doesn't sound like good news."

"It's not bad, if that's what you mean."

"What is it?"

"The painting must be done in time for the decoration ceremony."

Pieter gripped the railing of the bridge and looked down on Jan, who seemed to have shrunk. "Something doesn't quite make sense. The painting must be done in time for the ceremony. Isn't the ceremony scheduled for after the completion of the work?"

"Not exactly," Jan said. "You see, Juliana wants the restoration completed by a certain date; so does the Town Council and the Director General. . . ."

"That only leaves you, Jan. Are you part of this too?"

"I'm just the harbinger of bad news, but that's the way it's got to be. Juliana's leaving on some diplomatic business, and she has made it known through various channels when it must be completed. Even the TV and film crews have had to push up their schedules."

"I don't like this. I don't like being rushed." Pieter climbed down the steps, approaching Jan. Jan backed away as though he expected to be hit. "I'll tell you what, though. We're coming close to finishing. What's the deadline?"

"Two weeks from today."

"Jesus," Pieter said. "That's cutting things a little close."

26

Van Rijks loved to stand in the museum, with the warmth of bodies pressing around him. He loved the fine sweet smell of the women's perfume, the mustiness of rain-damp clothing, and, when someone came out of the workroom, the strong fragrance of wintergreen on a cool gust of air. As long as he stood among the spectators, he felt protected against the work that was going on behind that wall, safe from the people as well as what they were working on.

Standing in the gallery watching them work confirmed the fact that he had been alive, was still alive, and, for the time being, was well. It was as though the gallery were his only point of reference now. He was not confused, as he had been at his studio in Leiden, and with Neel, wondering if he had ever really left, because here was where all his past ended. He knew that. And from here, all that lay before him would begin. As long as he stayed on the medication, everything would continue to fall into place. The medication, for instance, had helped him know that he had been the one who had damaged the painting these people were gawking at. And right now he was bursting with that secret knowledge.

He remembered other things too. He knew that he had been dragged out of this very building. He could feel the strong grip of the guards' hands tightening on his biceps, their shrill whistle piercing his hearing, his arm twisted agonizingly behind his back. Then there had been the interrogation, the humiliating beating they had given him in that small green room, insisting he had been sent by some political group. At first he had not talked, and they kept him awake through the night with a bright bulb constantly burning and a dose of cold water when he became groggy. They had pressed their foul-smelling faces into his, distorted as though made from soft clay, stretching oblong, then sagging as they flung profanities at him.

The young, athletic-looking cop with the pink face and the perpetually moving eyes had finally backed off from him and said, "He's no terrorist; he's a bloody loon."

"It's no less a shame," the other said.

"Bug off," he told them both.

Then he had been given clean clothes and handled as gently as though this had all been a terrible mistake. He truly thought he was going to be turned out on the street again, to face whatever it was that had prowled so uncontrollably inside his head, that had erupted in such a violent frenzy that he had tried to *kill* a painting. But they had not turned him out.

The abusive, foul-smelling police were replaced by young men with kindly voices who dressed in white and smelled of isopropyl alcohol. They wielded supernatural powers in that they were able to propel him through antiseptic corridors by the mere touch of his elbows. When they pinched lightly, he simply turned like a horse under rein. He could never bring himself to challenge them.

Until they gave him his first taste of the pills. A heaviness crashed around his heart; he felt anchored to the floor by shuffling leaden feet. But with that heaviness came a certain clarity. He could almost sense the medication seeking equilibrium throughout his blood. He did not have the strength to raise his arms; he knew if he was foolish enough to lie down and allow the blood to settle along the underside of his body, he would never get up again. So he walked ceaselessly around the ward they had put him in.

It was then that the pills began quelling his turmoil. He remembered, days before, sitting in the empty courtroom, his arms pinioned behind his back, while three men talked quite reverently about what they would do with him. Finally, one of them rapped

206

a gavel against the hard wood of his desk and said they could take him to the State Psychiatric Institute. He could still hear the words, spoken in an even, unemotional tone: "W. van Rijks destroyed part of his nation's artistic legacy and brought disgrace upon himself, as well as the Netherlands, by so wantonly committing such a senseless act. However," the man continued, "this is no longer a matter for the jurisprudence system. There will be no trial; all records of this proceeding, and all subsequent information in this matter, will be sealed from the public."

As part of his therapy, they had let him wander the Institute in that thick fog that the pills imposed. He stole pills from the other patients in the ward too. They were such dullards. They hid them under their tongues, pretending to swallow. When the orderlies left, they secreted them under their mattresses or in the hollow post of their headboards, and he would slip around in the darkness, gathering them. Once, he had even managed to steal some off the tray a male nurse carried from bed to bed. In a short time he had amassed enough pills to continue his therapeutic walk right off the Institute grounds.

But the pills did not always work their magic, and he found himself standing in the gallery where his trouble had started, daring them to figure out who he was, and all the eternal destruction he represented. When he had slashed the painting, he had not been cognizant. And the police had done their best to hide him away, to force the world to deny his existence. This time, the world would rear up on its hind legs and howl at him.

Yet something in the bearing of that dark-haired man who directed this surgery threatened the accomplishment of his new plan. With the other spectators' shadows lying across him like a fine dark netting, he watched the man kneel and scrape and wax and iron. He noticed the man had taken to watching him too. He noticed it and loved it. He felt compelled to match the man's intensity. He saw the restorer as an arrogant miracle worker, trying to raise Lazarus from the dead, struggling to undo the mortal handiwork he had inflicted. He wanted to know what it was that would make this man attempt such an impossible task.

For it would be impossible. Even Christ could not give Lazarus immortality.

But the day they finally picked the canvas up from the floor and suspended it from cables in the ceiling, he saw that the impossible had, in fact, been accomplished. The first sight of the healed painting caused his tongue to dry and flatten in his throat. His breath slowed, and a throbbing pressure built behind his eyes.

He saw then, too, the damage he had inflicted on the painting, and part of him felt sickened by it. Yet someone, he knew, had to destroy what others loved, to play a vengeful God in the absence of a merciful one, to make people understand the meaning of loss strong enough to stop the world.

Hanging in the workroom, the canvas looked like a monster regenerated from dead flesh, its belly laced with scars. The people around him instantly multiplied into a crowd, and he saw the crowd of figures on the canvas. They were marching out of the darkness at him again. The light glimmering in the palm of Banning Cocq's extended hand enticed him. *Step right up. Here, take my hand.* He saw the eye too, that angle of face that gnawed his very center, that melted his will as entirely as flame melts ice. And there was little Johannes, innocent mischief twinkling in his eyes, as he fled the turmoil of marching soldiers. He felt the bouncing begin in the balls of his feet, small tremors moving up through his ankles to his knees and into his hips. He could not control it; the man on the work bridge stared at him, and he rushed from the gallery in a blind panic, knocking aside the people who stood in his path.

27

Pieter saw the man watching, but there was nothing he could do about it. He had just cleaned the surface of *The Night Watch* with a piece of foam rubber dipped in oil of turpentine, and he was applying stopping to the slashes on the front of the painting to bring them up to the original paint layer.

Demmie had not showed up, and that both puzzled and perturbed him. She had never missed work before, and her timing now was particularly horrendous. He had only Theillen to help him, and though he was determined to have the guards detain this man, he could not stop the work he had begun.

Almost as soon as he noticed the man, a strange-looking woman, leaning against one of the windows, caught his attention. Her hair was long and black; she wore large dark glasses, a ragged brown serge coat. She was making frantic hand gestures in front of her chest, and when she removed the sunglasses he saw that she had Demmie's eyes. And hands.

My God, he said to himself. This time she has gone too far.

Since van Velde had not found the man at the address he had given him, she must have taken it upon herself to play her own cloak-and-dagger game. It was not out of character for her, but as he looked at her, dressed in that amateurish disguise, he felt a sudden rush of anxiety.

The man stood behind her and to the left, separated by several people. He seemed unusually nervous. He rocked from foot to foot, fingering his heavy beard and shifting his hat, first back on his head, then low over his eyes. Demmie was casting sidelong glances at him. Pieter thought of sending Theillen out to drag her in, but decided he indeed wanted to learn about this mystery spectator more than he needed her in here working.

He and Theillen spent about half an hour putting the definitive first coat of varnish on the cleaned painting. Theillen performed Demmie's job of spreading the varnish in small patches, while Pieter came behind him with a wide, natural-bristle brush and smoothed it out. It was over this layer that he would retouch the slashes. Again he felt lighthearted in the work. The beginning of the end. The old varnish had darkened the paint considerably; now the faces seemed to glow with sensual yellow light, each patch of skin as luminous and vibrant as Rembrandt had intended. The ornamentation in the little girl's dress and van Ruytenburch's coat were no longer cast in light; they were clearly the source of light. He could even read some of the names carved in stone on the arch above the characters' heads. He sensed the drama, the coming to life of centuries of repressed energy at his fingertips, as he brushed the varnish.

When he got to the section that was high and to the center of the composition, he stopped. Theillen had climbed down and lowered the canvas so that he could reach this portion from the elevated bridge. He found himself staring into that eye, Rembrandt's eye, with the most incredible sensation of déjà vu. The portion of face seemed to glisten with a fresh wetness from the varnish now that the painting was once again cleaned. His head whirled momentarily, and he nearly lost his balance. At first, he thought it was a dizziness born of the varnish fumes, but the fans were on, and he was not crazy. He spun around to the gallery window. The man was bouncing up and down.

The bouncing. The wet glazed-looking eyes. His mind flashed with a series of memories that seemed to break from some unfathomable recess inside him. He saw the bright yellow cardigan, as profound as the sun itself, the wrestling match with the police at the Dam; but it was the bouncing that made him know with certainty who the man was.

Then they locked eyes. At that moment, it was as if his vision had been reduced to the foreshortened tunnel of his camera's viewfinder as he had focused on that face some months ago. He saw again the man in the yellow sweater moving at him through the crowd like a sea beast, while he focused on that face, held his ground, then got tromped on for that one final picture. How could he not have known?

Standing transfixed on the work bridge, he remembered Jan's words when he had asked him who slashed the painting. "Some fucking lunatic." And then the picture from *de Telegraaf* that he and Demmie had found at the Press Institute flashed across his mind. Why not? Goddamn it, why not?

"Van Rijks," he said aloud, shivering with the name.

It appeared to Pieter that van Rijks could read his thoughts, for at once, Van Rijks took on a sudden panicked look and ran out of the gallery, nearly bowling over a group of elderly people. Pieter saw Demmie hurry after him and yelled for her to stop, but his voice was contained by the thickness of the gallery walls. Theillen looked at him as if he were crazy.

"Demmie's not here," Theillen said.

"Yes, she is," Pieter countered. "She's in a dark wig, following that man. Run and catch her!"

Theillen did not move; his dark eyes showed only blank amazement. "Goddamn it, catch her!" Pieter commanded him.

Theillen bounded down the steps of the work bridge, but by the time he had gotten into the gallery and through the crowd of people, they were both gone. Pieter trailed Theillen into the hallway that opened onto the lobby where the sales desks were. "I'm sorry, Mr. Beckum," Theillen said, "but I really don't know who I was supposed to be looking for. I didn't see Demmie."

"Forget it," Pieter said. "Let's close up shop."

Pieter's first thought was to call the police, but he decided that he would give Demmie time to get back to him. Van Velde had wanted a criminal offense, and he and Demmie would lay this right in his lap.

Pieter went up to his studio and got out the pictures he had taken for the first-aid treatment of the painting—those original pictures of the slashing. He had kept them in a box in his desk. He picked out the few that had still been on the roll from the Queen's birthday.

Then he got in his car and rushed to the Press Institute, where he had the receptionist lead him down to the basement. He found the partial picture of the slasher in *de Telegraaf,* and after the girl had gone back upstairs, he tore it out and folded it into his pocket.

He drove back to his apartment, found the complete undeveloped roll of film from the Queen's birthday that he had thrown into a bureau drawer, and took it to a photography shop near the Dam. He offered the man two hundred guilders extra to develop the film immediately, and he waited until it was done at a café around the corner, drinking a glass of beer.

Finally, he went home to wait for Demmie. After an hour, he called her apartment.

"Why didn't you come back here?" he asked her. "I was worried, with you in that disguise. Do you know who that was you were following?"

"Pieter," she said, "that man scared the hell out of me."

"I think you should get over here. I have something important you should see."

After he hung up, he took some pins from the kitchen and began tacking the pictures of van Rijks all over the walls of his living room. With charcoal, he colored a heavy beard on some of them. There was one partly obscured picture he had taken—it must have been in a moment of great confusion, right before the man had started after him—that was almost an exact duplication of the only picture that had made the newspapers.

When Demmie came in, she looked around the room. Then, as she saw the newspaper clipping and the matching photo on the wall, she said, "Oh, my God. When did you figure this out? Where did you get all these pictures?"

He told her about the Queen's birthday, and about taking the pictures of the lunatic whom he had chosen for some imagined photographic essay he had never completed. "I had forgotten all about him in the turmoil that followed that weekend," he said. "It wasn't until this afternoon, while I saw him in the gallery again, that I knew our spectator and van Rijks were the same person."

"But I thought the police said he was dead?"

"They did."

"What's he doing here?"

"I'm afraid of that answer," Pieter said. *The Night Watch.*"

"Oh, Pieter." She was trembling as they embraced each other. She still wore the tailored shirt and mid-length dark skirt of her disguise, but the wig was gone and so were the glasses.

He sat on the couch with her, and he could feel her body quavering. "Don't be so scared," he said, stroking her back. "I'll call van Velde in the morning and ask him to come to the museum. He can trap van Rijks there." But he, too, was shaking.

"You don't know what happened," she said.

"What do you mean?"

"I followed him, you know. You saw my disguise. And I thought I found where he was living—on one of those deserted streets in the Jordaan. But when I came back here to wait for you, I got anxious. I went out on the porch to look down the street for you, and *he* was standing on the sidewalk below, staring up at me. He was smiling, or leering, or something."

"What?"

"That's right," she said. "He turned the tables on me. I guess he saw through my disguise and followed me. And I led him to this apartment."

Pieter remembered his first thought after seeing the torn canvas: How terribly strong the man would have to be to rip through all that canvas and varnish.

"I'm going to call van Velde now." He got up from the couch.

"Forget it," Demmie said. "I tried. He's out of the city until tomorrow."

He sat down again, and she tucked her head in the crook of his arm. Her hair smelled of baby powder. He asked her about it.

213

"I powder it," she said, "to keep from having to wash it so often."

"Why don't you fill up the tub and soak for a while?" he said. "It will calm you down. I'll go to the corner and get us something to cook."

"No, Pieter," she pleaded. "Don't leave me alone. You didn't see him down there. The look in his eyes. He scared me terribly. I waited till he went away and then went home to my apartment. I was afraid he'd come back."

"Relax. He's gone now. Besides, he can't get up here. He would have to ring the bell. Just keep the door locked, and I'll make sure the downstairs door is locked."

"How about if we live through the night on love?" she said. She tugged at her shirt and buttons popped open like snaps.

"That's a neat trick," he said. "I'll hurry back."

"Why don't I wait for you? We can soak together."

Her questions were coming out of fear, and they unnerved him, heightening his own anxiety. "No," he said. "I don't want a bath. Just go relax." He gave her a firm shove toward the bathroom.

"You're getting too used to me," she said, closing the door behind her.

Part III

THE DESTRUCTION

28

After he had forced open the door, his attention was immediately drawn to the sound of running water. It came from somewhere in the back of the apartment. At first, his steps were drawn in that direction, but for some unaccountable reason his feet stopped. He turned through a hallway and entered the living room, feeling as though he had been in this house before. Then he saw his face tacked up all over the living-room wall. Large black-and-white pictures: some were shot so close he could count the pores in his cheeks; others were shot from a great distance. A beard had been penciled on some of them. He was ranting at the throng of gaily dressed people gawking at him; he was being strong-armed by a couple of cops.

He began snatching the pictures violently from the wall. That bastard. These are pieces of me he's been collecting. He was so numb with rage that he started shredding the pictures. A part of his soul had been stolen in these moments. Now he had something to direct his rage against.

The water was shut off, and in the ensuing silence, a humming commenced, as sweet and piercing as a child's. His rage drained away, and he was suddenly happy, walking through his own hallway with the smell of Neel's potato casserole in his nose. Then he became frightened. It was part of their trap. Everything was part of the trap: the pictures, the child. They were agents of madness, taunting him. The humming intensified in pitch. It rose an octave, then seemed to rise another; he clamped his fists over his ears.

But nothing lessened the intensity of the humming. It broke off with a sound of a bottle dropping in water, and "Oh, shit."

When he burst through the bathroom door, he had a wad of shredded pictures in his hand. She was soaping her hair. She opened her mouth to scream, but he slid on one knee beside the tub and covered her lips with the palm of his hand. He flung the pictures into the water and grabbed a handful of her curly, wet hair.

"Don't scream!" he whispered into her terrified face. Her eyes were stretched so wide he thought they would pop out into the water and bob among the floating bubbles.

He looked her body up and down. He wished that he had a third hand, so he could touch her glistening breasts and stomach. And he wished he had a fourth hand, because with it he would touch her sex. And a fifth. . . . Slowly he let go of her hair and released the grip on her mouth. Her bottom lip quivered as though she were going to cry.

"Do you know who I am?"

"Yes."

"What are you doing with these pictures all over your walls?"

"It's not my wall. They're not my pictures," she said. Her eyes tightened fiercely. "They're Pieter's."

"Oh," he said, "they belong to your keeper."

"Eat it," Demmie said.

Van Rijks knelt forward quickly and pushed her head under the water. As her head went down, her back arched, her stomach writhed up, and her knees banged hollowly against the side of the porcelain tub. She was still thrashing when he let her up. She choked water and started to claw at him wildly.

"Are you crazy?" she screamed.

He laughed at her. The curls had all come unsprung around her face; her eyeliner ran like dark tears down her pale cheeks:

"Yes," he said. "Now get out." He tossed her a towel.

29

As Pieter inserted the key in the apartment door, he noticed it was ajar. He hadn't been careless; he knew he had closed it when he left. Climbing the stairs, he felt his stomach lurch, a dry feeling of terror rise to his throat. Now he took the stairs two at a time.

He pushed the front door gently and craned his head in. Photographs were scattered about on the rug.

"Demmie?" He set the package of food on an end table and tiptoed down the hall: someone might spring from a closet, or a corner of the dark bedroom. Van Rijks. "Demmie?" Christ, what had he done?

A ribbon of light showed in the crack under the bathroom door. His mind tripped with horror. He expected a grizzly scene, gouts of blood splashed about on the bright tile walls. For a moment, he hesitated to open the door. Then, when he did, he saw a towel draped over the tub, one end in the soapy water, a puddle on the floor. On the mirror was a message, lettered precisely in green acrylic paint, still wet: NO POLICE, WHOREMASTER. YOURS TRULY, VAN RIJKS, THE SLASHER. SEE NOTE ON TABLE.

What the hell was going on? "See note on table." Was this one of Demmie's sick jokes? It had scared the shit out of him. He would turn her over his knee when he caught up with her and give her the spanking she deserved.

The note was on the coffee table. It was in Demmie's handwriting, and beneath it was a picture of van Rijks that had been torn up, then put back together like a puzzle. The note read: *Pieter,*

*this is for real. Van Rijks took me with him. He says no police or
else. He says he will keep disappearing like he did the last time
... until the right time. He says he will return me afterward, maybe.*
She did not sign it. His first thought was to call van Velde, but
Demmie had said he would not be back till the following day.

Pieter slumped onto the couch. He didn't dare call any of the
other cops; he didn't trust them. He didn't know why he felt as
though he could trust van Velde, either. Van Velde was one of
them. Van Rijks might take Demmie's life. He was a lunatic. The
debris of pictures on the floor attested to that. But van Rijks could
not possibly be crazy all the time. No one was. He had moments
of lucidity. How else could he have calculated things to turn out
so? And when he was lucid, Pieter thought, he was very intelli-
gent, and very dangerous.

God, he wanted to know what made this man act. There was
no reason for this chaos to visit his life. And van Rijks wasn't dead.
The detective had lied. Pieter alternately raged at being lied to
and trembled with fear. What had been the purpose of lying to
him? They had even used him, during the first days of the press
conferences, to feed the public misleading information. And they
had succeeded in placing him and Demmie in far greater danger
with their stupidity.

He tried sleeping because he could think of nothing else. The
sheets and covers twisted around his legs. Demmie had been
kidnapped. The words finally registered in his brain with the full
force of a punch. She had been spirited away—stolen straight
from her bath—by a madman who left a cryptic note about "the
right time."

Pieter flicked the light on and picked up the note from the
nightstand where he had left it. He felt so utterly helpless. He
thought he might break into tears at any minute. He had seldom
cried as a child, and never as an adult. But now he felt it swelling
in his throat, closing around his neck like a pair of strong hands.
Demmie would be admonishing him now: Come on, Pieter, cry.
It's all right to cry, she would say; put yourself on an emotional

edge. He wondered how she felt about being on the edge now—the edge of something she could never have expected.

He called Jan, but he could not bring himself to tell him about Demmie. He had not felt this isolated since his childhood. He had no one to turn to now, just as he had had no one to share his excitement at the ballet. Except Demmie. And then, just as now, there was a tremendous chasm between them. He realized that at the first mention of kidnapping Jan would want to call the police or do something equally stupid, so he found himself passing the time with him, talking about his *Night Watch* exhibit. Pieter wondered if he wasn't going a little crazy himself, sitting on the edge of his bed in a bathrobe pretending to be interested in Jan's work while Demmie's life might well hang in the balance.

Abruptly, he said goodbye to Jan. Then, on impulse, he called Theillen and suggested they meet at a café for coffee.

"It's a little late, isn't it?" Theillen asked.

"Yes," Pieter said, "but come just the same."

As soon as he hung up, the whole terrible mess hit him. Van Rijks had come to the museum because he had tried to destroy the painting once and had been unsuccessful. He was going to try again. That was what he had meant by "the right time." Now Demmie was his insurance against failure.

Pieter threw on some clothes and walked, instead of driving, to meet Theillen. The night air was cool with mist from a light fog that hung above the streetlamps. Couples lolled in the darkness of doorways. Occasionally, a passerby nodded to him, but he did not acknowledge anyone's greeting.

Somehow the police had removed themselves from this matter. Everything was left up to him. He simply could not allow that lunatic to destroy the painting again. Perhaps this time the damage would be irreparable. If it was—if art could be so easily obliterated—what was the purpose, then, of the work he had given his life to? He had come to love the painting, as though that canvas were a part of him, and felt ready to enter into preternatural battle with van Rijks over it.

And where did Demmie figure in this? He knew that if van Rijks could destroy precious art—that which was so worth living for—then he could as easily destroy human life. For van Rijks, animation was the only difference between a slashed masterpiece and a slashed woman. He could accomplish either.

Theillen was waiting at a table outside the café on the Rokin where he had taken Pieter the day he was told of his rejection as an apprentice. Theillen had already ordered his coffee. He appeared to be brooding when Pieter approached.

"Sorry it took so long."

"Who were you talking to?" Theillen asked. "Your lips were moving for half a block."

"Were they?" But Pieter knew that they had been as soon as Theillen mentioned it. He wondered if he wasn't capable of a mental plunge like van Rijks's. He looked at Theillen's Anne Frank tattoo; perhaps Theillen, who had marked himself so thoughtlessly with such a profound horror, held that same potential for madness. He was sure it existed in Demmie. And if all these people were touched by it, how far out into the world did the circle extend?

"I'll start from the beginning," Pieter said after ordering his coffee. He related the story very precisely, though his words must have sounded delusional. When he finished, he expected Theillen to tell him to do the logical thing—call the police.

"What are you going to do?" Theillen asked.

Pieter thought a moment, as if in the pause an answer would descend upon him and his life would once again be simple.

"I don't know. I'm afraid for Demmie. My instincts tell me to wait, that he will be in touch with me. From there I might get some kind of lead on him. He is crazy, you know. I don't want to be the cause of her getting hurt. I love—" The words slipped so casually off his tongue; he stopped when he saw the pitying look on Theillen's face. Then he said it anyway: "I love her."

"I just thought of something," Theillen said. "Something you mentioned."

"What?"

"This man van Rijks found his way to your apartment by following Demmie. But she had followed him somewhere. Did she mention the address?"

"Not an address, but she did say it was on one of those streets full of boarded-up houses in the Jordaan."

"We could start there. We could search through some of those places, and we'd feel we were doing something, instead of just going home to bed."

"I didn't call you out in the middle of the night to conspire," Pieter said. "I wanted someone to talk with. You needn't get messed up in this."

"I'm your apprentice," Theillen said. "Tell me what you want me to do. Go home or come with you?"

"Come with me," Pieter said.

30

"I could torture you," van Rijks said to Demmie, laughing under his breath.

"Are you serious?" she asked.

"Does that terrify you?"

"You terrify me."

He made her sit on the metal bedspring he had taken from the trash. Her hair was still wet from the bath; it hung limp around her wide-eyed face, making her look childish. He wanted to caress her like a child, but he remembered how her body had risen out of the water and how the scrub of blond hair below her belly belied her innocence.

She had followed him obediently in the night and had stood behind him as he tore some of the boards off the front of the house to get in, then replaced them; and she had followed him —him with the eyes of a cat—as he led her through the pitch blackness without bumping a wall or a doorway while she stumbled over the debris in the abandoned house. Finally, they climbed a steep set of stairs, and he pushed open a bookcase which concealed a complete apartment on the other side.

The windows had been boarded, and for light van Rijks kept three candles burning. Each created a little pool of flickering yellow light against the darkness. He kept the candles separated —two in the corners and one on the small table in the center of the room—so that no light intruded on another. He barred the door from the inside and sat at a three-legged chair at the small table, sketching her as she had seemed to him in the tub. Empty food wrappers were scattered about the floor.

"Let me go, damn it," she said. "What the hell are you going to do with me?"

"Like I said, I could torture you." His hands were shaking, but not as badly as when he had been alone here. It was as though her presence kept the demons at bay.

"Don't be asinine," she said. "You don't mean that. I know you don't."

"You don't know anything of the sort." Her tone taunted him, just as Neel's had. "But you're right. I don't mean it, though it's something I've thought about."

"Torturing me?"

"No, fool. Anyone. It doesn't matter who. I just want to know almighty power as it really is."

He sat hunched at the table, meticulously drawing her. Her breasts were buoyed by the water in the tub; her belly, hips, and legs were rippled beneath it. Instead of the clusters of soap bubbles, he had drawn clusters of eyes. Her face, a perfect oval framed by matted bangs, showed her wing-shaped lips stretched with an intake of breath as though she had been startled. Beneath her raised brows, she was eyeless.

"What's the matter?" she asked.

He watched the wavering light of the candle in front of him. He held the flame steady in his eyes until he could feel the weak yellow light intensify, burn through to his brain. He shook his head violently to clear it all away.

"Shut up," he snapped.

"You don't frighten me," she said, getting up from the bedspring. "Let me see what you've been sketching."

He kicked the chair out from under him and lurched to his feet. "Shut up!" he shouted. "And don't ever get up, or even move, unless I tell you so."

Then he handed her his drawing. Even in the dim light he could see her face pale; the paper trembled in her hands. "This is horrible," she said. She began to cry softly.

"I'm sorry," he said. "I have an artist's soul, and the hands of a turd." Her crying seemed pitiful, as though his drawing were wrenching each hollow sob from her. "My hands could draw little before; now they draw less."

He took a vial from his jacket pocket, opened it, and swallowed a pill. He sat beside her on the bed, stroking her calf, and told her about Johannes. She stopped crying. She would not look at him, but she listened intently, as if she understood everything. She was so much better for him than Molen. He felt as if the weight might finally lift from him, until he finished and she said, "Why didn't your wife just have another child?"

Then he howled; his hand gripped her leg so tightly he felt the sharpness of bone beneath the layers of muscles, and she cried out. "Is that all life means to you?" He dragged her from the bed. "You don't understand anything!" he shouted. He pushed her to face one of his wall drawings, a self-portrait done in chalk, and held up a candle behind her. "See that pentimento? That's *his* face bleeding through on my cheek, and I didn't draw it. You think that's crazy?"

"But that's just some cracks in the plaster."

He shoved her back toward the bed.

"Why are you doing this, goddamn it?" She began to whine. "It's not my fault. You have no right . . ."

"I have every right," he said, coming at her. He moved his face close to hers. "I have the right to mark this world, to make it pay."

A laugh began to build in his chest; he felt as though he were going to lift right off the floor. He whirled, laughing now, to the table, and scooped up the candle. "It's as simple as the right to obliterate light." He blew the candle out.

Then he scuttled over to the corner, hee-heeing gleefully, and blew another out.

"What are you doing?" she cried.

"Exercising my prerogative," he said with the same breath he used to extinguish the last weak flame. "There are rats in here, you know. I've heard them. They come in off the canal, their little pink feet scratching the floor. And they only come in to keep me company in the darkness. You will appreciate the little creatures while I'm gone."

She was breathing as heavily as he was laughing. He could not see her in the opaqueness of the room, but he heard the rustle of her clothes as she drew her feet up off the floor, and he could feel the heat of her body. The man on the charger reared across his vision, blanching it white. Johannes's severed, voiceless head bobbed across the darkness. The floor drummed with marching feet.

"Give me some light," she begged, her voice quavering.

"No, bitch. The light is on the inside." He wanted to punish her for feigning understanding, for tricking him with sympathy, as though he were a weak, mindless fool. His voice dropped to a whisper. "This is all something you could never understand, son. Nobody can. A very personal and private convolution of sanity that only the marked can go through."

"I'm not your son," she corrected him vehemently.

"You'll try to escape," he said, giggling. Then, seriously, angrily, "But forget about it. There is no way to get out once I've locked the door and pushed the bookshelf back. I have a message to deliver to your whoremaster. Kiss the rats for me."

The whine of her voice trailed off as he pushed the bookshelf into place. He needed to find Molen too; he had an errand for the weasel. He pressed his ear to the wall and listened to the sounds she made. Food wrappers crackled and he knew she was on the floor, groping for the extinguished candles. She would have no matches to light them, though. He scratched the walls with his fingernails, imitating the scurrying sound of rats' paws. There was a muffled crash, as though she had fallen over the table. She yelped too, then found her way to the door and scratched against it. When he finally heard the bedspring creak, he knew that she had resigned herself to captivity. See how easy it is when you do it right. He chuckled to himself as he walked into the street.

31

They caught a tram back to Pieter's apartment so he could get his car. They would need it to travel across town to the street where Demmie had followed van Rijks. Pieter took Theillen up to his apartment and showed him the pictures.

"No," Theillen said as he flipped through the ones that hadn't been torn. "I can't recollect ever seeing him before. But I haven't paid much attention to the people in the gallery."

"Well, he's been paying attention to us. And if he knows Demmie and me, he knows who you are. Remember what he looks like."

"Can I have one of these pictures?"

In Pieter's car, they drove to a side street off the Prinsengracht, near the train station. It was now a neighborhood of junkies and runaways, thieves and stolen-car dealers. Periodically, the police raided these empty houses to roust the squatters from the neighborhood because tourists had been lured there and relieved of their money.

All the buildings had narrow brick fronts and high-gabled roofs. Most were boarded up, claimed by the government for future restoration. Demmie was in one of them, Pieter was certain, held captive by a madman.

They walked along the unlighted street, Pieter a step behind. Theillen's stocky frame rolled on the balls of his feet, the darkness diminishing the powerful compactness of his body. Now and then, a car zipped by, drenching them in momentary brightness, casting Theillen momentarily larger than life. Theillen, like Demmie, just *did* things—hiding the box of *Night Watch* documents without question; tattooing himself because he was so moved by Anne Frank's house that marking himself was the first, probably the only, way he thought of expressing it. Whereas Demmie's eccentricities had up till now seemed whimsical, Theillen approached his somberly, as though he expected quite naturally that any day the price for eccentricity could be stalking a madman in the night.

"What will we do if we find them?" Theillen asked.

"There's two of us," Pieter said. "I suppose we'll just force him to give her up."

"Does he have a weapon?"

"I don't know."

"Great," Theillen said.

"Well, he wouldn't have a gun, if that's what you mean. I don't think he's that resourceful. Besides, you can leave anytime you want to."

"I'll stay," Theillen said. "We should have prepared better, though."

Pieter stopped at the mouth of the alley and picked up a long stick. He handed it to Theillen. "Does this make you feel better? If he comes near you, swat him."

"That's not funny," Theillen said, but he did not drop the stick.

They broke into three buildings by prying boards off a door or a window, and walked as quietly as they could in the darkness. The floors were littered with wreckage—fallen chunks of plaster, splintered and collapsed beams, broken furniture, pieces of glass, bottles. Pieter felt frustrated, completely useless. They were making enough noise to be heard by anyone nearby, and if van Rijks thought someone was after him, Demmie would surely get hurt. "This is hopeless," he finally said. "We're just blundering around in here. Let's quit."

Pieter dropped Theillen at his apartment, and as he drove home it occurred to him that if they stood watch—Theillen tomorrow during the day, and he during the night—van Rijks would have to reveal himself. He had to have food, or water, or maybe just some fresh air. If van Rijks's madness was as compelling as Pieter thought it might be, he would have to come back to the museum now that *The Night Watch* was hanging. And to retouch the painting, Pieter wouldn't need Theillen's help.

A note was taped to his apartment door. On the outside of the envelope, the word *Whoremaster* was scribbled. He hurried upstairs and tore it open. *I know you are following me. You have done it before and you will try it again. But I have that which is precious to you and I will scar her, hurt her, and perhaps I will pretend she is the canvas. Get it? Go about your business as usual. No police, and I mean it. I shall come to the gallery to check on you. And leave the curtains open all the time. Yours in paint, Rembrandt van Rijks.*

Pieter crumpled the letter and threw it against the wall. He gathered up the pictures of van Rijks and ripped them in fury. He kicked over his coffee table. As he tore the pictures, he stomped on the pieces that had fallen on the rug. He wanted this man in his hands so he could tear him apart too. He wanted to break him and his madness, and all the madness of the world that allowed things like this to happen, that allowed this random violence to descend upon his life and wreak such devastation upon it. Why had it suddenly chosen him, and the woman he loved? It was as real to him as seeing Demmie's bath towel draped in the soapy water. And the *horror* of it was as tangible as the sickening smell of his own fear.

The sun was coming up, the darkness giving way to a gray light. He lay down on the couch. Morning traffic noise echoed up from the street below. The last thing he remembered hearing was the clang of the first tram's bell as it passed below his balcony; then he fell asleep. When he awoke, it was nearly ten-thirty. He felt as if he had been drugged, or that he was lost, and he could not bring himself to hurry.

He walked to the Café Nero on the Vijzelstraat and ate a croissant with his coffee. Willem, the proprietor, made small talk with him because there was no one else in the café. Willem questioned him about the restoration; Pieter tried countering his questions without being curt, but his mind was working so slowly that he had to ask Willem to repeat himself. Van Rijks's crumpled note was in his pocket. Van Velde was only a phone call away, but his mortal fear for Demmie's predicament left him unable to decide what to do. *No police,* the note said. It burned in his pocket now. *Perhaps I will pretend she is the canvas. Get it?* He wished he had slept longer, deeper; he wished he had allowed his lethargy to consume him so completely that he wouldn't have to make a decision.

Pieter opened the curtains as soon as he got to the gallery. He expected van Rijks's face to be among those looking in. Half of Amsterdam seemed to be there, but not that bastard, not now.

During breakfast, Willem had told him that the television broadcasts had begun announcing the completion of the project —no doubt, Pieter thought, at Jan's prodding. They had run update stories on the progress of the restoration, yet no station ever mentioned the vandal. It seemed to Pieter that everyone— the police, the press, and even he, until now—had denied the existence of van Rijks as if he had brought immeasurable shame on a people so sensible, so humane. No wonder he was out to get them all, to register, this time, his name and face so clearly that no one would ever forget. The press had made the slashing appear a catastrophe without a perpetrator.

Pieter consulted the laboratory report on the paint composition of *The Night Watch,* then laid out the oils he would use on a worktable. As he was putting on his white coat, Jan escorted the film crew into the gallery, gesturing regally like some minor ambassador. He watched Jan's jaw suddenly fall.

"Where is everyone?" Jan sputtered. "This work must be done by Friday."

"Demmie is sick," Pieter said, "and Theillen is up in the studio working on a piece that's been sitting around since this *Night Watch* business began. Besides, there's nothing they can do. Only I can paint."

"I don't like it," Jan said. "This is all very bad for my stomach, you know." He patted his belly.

"Don't worry, Jan. Everything will be completed on time." If you think you have an ulcer now, Pieter thought, let me tell you something that will make it bleed. He kept looking to the open curtains, hoping for van Rijks to show his taunting face. Theillen was stationed in an abandoned house near the Prinsengracht, waiting for van Rijks to move; and if the man showed up in the gallery, Pieter would have the guards swoop down on him.

Jan scurried about as the camera crew set up their lights and marked off distances for shots. The director asked Pieter to climb the work bridge and do some of the retouching.

"I can't do that," Pieter protested. "Not like an actor. This isn't a drama."

"Oh, come on, Pieter," Jan pleaded.

"No, Jan. Besides, I can't retouch with those lights. I need natural light."

The young director stepped in front of Jan, dwarfing him. "Could you climb up on the bridge and pretend to be retouching? We'll shoot the footage and edit it properly, so nobody will know we've staged it."

Pieter climbed the steps of the work bridge, shoved a handful of brushes into the pocket of his work coat, picked up his palette, and pretended to daub on some paint with a brush. As he touched the paintless brush to the cheek of Banning Cocq, his hand shook so violently that he had to take it away.

"Pieter, what's the matter?" Jan asked. "Your hand."

"Nothing," Pieter said, but the alarm in Jan's voice had been so pointed that it unnerved him. "Hand me that mahlstick."

Jan fetched the baton, and Pieter steadied one end in the crook of his elbow, the padded end against the canvas, and laid his forearm across it to keep his hand from trembling. But even as he held the mahlstick, his fingers danced hazardously with the brush. This is no way to begin the retouching, he thought. He made small imaginary dots, as though he were filling the slashes with paint; suddenly, it seemed to him that he might scream. This insanity had turned into the highlight of the Holland Festival. The gallery was packed; newspapers were doing follow-up stories; television announcers were heralding Friday's ceremony.

Jan and the Director General had surely done their jobs. Here was an attraction not to be missed by the throngs of tourists and locals. There was a little of everything: sex, with the young, curly-haired apprentice; violence, with the slack-jawed slasher; artifice by the restorers; and a little pageantry thrown in by the Royal Family. Who was the buffoon? He? Jan? Demmie? Juliana herself?

Yet the painting was the focus of all this center-ring attention. A common piece of canvas that had painted across it one of the finest masterworks ever created, and here it was now, subjected again to base theatrics, like some magnificent black bear reduced to pedaling a bike in a tutu. He was posing with *The Night Watch* for dramatic effect so that some media whizzes could sit over their film in a darkroom and put a story together. But the story, god-damn it, *was* the painting. Inasmuch as they were all intertwined with *The Night Watch*—in its whole or rent state—they were the living characters in the grand drama that the Master had begun three hundred years before. Wherever he was, he must be having one hell of a laugh on all of them. Art does not imitate life; nor life, art. They are inseparable in works of this magnitude. He could hear the motor of the camera whirring behind him; the heat from the lights burned his back. For an instant, he felt as if the camera were some technologically advanced machine that was imprinting his silhouette against the canvas, among the likes of Banning Cocq and Lieutenant van Ruytenburch, with his arm propped in mid-stroke.

"That will be fine," the director finally said. "We have ample footage."

Pieter laid out his brushes and palette, again checking the gallery windows for van Rijks. Then he climbed down. "I hope there will be no more posing, Jan."

"There won't be, Pieter, I promise that. And you've been a very good sport about it all. I want you to know that." Jan appeared to be studying him, trying to figure out a reason for the pronounced trembling that had so startled him.

"A good sport," Pieter repeated. Jan had had as much a hand in this lunacy as anyone. If there had been no gallery, no public restoration, there might have been no van Rijks to come into their lives. But there were always van Rijkses, he thought, and there always would be.

"And you will be done by Friday," Jan was saying. "I can confirm that with The Hague?"

"Of course."

"One more thing, Pieter. The temporary wall will be dismantled for Friday, to allow the ceremony to proceed properly. Your work crew can start the dismantling at the close of the museum on Thursday."

"The whole time they're taking it down, I want extra guards here."

"Why, Pieter? What's the matter?"

"Nothing, I told you. Just have the guards here."

"No problem." The film crew broke down their equipment, and as Jan and the film director left together, Jan cast a nervous glance over his shoulder.

Pieter cut a piece of blotting paper and taped it to his palette, then applied each color directly to the paper to draw out most of the oil so the paint, when applied, would dry quickly. He worked on the abraded areas of Banning Cocq's black suit first. Because his hand was still shaky, he allowed the brush to carry little paint and made brisk, light strokes. He would not use the mahlstick; he forced his concentration from the pit of his lungs, exhaling as the bristles, ever so delicately, licked the canvas.

The smell of paint filled his nose. He felt the gentle vibrations of the air conditioning through the planking of the elevated bridge; heard the sudden constancy of his breath against the absolute silence of the workroom. He did not think of Demmie then, or of van Rijks, as he moved to Banning's face and began dotting his cheeks with flesh-toned oils, but rather of each glimmering dot of paint as it made this painting whole once again:

234

Banning's dark ambiguous eyes, so complex in their wonder and their longing; his long nose so masterfully hued with light it looked like resilient flesh; the distinct shape of his goatee.

Then he moved on to Rombout Kemp's hat, to the dog snapping at the drummer boy, to the little girl with the chicken tied to her incandescent dress. He painted trancelike for hours, the tips of his fingers tingling with cool numbness, and he turned to the gallery window only when his concentration lapsed. Then hopelessness struck him like a blow to his sternum.

On the morning of the second day, he decided to call van Velde. It was stupid to have waited. At each thump or tap against the glass, he twitched. Demmie might be dead by now. When, finally, he climbed down from the work bridge to change his blotting paper, his heart heaved into his throat.

Van Rijks, his eyes as dark and distant and ambiguous as Banning Cocq's, was staring at the painting. Then he craned his head, looking puzzled that no one else was in the workroom. He reached into his jacket and pulled out a piece of paper. He held it up, motioned toward the door, and disappeared into the crowd behind him.

Pieter burst through the door, yelling, "Guard!" and ran into a solid wall of spectators. He tried pushing them aside, but they seemed to rush back in on him. It was like climbing out of a deep pit of sand. He saw a guard's bobbing cap; it was coming toward him, and away from the exit.

"Damn it," Pieter said. It was the young guard he had caught having coffee in the anteroom.

"Come with me. There's a man in a seaman's cap. Beard. Leather coat."

"Yes, sir," the guard said. "He gave me this."

The note was sealed with a piece of tape. "He said he had to run."

Pieter pulled the guard out of the gallery, and they hurried into the vestibule, to the head of the great marble staircase, but van Rijks had vanished. The guard began walking back to the gallery. "You left the workroom door open, Mr. Beckum."

Pieter tore open the note. *Pieter, I love you and I am all right. This loon will not hurt me, he says, unless you mess up. He's very single-minded in his—Enough of that crap. She told me about the Queen coming. I have a thing for the old lady and I want to be there. Arrange it. I'll be in touch. Best wishes, Rembrandt. P.S. Arrange it because you can't restore your whore.*

He worked for another hour in the gallery, expecting Theillen to show up. With Demmie. Then he went back to his apartment. When Theillen finally knocked, he knew without opening the door that she was not with him.

"Where is she? Didn't you find her?"

"No," he said. "Take it easy." Theillen fell into an armchair and put his feet up on the coffee table. "Can I have something to drink?"

"Did you see which house he came out of?"

"Yes. We were very close the other night. Only two houses off. But I searched the inside and couldn't find anything. I think this fellow's smarter than we anticipated. I don't believe she's in the house I saw him come out of. She may already be—"

"I'll get you a drink," Pieter interrupted. "Don't tell me that."

"All right," Theillen said. "But don't you think it's time we called the police?"

"No. I got a note from her today. That's why he left the house. She's all right; he doesn't want to hurt her. I think he wants the painting."

"You're not going to give it to him?"

"Of course not," Pieter said. "I couldn't if I wanted to." But he did not truly know if, given a choice between Demmie and *The Night Watch,* he would not throw the painting to the madman and let him have it. Demmie gave him more life—more immediately—than the lifetime of paintings on which he had labored. "Of course not," he repeated.

He poured Theillen a spa with a twist of lemon. "Why don't you go home now and get some rest? If we're going to finish the painting on time, we'll have to varnish after the museum closes."

"I still think the police could help." Theillen got up to leave.

236

"I'm sure they could," Pieter said, "but I don't trust them. Van Rijks wants to be there on Friday, and I'll notify van Velde Thursday. They can spring their trap when he shows. If I tell them too soon—" He stopped himself. "I'm just afraid of what might happen."

That night, Pieter, following Theillen's directions, entered the house under cover of night. He found the place where Theillen had watched, a wooden box by the first-floor window with two ragged blankets for cushioning. The stick he had given Theillen for protection was propped against the sill. He did not know what he was watching for: Van Rijks? A glimpse of Demmie? Theillen had already searched the place. There had been too much pressure on Pieter today, and his eyes grew tired quickly. After Theillen had left him, he had gone back to the museum to paint more. He hadn't slept in two days. He thought he saw movement from the corner of his eye, but when he focused his vision the darkness yielded only the slow, shadowed swaying of the full maple branches. He shifted his buttocks on the rough seat. The camera crew had irritated him beyond belief, as had Jan's constant, unsubtle pressure about the Queen. He felt smug, almost calm, knowing he was privy to the upcoming calamity.

Finally he could neither think nor watch any longer, and he gave in to his exhaustion, sitting bolt upright. He awoke on the floor with the first light. His clothes were covered with a thick coat of dust; his mouth was caked and his neck ached from the hard floor. He rushed home and changed clothes, but he did not shower, and when he showed up at the gallery, feeling as if he had failed Demmie miserably, Theillen told him his hair was matted with dust. "Cover for me, will you," Pieter said, "while I go upstairs and clean up."

32

Pieter watched the gallery windows as though he expected to see van Rijks standing there holding a stick with Demmie's head on it. Finally, he closed the curtains because he could not retouch the remaining slashes under such pressure. He had decided to let Theillen help him, and Theillen worked beside him, filling the long, arcing slashes in the dark area of Banning Cocq's leg with hundreds of tiny dots. If the boy made a mistake, Pieter could easily lift the paint off the thin layer of varnish covering the Rembrandt canvas and reapply it. He mixed Theillen's colors on a palette covered with blotting paper.

The skylight overhead was so ablaze with light that, in spite of the air conditioning, the air above the work bridge seemed dangerously hot for the painting. Pieter mixed yellow, white, and brown oil paints to match the glowing cream of van Ruytenburch's coat and began the laborious dotting of the slashes that raked his legs.

He and Theillen worked in complicitous silence, and only when Pieter descended the work bridge to draw the curtains did Theillen speak.

"How do you feel?" he asked.

"Nervous," Pieter said. "Fucking nervous."

By late that afternoon, when the strong sunlight waned, they had applied thousands of dots to fill the lines of the slashes. Pieter had opened the curtains periodically, but van Rijks had not been in the gallery. Nor did he really expect to see him after he, Pieter,

238

had burst through the gallery door like a wild man yesterday, shouting for the guard.

After closing time, workmen came in and with amazing speed took the wall of the gallery apart. They constructed a small stage in the center, over the space where Pieter had first laid the painting. Pieter told Theillen to remain with the extra guards Jan had sent for the security of the painting. "I'll be back in a while, and we'll put on a light coat or two of varnish," he said.

There was nothing more important to Pieter than finding Demmie, not *The Night Watch*, not his audience with the Queen. He was going to give himself two hours, and if he could find nothing, he would head straight for van Velde.

Before he left the museum, he stopped in his studio. He did not know if van Rijks was armed, but he didn't want to take any chances. Something told him he should have protection, so he put one of the razor-sharp scalpels he had used for scraping the canvas in his coat pocket. Then he drove through the darkness across town.

He found the house he had spent the previous night watching from, and positioned himself on the box by the window. The front of the high-gabled house across the canal—the house he was watching—was shored up by giant beams, and the waxing moon cast it in alternating stripes of shadow and silver light. What was he doing here? His life had become unhinged. Since he had fallen in love, things had begun to warp in perspective.

A sudden splash in the canal startled him. He strained his eyes in search of an accompanying movement, held his breath against the possibility of another sound; but concentric circles of stagnant water were the only movements he could perceive, and the drumming of his heart was the only sound. A tree branch, he told himself.

This was his own perverse night watch, he thought, generated by the life still held in that painting, made new and whole by him, then twisted by the muddled mind of van Rijks. Demmie was in that building; he knew it. He decided to give the house one more toss. Perhaps Theillen had not been as thorough as he could have been. Fear might have caused him to overlook something. But what about me? he thought. Don't I have fear? Wasn't it fear that shuddered through his legs right now as he stood up? It was, but altogether different. It was not the vision-blinding fear that bordered on panic, but a resignedness. No questions of success or failure weighed on his mind.

He took a flashlight from the glove compartment of his car and crossed the footbridge over the canal. The broad leaves of the maples along the quay gathered in the moon's weak light, and he used their shadows to make his way up the street. As he tugged at the wooden planking that covered the entrance to the house, he was surprised at how easily it came away. It was a sign that they were here. He carefully replaced the planking behind him.

Once inside, his vision was completely gone. He did not turn on the flashlight right away; rather, he squatted on his heels and waited for his sight to return. Gradually he could make out the lines of broken beams hanging to the floor, contours of shattered furniture, the dark hollows in the plastered walls.

As soon as he was certain that he was alone, he flicked on the flashlight and quickly scanned the room. It looked as though it had been ravaged by war. The shock of bombs might have shaken the plaster loose. An upturned card table with a hole torn through its center leaned against a fallen beam. These places had been the hideouts of his childhood, and occasionally the source of his adult nightmares. His dreams had been filled with the harsh sputter of machine guns; the red-yellow fire from their muzzles lit the night like some apocalyptic lightning. After the war, when so many of his school friends had played in the bombed-out ruins, he had stayed away, afraid that the killing was not really over, that it was just a foolish interlude while they made more bombs, more bullets. When the holocaust began again, they would not catch him in one of these hovels with the others. Even now, as he satisfied himself with Theillen's evaluation of the place, shut the light off, and waited for his eyes to settle with the darkness, he half expected to hear the pounding of hobnailed boots on the cobblestone street outside and found himself trembling with a dread he had not felt for over thirty years.

He moved to an uncluttered corner of the room and arranged the card table so that, when he squatted, it concealed him. He would wait here, not across the canal. Something did not make any sense at all. He could feel Demmie's presence—she had moved through this dingy room—but had he told anyone that, he would surely be thought crazy.

He placed the flashlight on the floor beside him and took the scalpel from his pocket. He wondered for a moment if he would use it. Only if I have to. That was bullshit of the first order. He could not kill. Like an artist, he was charged with giving life. But what if it meant that Demmie's might be at stake? Anything was possible, she would say. No, that was not true of him. He would have to be deranged to kill, and halfway deranged even to entertain the thought. He *was* thinking about it, though. And when he had made that special trip upstairs to his studio to get the scalpel, he had changed all the rules, regardless of what van Rijks might do. Kidnapping was one thing, killing quite another. A line from Goethe came to him as he sat in the darkness: *There is no crime of which I cannot conceive myself guilty.* That was madness, truly, he thought, but it was also truth. Demmie would appreciate that line.

He wished Theillen were with him now. Theillen. There was a strange case. So somber about his life. He could suffer any of the lessons in technique and artifice. He always dressed in the same drab colors; his hair was always unwashed; his arms were always kinked in some muscular flex or another. And that inexplicable tattoo: Anne Frank, 1929–1945, inexplicable even to himself. "I had it done for no reason." He could have used those muscular arms, though, Pieter thought, to back him up, perhaps to keep him from using the scalpel in his hands.

"Anne Frank," he said softly. He pushed quietly to his feet, gave his aching knees a minute to loosen, then started feeling along the walls in the darkness. He no longer believed that anything was impossible. He could not know which of the walls were hollow and which were stone. Anything could be an entrance. He came across a bookshelf and tugged at it, but it did not give. There were no trapdoors in the floor. He weighed the heavy flashlight in one hand, the scalpel in the other, then went back and tugged at the bookshelf again.

33

When van Rijks had come back earlier that day carrying two bottles of beer, Demmie had attacked him. She had been hiding behind the door, waiting silently in the dark where he had left her, and she sprang on him, screaming and tearing violently at his face. In that instant, he did not realize it was the girl. She screamed, "This is too much!" repeating it over and over again as her nails clawed at the soft flesh of his cheeks. Two thoughts clapped together with shocking clarity as the first throb of terror buckled his knees—that his torment had found substance and form and had dropped on him like a writhing python, and that he had been finally caught by the police. He screamed, too, and heaved her across the room. It seemed an eternity before he heard her child-like grunt as she hit the wall, then collapsed to the floor. The darkness had turned crimson in his eyes.

For the longest time afterward, she had sat whimpering where she landed, her breath competing raggedly with his. Slowly the darkness came back.

"I can't stand this," she said. "Why do you leave me in the darkness? It's cruel."

He could not answer her. He found the table, lit the candle. He had two pills left. He swallowed one, then drank some beer. He offered her the bottle, but she just stared fiercely at him.

He felt very tender toward her. And toward Beckum, for that matter. All their following and watching and subterfuge had scared him, and the fear made him start to use his mind carefully.

He realized that he could no longer afford to drift off. A mistake; they would catch him before he could complete his task. That was why he'd tracked Molen to the Café Zwart and made him sniff around the gallery for cops. To entice Molen, he had told him he could keep whatever money he got for the last drawings. "You've got a real talent for sniffing cops," he had said and Molen had grinned. So the restorers of paintings had inadvertently restored the madman who would destroy what had been restored. Van Rijks chuckled, pleased as much with the irony as with his ability to recognize it once again. He could not care less what happened afterward. There was no afterward.

He hadn't said a word to Demmie since she had stopped crying. She lay on the bedspring with her knees drawn up to her chest. He sat at the table, fatigued; his elbows felt as if they were filling with lead and his shoulders ached in the joints. He sang softly to himself, meditating on the lone pill in the vial. Finally, he addressed her. "It was foolish to attack me."

As if the sound of his words activated her, she pushed herself to her feet. "It was all I could think of to do."

Van Rijks heard scraping outside the wall. "Rats," he said.

"Why don't you ever bring food?" she asked. "I'm going to die from hunger."

"You'll not die from anything."

"Please. I can't go too long without food. I have diabetes. I can die. I can go into insulin shock."

"Lies," he sneered. The scraping again. She came closer. He lowered his eyes to the bottle of beer.

"That pill's some sort of key for you, isn't it?"

"Go to hell."

"Someone's out there," she said.

"Rats," he said again. She touched his shoulder, and he jerked as though a rat had just scampered up his trouser leg.

"It's help for me," she said. Then she screamed. He sprang backward, knocking over the chair, and as he moved she snatched the vial from the table and darted to a corner of the room.

He bounded over the table, but it was too late. She had popped open the vial and now held the white tablet in front of her, rolling it between her fingers.

"Stop," she said. "Stop or I'll swallow it."

She yelled again for help. He did not know what to do. His skull seemed to shrink, tightening around his brain; his vision dimmed. All he could see was a set of devilish eyes, glinting in the candlelight. The lips, framed by dark tendrils of hair, twisted in some final smirk. Her mouth opened, showing wet shiny teeth, knife sharp and jagged. Then the white pill floated up through the darkness that embraced her face and disappeared into the hollow of her throat.

He heard himself scream, "No!" as though he were dying.

His hands were on her neck; he thought he could feel the lump of the pill in her throat. His thumbs pushed into her larynx, and he became suddenly giddy. Then he released her, and she collapsed in a heap at his feet. Someone was pounding the door so violently that he thought the whole wall was going to collapse on him.

He dragged her by the hair across the room, picking up the empty beer bottle from the table on his way. *Do to her what you would to the painting!* a voice shouted inside him. *She's ruined it. She's ruined everything!* Another scream split the room, and he kicked her ribs to silence it.

Then he stopped again. But this time it was because the bookshelf had been torn from the wall and a concentrated beam of yellow light froze him where he stood, his heel suspended above Demmie's face.

34

The bookshelf was a mass of rubble at Pieter's feet; the door was to his back. And his hands shook so frenziedly that the beam of light danced all over van Rijks's surprised face. He crossed the scalpel in front of the light to make sure that van Rijks could see the yellow glint of the blade. "Back away from her," Pieter said.

Van Rijks's hand, gripping the beer bottle, twisted at his side.

When Pieter had heard Demmie's cry for help, it was as if no wall separated him from her. The scream had pierced him so quickly, so thoroughly, that he shot to his feet, tearing away at the bookshelf until it came free. He had not known he possessed such strength; he pulled at the bookshelf with the strength of the madman who had ripped through the impossible thickness of *The Night Watch*. Then the terror came. It rushed back on him, pounding against his ribs. He was here, face to face with van Rijks, and he hadn't the slightest idea what to do next. He was too afraid to take his eyes from the man to look at Demmie, who lay moaning at his feet.

Finally, he spoke. "Move against that back wall."

Van Rijks did not move. "Where did you get my pictures?" he growled.

"Against the wall!" Pieter shouted.

Van Rijks stepped closer, the bottle slightly raised. He crouched, then screamed at Pieter, "Where did you get my goddamned pictures?"

The shock caused Pieter to stumble backward. The light

246

dipped to Demmie's face; her eyelids fluttered, then closed. And in that moment, as he flinched from the scream, van Rijks was on him. From his crouch, van Rijks had flown like a disembodied spirit through the darkness, consuming the yellow light with his phenomenally long arms. Pieter fell backward—under van Rijks's weight—the man's arms closing around his shoulders like the jaws of a vise. His hand pushed outward and he felt the scalpel, buried to the handle, in van Rijks's soft belly. Then he pulled it out and thrust again. He smelled beer as van Rijks expelled a hot sour gust of breath. Pieter lay pinned under him, waiting to be pummeled with the bottle, or crushed, or somehow torn limb from limb. But van Rijks did not move.

Pieter pushed against van Rijks's limp, dead weight. The hand that had held the scalpel was warm and wet, and rapidly becoming sticky. He knew what it was, but he would not let himself think about it. Finally, he rolled van Rijks off. The man's head whacked hard against the floor, and he gave a breathless gasp.

Pieter scrambled to his feet, setting himself against another attack. He picked up the flashlight. "Are you all right?" he asked Demmie.

She tried to raise herself, but he held her shoulders to the floor. He thought her ribs might be broken and he would not chance moving her. As he reached to smooth the hair back from her forehead, he saw his hand, slick with dark blood. He wiped it frantically on his slacks, but the blood was already beginning to coagulate, and it smeared.

"I'm fine," Demmie said slowly. "I took his pill away from him. He went bonkers." She giggled. "Get me out of here, will you, Pieter? I've had enough of this place."

"Let me call an ambulance."

"No. I can't stand it here. He left me the whole time in the darkness. I don't even know what day it is. I thought he was going to kill me. Please take me out." She pointed to the outline of van Rijks's body on the floor. "I couldn't bear to be alone with him," she said. "Anyway, I ate his pill and it's starting to take effect, so moving won't hurt in the least."

"All right," he said. He lifted her, and she winced as he put his arm around her waist.

"I've never been kicked before." She bent forward with the pain, holding her ribs.

"Why did you eat the pill?"

"I was desperate," she said. "When I heard all the noise you were making out there, I knew it wasn't rats, and I took a chance."

"Rats?"

"Never mind."

They had to walk past van Rijks to get out; the sight of him lying there made Pieter shiver. The scalpel was sticking out of his stomach in a neat circle of blood, as if it had been jammed solidly into a block of wood.

"Oh, God," Demmie said, "I think I'm going to be sick."

He rushed her outside, into the air, and it was as though the briskness of the night restored her. She leaned against the side of the house, drawing deeply and wincing with each exhalation. "That was so awful," she said, looking at his bloodied hand. "Pieter, I'm so sorry for you."

She sounded as if she might cry, and he said, "Don't talk now."

He took her in his car to a doctor he knew who worked in the red-light district, and whose office, because of the hours most of his clients kept, was still open when they got there. After assuring Pieter that her ribs weren't broken, he wound an elastic bandage just under her breasts. Pieter washed the blood from his hands and called van Velde. He told him about van Rijks, that he could find the body in the old abandoned house, and that he and Demmie were leaving the doctor's office and would be home if he wanted to question them.

The doctor gave Demmie some more pills in case, he said, she woke up in the morning with stabbing pains in her side. As he said that, she looked at Pieter, her face draining of color.

When they got home, Pieter unwrapped Demmie's ribs and drew a bath for her. Her abdomen was already swollen, puffy and bruised blue with the accumulation of blood. Her speech had slowed so that she paused over each word. He wondered what it was she had taken. When Demmie had described the pill, the doctor had said it was one of the strongest barbiturates, manufactured for the control of deeply psychotic patients. It would be some time before it wore off.

As she lay in the bath, she kept dropping off. Her head would suddenly flop to the rear or to the side, with a clunk on the porcelain, and her eyes would roll up. He said to her gently, "Come on, Demmie. Don't fall asleep in here. I'll have you in bed in a minute."

And as she came awake with the sound of his voice, she lamented, "Poor Pieter. Poor, poor Pieter." It rolled from her tongue slowly, as though she were in some sort of delirium.

He struggled to help her out of the tub. Then he rewrapped her ribs as tightly as the doctor had. The bandage pushed up her breasts, making the nipples point directly to the ceiling. She jumped once from the pain.

"Poor Pieter," she kept saying. He carried her from the bathroom and carefully laid her in his bed.

"Why 'Poor Pieter'?" he finally asked as he drew the cover over her.

"Because," she said, her eyes fluttering with exhaustion, "because you just killed somebody."

Her words, slow and lifeless from the drug, startled him. He *had* killed a man. He could see the scalpel sticking out of van Rijks's stomach in the dim light of the room, and he could still smell that last foul gust of his breath. It was true. He was poor, poor Pieter. But he had not really killed van Rijks. Van Rijks had willfully killed himself by jumping at him, just as van Rijks had willfully stolen Demmie away from him. But he wondered, too, if, standing there, anticipating the jump after being so startled by the scream, he could have moved aside, or turned the blade down to the floor. He became weak at the thought that as soon as he had felt van Rijks's hot smothering weight descend on him, he had pulled the scalpel out and pushed it through the pliant belly flesh, with a second, twisting thrust, till it snagged on something solid.

He sat in his dark living room, waiting for van Velde to come and finish all this off, to ask the questions that had to be asked, so that he could sleep. He would phone the Director General and have them put off the ceremony for a day while Demmie recuperated and while he put the finishing coat of varnish on the painting. He would tell the Director General that Juliana could damn well wait a day for her pin-sticking exercise.

Pieter dozed off, and so was slow to answer the pounding at his door. By the time he had got off the couch, he was startled by the looming figure of van Velde standing inside his hallway.

"You ought to keep your door locked," van Velde said. Stubble shadowed his cheeks; the whites of his tired-looking eyes were laced with pink.

"I was too confused when I got home," Pieter replied. "I forgot to lock it. Did you find him?"

"No. That's why I said you ought to keep your door locked."

"What do you mean? I left him there on the floor. There was blood. He wasn't breathing. I'm sure of it."

Van Velde sat in an armchair and Pieter fell back onto the couch. "Did you check to make sure he was dead?"

"No," Pieter said. As soon as he had rolled van Rijks off, there was something revolting, gut-rending about touching him. He had hurried Demmie away as much to avoid that responsibility as to get her air.

"He must have gotten up and wandered out of there," van Velde said. "I've notified headquarters, and they have put out a description. I'll give them some of your pictures. Would you get them for me?"

Pieter gave van Velde the pictures that were left, the few that he and van Rijks had not torn up. He also gave him the notes van Rijks had threatened him with, and van Velde studied them in silence. Pieter waited for the inspector to begin the lecture that he dreaded. The police should have been called. Why had he been so stupid? But van Velde just shuffled the pictures and grunted. Perhaps the detective had taken into account what he and Demmie had been through and decided enough had been learned.

As van Velde left, he said, "I have positioned a police officer downstairs. Until we catch van Rijks, don't answer you doorbell. Good night."

Pieter shook the detective's hand. "Inspector," he said, stopping him at the head of the stairs. "Didn't you know van Rijks had escaped from the Psychiatric Institute?" Pieter had not planned to ask the question. But somehow he wanted the blame for all that had happened to rest somewhere other than on his shoulders.

"We knew," van Velde said flatly. "But we were trying to capture him without a lot of fanfare from the press. Blow him up like they do in America and we have a country full of misplaced heroes. We've had more than our share of trouble from the Moluccan terrorists. His was a disgraceful crime; he wanted publicity all along. And that was precisely what our psychologists told us to deny him." Van Velde looked at Pieter blankly, scratching his bristle of gray-black hair. "But, oh, he was smarter than our psychologists and we simply bungled it," he said.

"Good night," Pieter said, as the inspector started down the stairs. Then he called out, "You simply bungled it?"

"Good night," van Velde said.

35

When van Rijks opened his eyes, he was alone. He lay on the floor, listening for them. The last candle had burned to a small puddle of wax with a sputtering wick pitching its feeble light against the shadows. Beneath the shrill ringing in his ears, he heard a voice chanting. And more—one was singing some silly nursery rhyme about a cat. His belly ached. He lifted his head and saw the scalpel jammed in his stomach. His stomach muscles tightened around the knife, and he groaned. He lay back and felt for the knife with his fingertips, then slowly drew it out, fearing his entrails would follow.

He fingered the hole in his stomach and sang the nursery rhyme. It did not hurt too badly, although it did feel as though someone had trickled salt in it. He rolled to his feet. He had no idea how long he had lain there, but they were gone and he had to move.

He balled up an extra shirt and shoved it inside the one he wore, over the wound, then changed jackets. He could feel the effects of the pill beginning to wear off, and as the medication diminished and the pain came, he felt as though he were going to lift right out of his body. A thousand tiny flutterings coursed his veins and arteries, flutterings that would soon take over his heart and head. Then he would be perpetually lost. He knew now that the pills had weighted him down, had given him center and gravity. But that bitch, that whore of the restorer's, had queered it all, had eaten his last one, the one he had marked for the Queen's party. He was seized by the urge to howl.

Where was the party going to be? he asked himself. Where else, asshole? She had said it, the curly-haired whore had said it, and he had told Beckum to prepare him some way of being there. But where? He couldn't remember. All he could think of was the oozing at the hole in his center. You need this patched, he said. You'll dribble out all over the floor and there will be nothing left but the sack of your empty body.

He spotted Demmie's purse and picked it up. She had grabbed it so casually as he ordered her out of Beckum's apartment. And now, in her haste to escape, she had forgotten it. Take it and run. They have gone but they will be back, and they'll bring others. They need witnesses for their handiwork. All killers do.

He wished, just then, as he made his way out of the house, that the confusion would stay away. He knew full well what he had to do; only now they would all be on to him, setting their little traps against him.

He moved to another house down the block, where he hid in the cellar. The pain in his stomach was worse. As it became the focal point of all his attention, he realized he could use the pain, as he had used the pills, to see him through till morning. The pain was better than the pill, he thought, laughing, if only it would get worse. He had fooled them by growing the beard and adopting the hat. He had dared to look them in the face and still they did not know him. Nobody knew him. Then the pain stung him as pointedly as if he had been stabbed again. What mattered? The painting.

He could almost say why. The answer lurked somewhere along the back of his tongue, where articulation could not reach, and frustrated him; it was like searching for a color that did not exist. The thought of *The Night Watch*, the mere recollection of it, caused a constriction in his throat that traveled to his stomach. It was as if, by killing the painting, he could kill a piece of everyone. Then they would all be on the same terms again.

He went through Demmie's purse looking for money. It would feel very good, very right, to hold some money in his hands. When he pulled her wallet out, a set of keys on a small ring jangled to the floor. He saw *The Night Watch* suddenly illuminated before him in the darkness. It shone bright and bold, a flurry of heightened color struggling to burst out of the engulfing shadows. Another spasm racked him. He imagined appendicitis must feel like this. But the keys, he thought, the keys would get him into the museum. He left the cellar of the abandoned house and made his way unnoticed across the city by tram.

He had watched Demmie and Beckum enough to know that they used neither of the giant brass doors at the base of the towers but a smaller, private door in the back of the museum. After trying three different keys, he found the one that opened it. When he stepped inside and closed the door, he began to laugh. He was standing in a long, damp, cement-walled corridor, lit only by weak amber bulbs. He had no alternative but to walk straight ahead. He found another door, tried a key, and pushed it carefully. It was the hallway that led to *The Night Watch* gallery. Two guards stood at the far end with their backs to him, talking. He quietly ducked back into the corridor.

The more he walked, the more the wound hurt him. But he wanted that, didn't he? He needed the pain. If that had been the main hall, then the elevator Beckum used should be right through this alcove. There were no buttons on the metal plate by the elevator doors. He used one of the keys. There were no buttons inside either, so he used the same key that had gotten him into the elevator and felt himself rising. The first leap of the car made his stomach tingle with pleasure, but the pleasure dissolved quickly.

The doors opened and he had to let himself out of the barred gate with still another key, and through several other locked doors. Then he was standing in the east tower, looking out at the streaking headlights on the Stadhouderskade below. He was laughing again. I am here, he said. Paintings were all around him. Some hung on the walls; some were wedged onto giant easels,

their frames stripped away. Amber bottles lined the shelves; pa-
lettes were suspended from nails against the wall. A desk and a
chair stood by the door. He rifled the drawers and came out with
an envelope. *Pieter Beckum, Weteringschans 293.* That was
where he had been to get the girl, and this was *his* desk. The same
numbing rage that had come over him when he had seen his
pictures tacked up all over Beckum's walls churned in him now.

But now his insides were hurting unbearably. He had to do
something about it. He found a large roll of canvas and cut a
couple of squares with the scalpel. Then he groped among the
amber bottles, sniffing first one, then another, until he found
some peroxide. As he bubbled it on his stomach, he saw two holes
and he became furious. That murdering bastard! he howled to
himself. The cold peroxide ran down his hips to his legs, soaking
his pants. It bubbled so much that it looked as if it were eating
his flesh. Finally, he searched out a hiding place.

36

The phone rang early in the morning. Before Pieter answered it, he checked on Demmie in the bedroom. She lay immobile from the drug she had eaten, the covers drawn up about her face, the raspy sound of her breathing filling the room.

"What is it now, Jan?" Pieter asked.

"I'm so sorry to hear about Miss de Graaf," Jan said. "I had no idea—"

"Get to the point, Jan. I haven't had much sleep."

"Juliana agreed to hold off the ceremony until tomorrow. But she really does have to leave the country, so the ceremony has to go on, you see."

"It can't go on," Pieter corrected him, "without bodies to pin the medals to. But we will be there tomorrow. You can assure the Town Council of that, and Theillen and I will come in today to administer the protective varnish to *The Night Watch.*"

"Thank you, Pieter. I know what you have been through. And if you'll pardon me for saying so, this ceremony will help the museum immeasurably."

"Sure," Pieter said, hanging up the receiver.

Theillen met Pieter in the opened gallery. The wall had been taken down last night, and a small stage, with a podium centered on it, had been assembled in front of the canvas, which hung from the cables in the ceiling. The television and film crews had set up their cameras, microphones, and lights in the rear of the gallery. Museum guards, dressed in their black uniforms, hovered in pairs like expectant buzzards inside the gallery doors to keep spectators away.

Pieter's worktable had been left in the corner. He mixed the quick-drying varnish from the dammar resin and oil of turpentine, while Theillen flexed the bristles of the wide brushes, softening them for the application of varnish. Pieter and Theillen climbed onto the stage. Two guards worked the cables, lowering *The Night Watch* as he and Theillen applied the first, preliminary coat over the retouched surface.

Theillen went first, slathering the face of the painting with the evergreen-scented mixture. Then Pieter, with brisk, overlapping strokes of the wide brush, smoothed it. In twenty-five minutes, they had finished. When Pieter stepped down from the stage, he saw that the varnish already gave fuller value to the colors—intensifying the ornate cream-colored attire of van Ruytenburch and the little girl, the pools of iridescent light at their feet, the fleshy tonality of their faces. And the slashes, even from this close perspective, were rendered totally invisible.

"This is how Rembrandt saw it three hundred years ago," Pieter said to Theillen, who beamed with satisfaction. He stood so close to Pieter that their shoulders touched.

In three hours, the varnish had dried and they applied another quick coat. They would have to put several more coats on later, but for the time of the ceremony, during which there would be no controlled humidity and hundreds of people would be nearby, *The Night Watch* would be safe. They had completed the restoration in spite of everything, and now the gallery, with the guards suddenly expansive in their chatter, pulsated with excitement. Pieter and Theillen embraced; the guards, each in turn, shook their hands.

Demmie was still sleeping when he got home. He began reading a newspaper but fell to reminiscing about their trip to Italy, wanting desperately to make love to the woman who was lying in his bed. As he took a sandwich and a bottle of beer to the police officer stationed downstairs, his own expansiveness faded with the recollection of van Rijks, still at large, stalking the streets of Amsterdam with destruction his only preoccupation.

When Demmie first called to him, he brought her some soup he had made. He wanted to pamper her, but he could not think of enough ways. While she spooned the soup into her mouth, he opened her shirt to look at her ribs. "Really, Pieter," she said. "Can't you wait?"

He laughed. The bandage had shifted slightly during the night, and her nipples, pointing upward, had taken on a cross-eyed look.

"Don't laugh at me," she said, jerking his pajama shirt closed around her and spilling some of the soup on the bedspread.

"How do you feel?"

"Groggy," she said, prodding her side with her fingers. "But not bad." She handed him the bowl and threw the covers aside. "Let me see how this feels." She stood up.

Pieter told her that van Rijks was not dead. She looked both disappointed and dismayed. Then her eyes suddenly changed. "I'm happy for you, though, Pieter." She reached for him and they hugged lightly. He felt a great buoying in his chest. "And it means I don't have to fuck a killer." She padded out of the room to the bathroom, laughing.

"Bitch," he called after her.

She threw together a big salad for dinner, and they ate it with wine and bread at the table on his balcony. An incessant din of cars and trams streamed underneath. She was looking over his shoulder, the wineglass poised at her lips, when a chill coursed her, almost tipping the contents of the glass.

"What's the matter? Cold?"

"No," she said. "It gives me the creeps sitting out here. I keep expecting to see his face down there on the street."

"Try to relax."

"You didn't see him lurking down there? Pour me some more wine, will you, Pieter?"

She went inside, and when she returned, she had a pill the doctor had given her for pain. She washed it down with a swallow of wine.

"The light's on in the studio," she said.

He turned, and against the silhouette of the spires in the distance he could see the faint fluorescent light go out.

"Theillen?" she asked.

"Probably," he said. "I gave him some cleaning up to do."

"Can we go inside?" she asked. "Sitting out here gives me the creeps. I feel so exposed."

"I never thought I'd hear those words from your mouth."

"Don't joke," she said. "I just don't want to think about it for a while. What we've been through would have been hard for anyone to handle. I don't think I'll ever take a bath here again."

"Don't say that."

He brought her inside. She unwrapped her ribs, and they made gentle love on the living-room floor. When it was over, he said, "We'll be heroes tomorrow."

She giggled like a child.

37

No one had come up all day, and van Rijks was furious about hiding for no reason. He had found himself a little corner, a structural irregularity in the woodworking room where the giant table saws were, and where the floor was thick with orange sawdust. He crept into a small niche and pulled a roll of canvas to cover him. Either everyone was downstairs or they were not coming. He couldn't figure it out at all. Occasionally he went to the windows, expecting to see the procession of long black cars and the crowds of people. He became hungry, then furious again when he could not find even a crust of bread in any of the trash cans.

That night, with Demmie's keys, he sneaked through the labyrinth of corridors in the museum, checking first one hall, then another. The keys opened some doors, while others refused to yield to him. He made his way to the first floor, down the set of dark winding stairs that opened to a corridor behind the great exhibit halls. He found the mirrored door that he had noticed on those days he'd stood behind the gallery window. Beckum had often disappeared through this door, and he was amazed that he could see out from this side.

He saw the stage, the steps leading up to it. Two cameras stood sentinel in the corners; lights were positioned all around; thick, snakelike cables wound across the floor. Two policemen sat on the stage, smoking cigarettes, and through the glass door he could hear their laughter. He quietly slipped a key into the lock to see if it would turn.

The canvas, as big as a wall, dominated the room. It hung suspended from cables and all he could see was the back of it. The stitches were gone, covered with the new canvas. He heard the marching of feet above the policemen's laughter, echoing through the walls as though an army approached. The policemen snapped to attention at the approach of a third man, older, with a gray, moribund complexion and a bristle of salt-and-pepper hair. He wore a threadbare brown suit. They exchanged some sort of amenities, and the older man left. The policemen stood at attention for a minute, no doubt making sure their superior had indeed gone. They appeared to be in some sort of trance, both turning to stare at the painting.

He heard singing, the nursery rhyme about the cat. A child's voice. His hands were on the door and he was about to push it open. No. Don't go. Not now. They will catch you like they did the last time, and you'll never have another chance. Then it seemed as though the entire gallery had been momentarily cast in a pall of darkness, and he backed away from the door. There emanated from the front of the canvas an unexplainable beacon of light, as definite as the beacon from the flashlight that had blinded him in that house. Dust motes even swirled in the beam. He wanted to rush from behind his cover, around to the front of the canvas, just to see what was so clearly pulling at his center. Stop. You know. It was the devilish eye that had complacently watched Johannes burn himself up and that had followed him, taunted him, consumed his drawings, and mocked him in the process. He fingered the scalpel in his pocket, the scalpel so generously left behind by that murdering bastard. He could get to the eye easily this time, carve it out. But that was hardly the point. Juliana had to be there, the Queen mother, to witness, as he had witnessed, heart-rending pain so profound that it dissolved the world around him. His belly ached with the excitement he felt, and he crept back up to Pieter's studio, carefully memorizing the route that had brought him to the gallery.

He knew what the cops were doing there. They were not the museum guards. She was coming, just like that whore had said.

The Queen. The cameras and lights in place. It did not happen today, no, but it would tomorrow.

By the time he finished the climb to the tower, his stomach was aching so intensely that it was all he could think about. He groped through the shadows of the studio for the bottle of peroxide and, this time, for some alcohol. He found the peroxide where he had left it; it soothed him for a brief instant. But what he poured on after that was not alcohol. He could smell his skin burning. He screamed out and folded in half as if he had been stabbed again. And again. Pain raced like the point of the scalpel slicing open his leg. He flicked on the light to stare at the purple and white gurgling in his stomach. Acid, you stupid bastard. He ran howling into the apprentices' studio, to a sink, where he splashed himself till his pants were soaked to his skin. He cut a piece of clean canvas, wet it, dropped his pants, and patted himself wherever he burned. It felt as if one of the soldiers had marched right out of the darkness of the painting—an assassin, as Beckum had been —and speared him in the side. There would be no more attacks, though, no more mistakes. He found the alcohol and shut off the light. He decided he would stay up all night, with the pain, and watch for their attacks.

38

Saturday morning, Pieter dropped Demmie at the back entrance to the museum so she wouldn't have to walk, then drove off to park. Cars were everywhere. The spaces close to the museum where he usually parked had been taken already. Disregarding the prickle of uneasiness he felt in his spine, he laughed at the success of all Jan's publicity. He expected Demmie to be inside when he got back, but she was waiting for him at the door with a foolish look on her face.

"Why didn't you go up?" he asked.

"I lost my purse," she said.

He let her in, and as he locked the door behind them, he said, "I suppose now we'll have to change all the locks."

"I'm sorry, Pieter. But so much happened so fast. . . ."

"Forget it," he said. "I didn't say that to make you feel bad. It was just a thought that popped out."

He walked through the corridors with his arm around her shoulder. If the museum staff gossiped, he no longer cared. They went up to the studio to drink coffee and wait for the Queen, and Jan, and whoever else was participating in this fiasco. After the ceremony, once the painting had been sealed off again, he would have the final protective coats of varnish put on.

The bright morning air cut through his high studio windows at a sharp angle. The light's intensity would be good for the skylights above *The Night Watch*. Everyone could see, before they turned on those horrendously bright television lights, just how magnificent the painting was in its new state. Not since Rembrandt had painted it, he imagined, had it looked so brilliant. When the old varnish had come away, the painting seemed to have gathered all the original light about itself and amplified it.

Demmie sat at his desk chair while he made coffee at the hot plate. "Do you smell anything peculiar?" he asked.

"A little," she said. "Like alcohol."

He looked over the shelves for a broken bottle, but he couldn't find one. He had asked Theillen to straighten up here. He would certainly speak to him about the mess he found. The smell, shreds of canvas on the floor, the shelves in disarray. What had he been doing here last night, if not cleaning?

"Theillen will probably throw his in the canal," Pieter said.

"What?"

"Oh, sorry. I was thinking about the job Theillen had done for us and wondering what he would do with his citation."

Soon the smell of coffee canceled the smell of alcohol, and Pieter and Demmie stood at the window of the tower, watching the cars pull up in front of the west wing entrance below.

"I think she's in one of those limos," Pieter said.

"Do you think this will take long?" Demmie set her cup down and tried to lift her leg to the sill. "Ouch," she whispered. "I guess I won't be dancing for a while."

"Do you hurt badly?"

"No. I just shouldn't try to stretch."

The phone rang. It was Jan. He said they ought to be down in the gallery now. They were about to begin auctioning the replaced canvas, and the gallery was filling up. Pieter and Demmie rode the elevator down the front way.

At the first sound of footsteps, van Rijks had pressed himself deeply into his hole. The workroom where he lay hidden was off the hallway, beside Pieter's office. He had heard them mention the alcohol, and someone named Theillen—probably that rough-looking young man—and how long it might take. The sound of their voices irritated the wound in his stomach. He heard the phone ringing. It would be soon now. Everyone was gathering. Then he heard them giggling, and the rustle of clothes, and the shuffle of two people locked and off balance, moans issuing from the office. He heard, too, the sound of feet as they went down the hall chuckling to themselves like the two stupid lovers they were.

He clutched the knife in his hands in case they discovered him. His body hurt so much that he couldn't have run if he'd had to, and so he twisted the handle of the knife, hoping against having to use it too soon. He had been so foolish, dumping the acid on his belly. It was swollen blue now, and a yellowish pus oozed from it. He had covered the wound with a square of canvas and taped it in place. When he was sure they had gone, he walked back into Pieter's office and picked up the bottle of acid on the shelf. He stood there a moment, weighing the thick amber bottle in one hand and the scalpel in the other. Then he removed his shoes and left, using Demmie's set of keys, to join the party.

Jan had placed a table on the stage. Neat pieces of canvas, shaved from the back of *The Night Watch,* were piled on the table. The newer canvas was in one pile, and the canvas that had faced the back of Rembrandt's canvas was in another. They would bring prices according to their age.

Pieter, Demmie, and Theillen sat in straight-backed chairs behind Jan as he explained that the bids offered for these pieces of canvas would go for the construction of more adequate security for such treasures as *The Night Watch.* He went on for five minutes, trying to make everyone feel guilty about the vulnerability of such treasures, and the disgrace such vandalism visited on all their heads. The first bids—the ones for the newer, almost worthless relining canvas—came in high. Hundreds of guilders were being spent for what Pieter had simply considered refuse. Two men in the front row began arguing when their bids exceeded their pocketbooks. "They're bidding for splinters of the crucifix," Demmie whispered, leaning toward Pieter. The television cameras whirred behind the blinding lights as Jan held up strip after strip of canvas. The room became exceedingly hot.

265

Pieter poked Theillen in the side. "You did a terrible job of cleaning the studio," he said. "I forgot," Theillen said. "Sorry. By the way, do we get any commission on this sale?"

The cold stone of the stairs numbed van Rijks's feet as he sneaked along the corridor. Nothing hurt now. Every nerve in him prickled, and he felt, oddly, as if he no longer had a body but was an invisible sphere of fluttering energy.

He stopped suddenly when he saw the policeman with his back to him, standing where he had stood last night, looking, through the mirrored door that he had looked through, at the ceremony beginning in the gallery. The policeman turned, as surprised to see van Rijks in the corridor as van Rijks had been to see him.

"Hey, what's going on here?" the cop said, reaching for his whistle.

Van Rijks jumped on him as he placed the whistle to his lips. He drove the fist that clenched the thick amber bottle of acid into the cop's face, smashing the whistle into his mouth with a sickening, tooth-shattering crunch. The cop bounced off the concrete wall, his eyes already glazed and rolling, the tip of the whistle glinting like a silver tongue in his throat, and van Rijks dropped him with an elbow shot to the point of his chin. He stood over the cop, waiting for him to move, ready to strike him again.

Then he looked through the door at the short balding man—the one who'd lectured the spectators in the gallery—as he exhorted the jammed gallery in some mad confusion of sun-bright lights and popping flashbulbs. He was holding up pieces of canvas. People were raising their arms, yelling at him. He saw Beckum, his whore and his lackey flanking him, sitting behind the table of canvas scraps on the stage. At once, the brightest of lights dimmed, and another explosion of flashbulbs lit the gallery; their strobing sent concussions pounding through the door he stood behind. His throat closed, and the base of his head tingled with electricity. He knelt over the cop and began removing his uniform.

Jan's auction finished with a flurry of arguments among the people who wanted the last piece of canvas, and two of the police in the crowd stepped forward to settle the dispute. Pieter was relieved to see them there. Two policemen were positioned at each door. One stood just inside the mirrored door behind him. He saw van Velde's bristle-top head, bobbing continuously among the people. Van Velde had called him that morning, before he and Demmie had left, to assure him that they would be watching for van Rijks. They would even have some plainclothesmen peppered throughout the crowd. They did not know what to expect from van Rijks, but they expected the worst. Pieter had had the same feeling ever since van Velde had told him that van Rijks was not dead. He was out there, waiting, as he had been all along, and Pieter, sitting so prominently on the stage, felt like the last shield in front of all that was worth saving.

"That's enough," Jan said, clapping his hands. Some workmen in blue tunics removed the table and positioned the podium and microphone in the center of the stage. A museum guard approached Jan and whispered something in his ear. "In the meantime . . ." Jan said, straightening up and pointing beyond the people to the gallery doors. The doors opened slowly, and a column of soldiers filed in to part the spectators. The bright lights for the cameras sizzled on, as though someone had let the sun into the room again.

Cameras clicked, each flash taking away a little of Pieter's breath. He had expected some fanfare, a little pageantry, but now everybody was clapping and pushing forward to get a look at her.

"Where's the music?" he asked Demmie. She gave him a quick, nervous smile, and that reassured him.

Queen Juliana stepped sprily along the aisle of parted spectators. She was wearing an aquamarine suit, with a matching broad-brimmed hat. Pieter felt suddenly cheated. She was so small, so frail-looking in real life, yet she looked so large in the newsreels and on TV. Even that day on the gazebo she had appeared larger than this. Why, to look at her now, she could easily be his grandmother. She ascended the steps, immediately approaching

Pieter to shake his hand, and he looked down on her little hat. She looked half at him, half at the crowd, and mumbled a precious "So pleased to meet you."

God, she even smelled like a grandmother, he thought. Flashbulbs popped around them. He wanted her to smell exotic—she was the Queen—but for the life of him he could not clear his nose of the faint smell of mothballs.

Queen Juliana, her voice small in her throat, read a speech into the microphone at the podium. She presented a medal to the guard who had prevented further damage to *The Night Watch* at great personal risk. She was apologetic that such an act of vandalism could have happened at all. Then she presented Pieter, Demmie, and Theillen with their awards. She pinned Pieter's medal on last, and there was a rash of picture-taking. Juliana's hands lingered on the lapel of his coat as she held the pose.

Jan had prepared a speech for Pieter, and as he read it a slow panic rose in him. The words that issued from his mouth did not register. He was commending the Town Council for their efforts throughout the long months. He explained how the restoration techniques he had used—aptly called "the Dutch method"—were completely reversible in case future generations found need, or technology, to do a better job. But all he could think about was the incongruous smell of alcohol. Juliana had put him on to that. She had disappointed him with her flat fragrance, and his mind had locked on to the pungent smell of alcohol in the studio. Then, as he continued reading, he remembered seeing the light in the spire last night, and recalled that Theillen had actually forgotten to clean the studio. He was running out of words in his speech, but his mind was racing beyond, to an inalterable conclusion. He realized he was completely dumbstruck, standing there, facing all those empty eyes as they waited for him to continue. He heard the click of the door behind him and, out of the corner of his eye, saw the policeman approaching the stage. Demmie's purse was gone too, and the keys, and the light, and *he* was not dead, and now he could smell the alcohol so sharply that he cringed.

He turned to Demmie, but no words came. Juliana shifted uncomfortably in her seat. Then he saw van Rijks in the policeman's uniform, the hat pulled low to obscure his face, standing at the foot of the steps beside the oblivious museum guard.

Pieter cried out, and the entire gallery, as one body, seemed to shrink backward. The guard at the steps spun to where Pieter pointed. With a glinting arc of van Rijks's uniformed arm, the guard fell to his knees, clutching his spraying throat, a horrible whistling coming from beneath his bloodied hands. His eyes narrowed uncertainly as he fell forward.

Van Rijks leaped onto the stage, and all Pieter could smell was the alcohol. Two soldiers sprang onto the stage and fell on Juliana. Flashbulbs thumped the air like small explosions. Soldiers and police, separated by panicking spectators, rushed for the stage.

Pieter lunged in front of van Rijks, and in that instant their eyes caught. The scalpel, streaked red, as was van Rijks's hand, flashed before Pieter. Crystal droplets from an uncapped amber bottle flew above him, catching fire in the bright lights. The droplets bit into Pieter's cheek and ear as he tackled van Rijks to the floor. His right arm wrapped van Rijks's waist, and he felt the unbearable sting of the blade, pounding again and again into his arm. A deafening thunder of footsteps beat the floor around him. He saw a boot, a woman's boot—pointed and dark leather—kicking into van Rijks's face as he crawled forward. Pieter's right arm was losing its grip; his fingers were cold and twitching uncontrollably and he squeezed with all his might. He could feel the phenomenal strength convulsing van Rijks's body, like some beast in its death throes, as he clung to him. Somehow, van Rijks had gotten to his feet; Pieter's hand was caught in his belt and he was being dragged on his knees. Everyone was screaming. Demmie fell over him, and he saw it was her pointed boots that had gouged van Rijks's face. The scalpel came up, van Rijks bellowing some inhuman roar, and Theillen plowed into him, but still he did not go down. They were all being dragged toward *The Night Watch.* Then suddenly there was a thunderous, earsplitting clap. The room fell numb, as if "Enough!" had been shouted from the heavens, and van Rijks collapsed on the stage at the foot of the painting.

Pieter tumbled beside him, and the crowd surged in. Van Velde and his men worked the people back. Pieter's brain felt stunned. That guard's throat had been slit; he was dead before he ever dropped to his knees. Pieter started sobbing. "The Queen?" he asked van Velde, who knelt in front of him.

"Gone," he said.

Pieter blew his nose on his coat to clear away the smell of alcohol, but it didn't work. His cheek burned as if someone had branded him. Van Rijks. The man had a small, clean hole right where his neck joined his head. There was very little blood. Then it occurred to Pieter to examine the painting. He rolled slowly to his feet, and his knees buckled. He thought he would vomit, and he staggered from the stage into a small washroom. When he looked in the mirror, dark blood dappled his cheeks. Gouts of it reddened his shirt. His right arm was so heavy he could not lift it. With his left hand, he splashed water on his cheek and was relieved to see the blood wash away. He splashed more water on the puffy blooms made by the acid burns. Then his legs began trembling, and he fainted.

39

The next thing Pieter knew, he was lying on the leather couch in Jan's office. Demmie sat beside him, smoking a cigarette.

Van Velde came in. "Well, he got what he was after. In the morning, his picture will be splashed all over the pages of *Der Speigel, Paris-Match,* and a dozen other tabloids. Just as he lies there."

"Who shot him?" Demmie asked.

"I did," van Velde said, turning away from her. "How is your arm?"

Pieter looked down and noticed the bandage for the first time. "All right, I guess. Who gave me an injection? It's all numb."

No one answered him.

Van Velde said, "I think the Queen wants to give you another medal. For the tackle that saved her, and probably the painting too."

"Tell her I don't want any more medals," Pieter said. "I wasn't trying to save her anyway." He sat up, and his arm swung limply by his side. He used his left hand to lift it and place it on his lap. He was dizzy from the loss of blood and concerned about the numbness in his arm. He stood, steadying himself by the couch, and asked Demmie to come with him.

"We have to wait here," she said. "Jan called for an ambulance."

"I don't have to wait," he snapped. "I want to see the painting."

She helped him walk down the flight of stairs to the gallery. At each step she took, he saw again the sharp, pointed toe of her boot as she hysterically kicked at van Rijks's face. The toe was scuffed with teeth marks. Everything had gone insanely wild in that instant. The screaming. The way they tore at each other, and at him. He realized that Demmie had been trying to kill van Rijks. And the sound of the gunshot repeated itself in his head.

It should not have turned out this way. He had not wanted the man killed, then torn half to pieces by the cultivated madness of the crowd. But it had happened here, he thought, in the National Gallery, in the face of *The Night Watch,* in the heart of the museum, where violence and destruction held a rightful place only in the imaginations of artists. It was sacrilege of the highest order, and he felt he had been among the few who had not contributed. He had tried to stop the slashing and had taken his punishment in the bargain. But he had not tried to kill—not this time, not in the museum.

The police had cleared the gallery of people. Debris was scattered over the floor. Even the scraps of canvas the bidders had bickered over earlier were left forgotten. And there, on the rug of the stage, below the foot of Banning Cocq, was a neat circular bloodstain.

Pieter climbed the stage and faced the painting so that he could see none of the mess behind him. In the radiance from the skylight, he became exhilarated once again by the painting's magnificent beauty—the brushstrokes so brilliantly alive now, the chaotic folly of this group of people so masterfully subdued. He checked for acid burns in the varnish, but there were none. Demmie stood at the foot of the stage and watched him. He felt compelled to apologize to the spirit of Rembrandt: for van Rijks's stupidity, for his own and Demmie's, for all of them who had become aware of what the painting represented and who had not cherished it.

He turned to her. "You and Theillen are going to have to finish this."

"No," she said. "Why?"

He lifted his arm from his side and let it drop. "Because the nerves in my arm are cut."

She looked on the verge of tears; her face was drawn, and the delicate wings of her lips quivered.

He laughed. "Don't look so hopeless. I don't mind its being done with." He felt delivered from it all. And, he thought, he had been delivered by the same mad slashing that had initiated it. He began to point out that irony to Demmie, but she stopped him with a question.

"When we finish, can we go on another holiday?"

Ever a surprise, he thought. "Yes," he told her. "A nice long one."